Black Heart Auctions

BUYING TIME

JAYCE CARTER

Buying Time
ISBN # 978-1-80250-581-8
©Copyright Jayce Carter 2023
Cover Art by Kelly Martin ©Copyright October 2023
Interior text design by Claire Siemaszkiewicz
Totally Bound Publishing

Published in 2023 by Totally Bound Publishing, United Kingdom.

Totally Bound Publishing books by Jayce Carter

The Omega's Alphas
Owned by the Alphas
Shared by the Alphas
Saved by the Alphas
Protected by Her Alphas
Caught by Her Alphas
Tamed by the Alphas
Claimed by the Alphas
Exposed by Her Alphas
Trained by the Alphas
Reclaimed by Her Alphas

Ready or Not
Fake It 'til You Make It
Opposites Attract
Third Time Lucky
Enemies Closer

Grave Concerns
Grave Robbing and Other Hobbies
Hell Raising and Other Pastimes
Saving the World and Other Bad Ideas

Dark Sanctuary
Bound by Fear
Trapped by Doubt
Buried by Despair

Nemesis
The Corpse Princess
The Resurrected Queen

Larkwood Academy
Silenced
Whispers
Screaming

The Devil's Luck
A Devil of a Time
Devil May Care
Run Like the Devil
The Devil's Due

Black Heart Auctions
Selling Innocence
Buying Time

Collections
Sun, Sea and Sinful Delights
Secret Santa: To Catch a Fox
Cupid's Academy: Stolen
Hot Bite: Summer Trips and Other Reasons to Get Naked

BUYING TIME

Dedication

To my husband, who still grabs my butt
even after twenty years together.

Chapter One

Kenz

Well, I'm fucked.

If only I meant it in a more literal way. Instead of me getting to finally ditch my virgin status, however, I was just in trouble.

Again.

Hayden, Tor, Char and Vance hadn't said anything else to me on the ride home, but had they really needed to? Hayden had uttered my most closely guarded secret, calling me by my *real* name, Mackenzie Williams.

The silence in the car crushed me. I struggled to breathe deeply, as if the air had thickened until it became too heavy to draw in. Despite that, even when the car pulled to a stop in front of the house, I didn't move.

I didn't reach for the door, didn't make any attempt to exit. Even when the others got out, I sat there, frozen, staring down at my own lap because I couldn't bring myself to look anywhere else.

Was this it? They knew who I was, knew how they could use that. If only I'd moved faster, avoided Jarrod, left that damn bugged reader behind, I wouldn't be here. Now I'd potentially put Nem and the others in danger because I hadn't been smart enough.

Here I am again, screwing up everyone else's life.

The door opened, and I expected to find Hayden there. He was usually the one who escorted me, who watched out for me.

Instead, a dark hand appeared in front of me, waiting. I glanced up to find Tor staring down at me, his expression unreadable.

I'd caused enough trouble, so I set my hand in his and got out of the car. The slamming of the door felt like a warning shot.

We went inside, and I knew damn well I wouldn't be allowed to go to bed. No matter how tired I felt, how much I wanted to lie down and sleep, it wasn't possible.

Interrogations are better done when the subject is tired. I recalled Dane telling me that once, when he'd been trying to find out where I'd hidden some candy I'd stolen from the kitchen.

The memory made me smile, even as my eyes stung.

Tor released my hand and gestured at the couch. I'd done enough to piss them off, so I did as he asked, sitting like a good girl.

Why do I keep failing at that? Even when I want to do well, I still don't measure up.

It seemed my path in life.

A mug was set on the table before me, the wonderful scent of coffee streaming from the top. Char pushed it toward me on the table with a single finger.

"Thanks," I whispered and picked it up. The warmth seeped through the ceramic and into my palms, easing that tightness in my chest.

The others filtered in from the kitchen, one at a time, each with a cup of their own. It seemed we *all* needed the caffeine. Then again, I had no idea when they'd realized I was gone, so I didn't know if they'd slept at all.

When they sat, however, the juxtaposition struck me. How many times had we done this?

"What are you smiling about?" Char asked, an edge to his voice.

"I was just thinking about how we've sat here just like this so many times. It's weird to think it's only been a few weeks."

"And we almost never did it again," Vance muttered, anger simmering in his tone.

"Getting right to it." I took a sip of the coffee, the taste of the sugar substitute familiar and welcome. "So you know who I really am?"

Hayden nodded, the look on his face already a familiar one. He had the expression he wore when he was trying to stay calm, to be the adult in the room. "Yeah, we know."

"How much do you know?"

"Enough," Char snapped. "Even this far away, the Williams family is well-known. Of course, as far as anyone knew, Mackenzie Williams, the last legitimate heir, was killed about a year ago."

Tor's gaze dropped to my stomach as he narrowed his eyes until the gold just barely peeked out.

"Yeah." I nodded and touched the scar through my shirt. "I wasn't lying about that. This is where my father shot me."

"Why fake your death?" Hayden asked.

"Because it was the only way for me to have a life. Otherwise, people would try to use me. I wouldn't be able to go to school, to have a real life, because people would constantly be trying to make use of my name and my bloodline. My father was Kyler Williams and my mother Caroline Hester."

Hayden cursed beneath his breath, the word vulgar enough to take me by surprise, given he didn't typically say such words. "So you're essentially a Mafia princess, huh?"

"You see why I lied. If anyone knew who I was, I'd never be free, I'd never get to live my life how I want My father used me all my life, caring only about how he could sell me off to benefit himself. I didn't want that future."

"There are rumors that the girl who took over Kyler's spot was related to him, but it's not easy to get anything specific."

I couldn't stop myself from seeing Nem's face then, from seeing the way she scowled, or better, the way her expression softened whenever she looked at me. "Nem. She's my sister — well, half-sister. We share a mother, but her father wasn't Kyler."

"Fucking hell," Char whispered. "You're telling me that your sister is *Nemesis*? The psycho bitch who runs the West Coast?" He paused, then let out another string of curses. "Which means those bodyguards you talked about, you're saying they're the Quad?"

I laughed softly at his tone. It was far from the first time people had reacted in such a way when they figured out I knew the Quad. Normally, it amused me. The flash of fear when the recognition hit.

This time, my laughter felt hollow.

"Yeah," I admitted. "They're like brothers to me."

"And who were you talking to in that alley? I didn't recognize the voice and it doesn't seem from the conversation that he was one of the Quad," Hayden asked, his tone one of barely contained anger.

In for a penny. I had no reason not to tell them, did I?

"He's a fixer. He goes by the Fox."

"Jesus," Vance growled out. "Even I know about him."

"I guess this explains why getting attacked didn't freak you out," Hayden said. "Why would it when you were raised as a Mafia princess surrounded by the worst of the worst, when your family has the most dangerous killers in it?"

"It's not like that," I said.

"Not like what?" Char asked. "Because I've worked in the shadows long enough to hear plenty of stories. Are you going to tell me they're killers with a heart of gold or something?"

I shook my head. "It's not that. I know how dangerous they are, but that's not who they are *to me*. To me, they're family. To me, Nem is the woman who could have left me to my fate, to be sold off by my father and killed, but she didn't. She risked everything and came back to rescue me. The Quad are my brothers, men who put themselves between me and danger time and time again. They're overbearing and annoying, but they care about and look out for me and gave me stability in life when I didn't have any. Even the Fox— he stepped in like a father for me when he had no reason to. I'm not stupid. I know people fear them, but to me? They're just my family."

Hayden let out a sigh that implied he thought me stupid. "You're naïve, Kenz."

"I'm really not. I didn't grow up nearly as sheltered as you seem to think. I've seen my share of terrible things, I've seen people killed, I've been targeted, I even know what it's like to feel my blood leaking away and think…this is it. It was the Fox who carried me to help, who saved me, and it was Nem who took over for my father to ensure I could leave and get away from that life. I know exactly who and what they all are."

Silence descended on the room, but it held less tension than before. It seemed like they each thought hard, like they worked through the pieces I gave them.

"Does Lorien know who you really are?" Char asked.

I nodded. "He does. He said it on the phone when we spoke alone."

"So that's why he wants you?"

I shuddered as I remembered the way he'd called us soulmates. "He said he loves me. When you were out of the room, he said that my real identity was why his family supported him going after me, but that he wanted me because we're soulmates."

A strange chill crept over my skin, and when I looked toward Tor, a darkness in his eyes made me want to curl in on myself. He blinked quickly and ripped his gaze from mine, as though shielding me from it.

"Doesn't that mean you've met him?" Vance asked. At my look, he shrugged. "If he claims he loves you, he must have met you. He came back specifically for this auction, for the one where you were set to be sold. He had to have met you somehow then, or he wouldn't have had any reason to target you."

"He used a voice changer on the phone," Char pointed out. "Even if she knew him, she wouldn't recognize his voice."

Hayden set his coffee down, most of the drink gone. "His family here is almost as big as the Williams family on the West Coast. It's possible he met you at an event sometime. Maybe he became obsessed then? While his family is important, it's too far for him to have had a hope of getting you from your father, but once you weren't protected? If he figured out your death had been faked, he might have just kept searching until he found you."

"Maybe," I said, unable to deny it. "My father knew a lot of people, after all, and I met more than I could hope to remember at parties." I rubbed my eyes, the coffee not doing nearly enough to keep me awake.

Then again, I'd snuck out the night before, which meant I hadn't managed any shut-eye. The idea of going to class today felt wholly impossible. How could I force myself to get up, put on a fake smile and see anyone?

"You should sleep," Hayden said.

"No, I'm fine."

"You aren't fine. You're going to pass out on the spot." Hayden took my mostly untouched drink from my hands. "You can miss your classes today and rest. You won't be any good in them anyway."

"I'm supposed to meet up with my adviser," I said.

"That's at four this afternoon. If you sleep now, you'll get a few hours before you have to go."

"So I can still go?" Hope sprang inside me. I'd thought after this fiasco he'd end up locking me down. I figured they wouldn't let me do anything after this whole mess.

"Yes," Hayden said, but the harshness in his tone said he I was far from being off the hook. "And tonight, after you're back, we will have a *very* thorough conversation on exactly what you did wrong, Kenz."

And here I thought I'd gotten off lightly…

＊ ＊ ＊ ＊

Hayden

"She asleep?" Vance asked when I got back to the living room.

"Yeah. I didn't know if she'd fall asleep, so I sat there for a few minutes, but she was out fast."

Char let out a long sigh, annoyance tinging the sound. "Well this sure all went to shit, didn't it?"

I couldn't argue with that. We'd thought we had some rich, spoiled brat in our custody, but come to find out we'd been really damn wrong. Who knew we'd had the pup of an entire wolf pack?

I sure don't want to tangle with that pack if they come looking...

I drew my hand into a fist as I thought about how close we'd come to serious danger without even realizing it. If the Quad had found out we'd all but abducted their little sister...

I shuddered to think about the hell they'd rain down on us.

Not that we couldn't handle it, but if we hadn't even known? It could have easily turned into a bloodbath.

"She didn't rat us out," Vance said. "When the Fox asked her about us, she could have told him what we'd done, could have asked for help, but she didn't. She lied to him and said we hadn't done anything to her."

Which brought up the *other* thing she'd said, the part none of us had mentioned.

Her words still echoed in my head, the ones that had come through our bug. *I love them.*

She loved us? I shook my head at the foolish idea. She didn't love us—she didn't even know what love was. Even if she did, she was far too young and trusting to be making such claims.

"It's just more proof that she's too innocent," Char said. "She should know better than to fall for people like us. She stupidly protected us instead of herself."

"And she was turning herself over to Lorien for us, too," I pointed out. "She was headed for that hotel just to keep us safe, to make sure Lorien didn't target us."

Just saying that made my temper sour, and I was glad she slept soundly in the other room instead of seeing my expression. Just the *thought* of her handing herself over made me feel as if I'd lose my sanity. What would that piece of shit do to her if he got his hands on her?

I won't let that happen.

But how was I supposed to deal with a girl so ready to sacrifice herself? How was I supposed to protect someone who didn't seem to give a damn about her own life?

My clients hired me because they wanted to live, typically, and they did as I said because they valued their lives. Did she not care about hers?

No, that wasn't it. That was my frustration speaking. I knew she valued her life, but she valued ours more. Maybe she understood love better than I did, then?

"So what now?" Vance asked. "We know who she is, have a better understanding of why Lorien is after her, but what does it change?"

"Not much," I admitted. "It doesn't give us any real leverage. If we expose what we know about her, it'd only put her in more danger. Instead of one psycho after her, she'd have countless ones."

"Kyler Williams' fucking daughter," Char muttered to himself, as if he'd yet to fully come to terms with that revelation.

"She's not much like him, is she?" I said.

"You knew him?" Vance asked.

"Not much. I'd met him before, on a few jobs. I've done security work on the West Coast, and some of my clients weren't the best people. I ran into him from time to time. He was a serious man with cold, calculating eyes. I've heard plenty about him, though, and none of it's been good."

"Yeah, well, he's nothing compared to Nem, who took over," Char said. "Maybe the apple didn't fall far from that crazy tree. I wasn't kidding when I called her a psycho. Her territory is peaceful, but that peace comes at a steep price. Anyone who causes trouble is dealt with in a very bloody way. I heard about someone who got into trafficking young girls, and my understanding is that they're *still* finding pieces of him all over that city."

I tried to picture Kenz surviving among people like that. I thought about her sweet smile, about the way she seemed entirely defenseless, and that didn't fit at all with the people I knew about. How could she keep being the person she was after living with and being raised by monsters like that?

How had she not turned into the same?

"Nothing changes," I finally said. "Her history helps us understand why Lorien wants her, or at least why he's targeted her. We've got to buy time and make sure Kenz doesn't do anything as stupid as this stunt again."

"Then what?" Vance asked. "Delaying only pushes the risk down the line. We still have no way to draw him out since he wants to make the exchange at a hotel. He's too smart to fall for the bug or tracker trick, either, so it's not like we can use her as bait and just follow her."

We are not using her as bait. The words scrolled across my screen from Tor after my phone chimed.

"I'm not planning to use her as bait. I don't think any of us are okay with that idea anymore."

Except Kenz. No doubt that girl would have done it in a heartbeat if we asked her to, which was the exact reason we had to keep her away from this.

"So what else?"

Give him what he wants.

The words on the screen had me turning my gaze on Tor. "Excuse me? I thought you just said we wouldn't use her like that."

He shook his head, his fingers moving quickly across his screen. *He thinks they're soulmates, right? People say that when they want to believe in love and romance. Give him the chance at that.*

The point remained lost on me.

Vance chuckled softly. "That's not bad, Tor. Never would have figured you for one to play that sort of sneaky game." He turned his gaze on me, his lips pulled into a smirk. "Lorien wants to believe they're going to fall in love. He seems to care what happens to her and what she thinks of him, right? What if we tell him that she wants to talk to him? That she's afraid of him right now, but if they talk, she might change her mind."

The pieces came together. It wasn't the worst idea I'd ever heard…

"So you think he'll agree to that, and he might let something slip?"

"He's arrogant and in love — at least, he thinks he is. That's a recipe for loose lips. Give Kenz the chance to talk to him and we might just find something to use against him."

"What if he gets his claws into her? She's already willing to sacrifice herself for us—clearly she doesn't make great choices when it comes to men. What if he tricks her and she decides life with him might not be so bad? What if she betrays us?" Even as I said that, I didn't quite believe it possible. Kenz was sweet and trusting, but I didn't think betrayal was in her nature.

However, that trusting nature could lure her into confusion, into making a choice because she thought it the right one.

She's smarter than that, Tor texted. *She can do this.*

When I couldn't come up with a better plan, I nodded. I didn't love putting Kenz in the line of fire, but I had to trust we could keep her safe.

All our lives were on the line, after all.

"And what about the other thing?" Char asked.

I love them. Those words echoed in my head again, precious and frustrating and proof of all the reasons we needed to be careful.

"What about it?" Vance asked. "She's young. It isn't shocking that she'd confuse reliance with love. Lock up men and women together and eventually they'll think they're in love. Just basic human instinct."

I hated Vance's words, but he wasn't wrong. It wasn't like we could indulge in anything. Our time was limited.

We knew it, had made our choice five years ago, knew that our lives were over one way or another when we finished this.

If we gave in to Kenz, if we let her think for even a moment that a future was possible, she'd be the one to ultimately pay the price. At the end of it all, she'd be the one to remain, to live on with that pain, and that wasn't fair.

"So we all agree, right? No one touches her," I checked, my gaze hard.

These men were almost brothers to me — with just as many complicated feelings between us — but I had no problem putting a bullet in any of them who dared to make a move on Kenz.

They each nodded in agreement, though the same shadow rested in each of their eyes. It was a desire for what she offered, for the fantasy that we could have some happily ever after with a girl like her.

But that wasn't possible.

We were broken, just moving along a path to finish this, and at the end?

No matter what happened, we couldn't hurt Kenz by leaving her to pick up the bloody pieces. It meant no matter how hard it was, how much I wanted to taste what she offered, I couldn't.

I had to focus on the task and nothing more, and that might just be the hardest thing I'd ever do in my life.

Chapter Two

Kenz

The sleep had done more good than I'd expected. I had no idea how I'd fallen asleep so fast, but somehow, I'd slept deep.

Hayden had sat on the side of my bed, not leaving me alone in the quiet room. When I'd woken, he'd been gone already, but that didn't change the warmth I'd felt from him staying. After everything had shifted the night before, that sense of security had helped.

The car moved smoothly through the crowded parking lot until Hayden pulled it into a space. His driving was, as always, flawless. It amazed me that he could drive so carefully—it was like he never missed anything.

How could someone be so aware of his surroundings? It was like he saw everything.

"You'll make me nervous if you stare at me like that." He turned toward me, catching me in the act. Tension lined his features that hadn't been there before.

20

I pretended not to sense the change and smiled. "Sorry. I'm just impressed by how in control you always seem. It doesn't matter where we go or what we do, you always seem to have a handle on it all."

"I've done security for a long time—it's second nature. In fact, the few times I go on vacation, I can't relax and take it easy. I'm always looking at exits and escape routes and details like that. I went on a trip with a girlfriend years ago and she ended up leaving me halfway through because she said I could never turn that off." He let out a self-deprecating laugh.

However, his casual mention of a girlfriend managed to bump my anxiety right on up. It was like the word had driven a splinter right into my nail bed, a sharp pain I couldn't pull out or lessen.

It reminded me of what else I'd said, what they'd heard but hadn't mentioned.

My little confession…

I guess it didn't take a rejection, did it? I hadn't told them because I knew they'd reject me, anyway.

I mean, what did I have to offer them?

Beyond what immediately could be useful to them, I had nothing. Just a name, a bloodline, and unless it helped them get their revenge, they didn't need it.

Instead of letting on about how dark my thoughts had grown—because Hayden would notice—I moved back to the topic at hand. "I'm always running into things and missing stuff, so I guess it impresses me that you're so focused all the time."

Hayden nodded, then slid from the car and came around to my side. He opened my door, the action normal already. It wasn't romantic, simply a matter of security, but my heart still sped when he did it. When he moved to walk on the side of the road, when he held doors open for me, my stupid heart took those as acts of affection instead of his professional obligations.

Don't be an idiot.

We headed into the building, and I always relaxed when we got here. This college was my sanctuary, the only place I felt free. It was like my wings weren't clipped anymore when I arrived, like the chains that bound me broke.

"I won't take long," I told Hayden as he took position by the door to Grisham's office.

"Take as long as you need," Hayden assured me, a familiar kindness in his expression that hurt.

I knocked, then entered when Grisham called for me to come in. I closed the door behind me and took the seat I always sat in, my sketchbook in my lap.

I'd been busy, but I'd worked over the past few days, trying to put the suggestions he'd given before to use. It was strange, given all I'd been through, that I could still focus on my art.

The truth was it felt like the only thing that saved me, the only time when I wasn't caught up in my head about my future, about what I should do, about the mess of my life.

"You look exhausted," Grisham said, a line appearing between his eyebrows.

Great, now I'm even worrying my adviser.

"I've had a lot going on," I admitted. I couldn't tell him much, but that was fine, right?

"I can tell. You've been looking more and more rundown every time I see you. Is it the exhibit you're worrying about? Because focusing on it and stressing will only ensure you can't get anything good done."

I shook my head. A part of me so badly wanted to spill what I was going through. I'd dealt with him for the past year, had relied on him for his guidance and advice, which made the temptation all the harder to resist.

But I couldn't. It wasn't the sort of problem a person could share with just anyone. Normal people couldn't fathom going through what I was and telling him would only burden or threaten him.

"You can talk to me, you know." Grisham got out of his seat, then came around the desk and sat in the chair beside me. He set his hand on top of mine and squeezed gently. "I've known you for a year now, Kenz, and I want the best for you. I'm your adviser here, so it's my job to help you when you're struggling."

"It's not about my art," I whispered.

"So? You know as well as I do that art isn't just what we put on paper or make out of clay. It's wrapped up in everything else in our lives, in our joy and our sorrow and our fears. It's all intertwined and impossible to separate. Believe it or not, I'm a good listener. Maybe if you talk about what you're dealing with, you'll be able to wrap your head around it?"

And damn, was that tempting. Everyone in my life had their own agendas. They wanted me to do things for their own use, had their own opinions, had too much background. It wasn't that they didn't care about me, but it was shaped by their own lives as well. Talking to someone entirely outside of it would be so nice, to pour out all the details without any background, without them having a dog in the fight.

I always had to hide my real feelings. Everyone worried about me, but they all had their own problems. I ended up trying to be what they needed me to be, what I thought would make things easiest for them, and that exhausted me.

Yet here I had the rare chance to just vent, to tell someone who didn't know the background or the people involved...

"I just have a lot I'm dealing with," I said softly. "I need to work on my exhibit pieces, but I'm so distracted by everything else. It's hard to focus." I stared at where he held my hand, his grip warm.

It didn't feel like when Hayden did it now and then, didn't make my stomach flutter. It felt reassuring, but that was it.

Grisham released my hand and pulled my sketchbook from my lap. He flipped it open to near the back, to the newer pages. He worked his gaze over the most recent sketches I'd done.

The same old pit in my stomach opened, the fear of rejection that sat with every artist when someone else looked at their work — especially unfinished work.

Grisham turned the sketchbook toward me, resting open on both our knees. "Do you know your biggest problem? You get focused on things you *think* matter and miss the rest. See this?" He tapped an image I'd done a few days before. It was a silhouette of the men out back. I'd seen it from my bedroom window, taken by the way they had appeared like living shadows before the colorful sky as the sun had set. None of them could be made out, but I'd wanted to show a side of them I didn't normally see.

"Yeah?" I asked to prompt him to go on.

"You spent far more time sketching the sky here. You layered in the pinks and red with your colored pencils, but you spent no time on the figures."

"But the sky is prettier," I said with a frown. "The figures were just shadows."

"Shadows have details, though, they have depth. They aren't just the absence of color or light — they have purpose. Tell me *why* you drew this. What made you want to use this as inspiration?"

I thought back to that moment. It was after they'd told me their pasts, when they'd laid bare their pain. I'd understood how difficult it had been, but they'd done it for *me*.

It was when I'd decided to do what I did, to turn myself over for their good. Looking at them, I'd thought about just how precious they were, how much their happiness meant to me.

"I wanted to show how set apart from the world they are, but how important. I wanted to show the beauty of figures who exist in the darkness, in the places others don't tread."

"Good. I see a glimpse of that here, but you lose your way. You lost your confidence. You saw the sky and thought that was the easier target, the easier thing to capture, so you veered from what you wanted to say and went with that you thought others would want. I have a feeling you do that a lot."

I frowned, ready to tell him he was wrong.

Except…I couldn't. I thought back to all the times I'd swallowed down what I really wanted and given it up to be a good girl. I might have complained, but in the end? I gave in.

I did as I was told.

"Maybe I do," I whispered.

"That's your biggest problem, Kenz. You need to look at what *you* want and stop letting other things distract you. Stop doing what you think you should, what others tell you to, what's expected of you. Those things are going to turn you into a clone of everyone else. You have talent, Kenz. I've been telling you that for a year, now. You can do so much more, be so much more, if you just stop trying to live by everyone else's rules."

I lifted my gaze, shocked to find him so close. We'd leaned in to look at the sketchbook, to study the image, and it had so engrossed me that I hadn't recognized we were only a few scarce inches apart. He was so close that I could feel his warm breath on my lips.

And there was heat in his eyes. I recognized that easily, and for a brief moment, the temptation felt like too much.

I wanted to feel wanted. I wanted to feel normal, to feel like any other nineteen-year-old. No matter how hard I'd tried, though, I hadn't been able to find that.

If I just closed my eyes and leaned in, I could have a *real* first kiss. I could experience that rush, that passion I'd heard about but never felt myself.

But before I did, the memories of the way Hayden had protected me before hit me. I saw Tor's golden eyes, Char's sarcastic smirk, Vance's arrogant expression.

Giving in to this would be like eating sand when hungry. It would only end up hurting me, wouldn't make me feel satiated in the least. It wasn't what I really wanted—just a cheap substitute.

So I pulled back, putting distance between us.

He sighed softly, though it didn't sound surprised. "I understand. Just remember that I'm here, Kenz, and I want the best for you. You're on the right track with this"—he tapped at the sketch—"but make sure you focus on what's important, not what *seems* best to others. Don't lose sight of yourself."

I nodded and took the sketchbook, then fled the room because he saw too much, because what he offered was just too tempting.

The fact that *someone* wanted me soothed a deep part of me, that little girl who'd always craved affection and attention and unconditional love but hadn't found it, it all clouded my head.

Wasn't it hilarious that when someone offered me what I thought I wanted, I just couldn't get myself to accept?

* * * *

Char

So here we are, pretending yet again. It was funny that I was usually so comfortable in that position. I slid into my personas with an ease that made me safer. Those other personalities of mine, the people I created and wrapped around me like a second skin, they were safe.

They made it so people couldn't touch *me.* They only saw or interacted with the false masks.

So why was it that all of us sitting here at the dining room table like nothing happened bothered me so damn much?

Kenz had said she loved me—that she loved us *all.* I could spot lies, and Kenz wasn't even a good liar. It meant I knew she meant it.

It wasn't truly love, of course—I didn't believe in that. However, she sure as fuck thought she loved us.

And instead of addressing that, the clinking of our silverware against the plates filled the room like some family dinner.

Lies and make-believe. Maybe that's what makes a real family dinner.

"This is good," Kenz whispered, her voice strained.

So she feels this too, huh? At least she's that smart.

"Tor's a pretty good cook," Vance said. "He doesn't do it much, but when he does? It's worth it."

I didn't much care for complimenting others — especially these assholes — but Vance wasn't wrong. Tor had gone all out, making a delicious Italian meal. Pasta, breaded chicken cutlets, even fresh bread from scratch. The bastard could whip up one hell of a meal when he wanted to. In fact, even if I'd wanted to hide out and keep to myself, the smell of this food alone would have drawn me out.

Kenz looked over at Tor and gave him a soft smile. "Well, thanks. It's really good."

Tor nodded, though a softness in his eyes sat at odds with his otherwise blank expression.

So the kitten can charm even that killer?

Then again, from what I'd heard about the Quad, it seemed she'd been charming killers her whole damned life.

I couldn't get that out of my head, either. I knew *all* about the Quad. Given I worked as a conman, I'd run across them a number of times. Never in person, never as their enemy, since I was far too smart to make a mistake that stupid. I wasn't a killer generally, at least not outright, but they were. They had no problem removing obstacles, which meant I'd kept myself from becoming their enemy.

And to think Kenz had *lived* with them, that she saw them like big brothers?

She really is a blind fool, isn't she?

"Stop sighing."

I lifted my gaze to find Kenz frowning at me. "I wasn't."

"Yes, you were. You've sighed at least six times since we've sat down."

"I'm just breathing," I snapped and shoved a piece of bread that was really *far* too large into my mouth. I chewed and chewed, but quickly it became obvious I'd really overdone it because she'd flustered me.

I grabbed for my glass of water to help wash down the wad of bread, coughing for a moment, and worse? When I lifted my gaze, I found Kenz struggling and failing miserably to hide her laughter.

"So are we just going to ignore all this?" I blurted out since the whole pretend and act mature thing wasn't going well.

"Char…" Hayden warned, censure in his tone.

"No. We're stuck together for another few weeks. We're supposed to rely on one another, so we can't just fucking pretend shit wasn't said."

Red colored Kenz's cheeks, and fuck did that drew me in. I wanted to pull the neckline of her sweater to the side and see just how far down that flush went. Some women, when they came, ended up with their skin pinkened over their chest, their throat, their back.

Kenz had pale skin — would she blush like that?

Focus! If I'd learned one thing in my years of being other people, of reading other people, it was that nothing good came out of a person's mouth when their cock was hard. There was some truth to the old saying that a man could only operate one at a time, and it was wherever the blood was.

"There's no reason to do this here," Vance said, a surprising amount of kindness for the notorious playboy. Then again, he might throw women away quick, but he was still nice to them until that point.

Who would have figured that a gentleman man whore existed?

"Of course there is," I said. "She needs to understand where we all stand. We're stuck together

29

for now, and it'll only hurt her to keep this fantasy of hers."

"You really are an asshole," Hayden muttered softly, but he didn't stop me.

Because I was right. He knew it even if he didn't like it. A moment now to get it all out in the open would hurt *far* less than letting her continue like this, than letting her fall any deeper into this delusion of hers.

I looked directly at Kenz, and her expression said she knew exactly what I wanted to say. Then again, the girl was smarter than most people would have figured at first glance. "You know we had that bug on you, which means we heard what you said."

"Yeah, I know. You know who I really am."

"I said *everything*." I lifted my eyebrow to call her out.

She blew out a sharp, unhappy breath. "Hayden's right. You really *are* an asshole."

"Yeah, I really am. This is the real me, so deal with it. You don't love us, Kenz."

"You don't get to tell me how I feel."

Her response took me by surprise. Kenz tended to let things like that go, to stay quiet even when she didn't agree.

"I'm helping you here, Kenz, even if you don't see it. You're mistaking the fact that you're trapped with us for love. That's it."

She shook her head. "I know how I feel. I'm not some idiot."

"You're still young," Hayden said, his tone unbelievably kind.

"I'm not that young," she argued. "Don't treat me like I'm just some kid."

"You're twenty-one—" Hayden started.

"No, I'm actually nineteen, and so what? Why does that matter? Why do you think that my age has anything to do with how I feel?"

"You're going through a tough time," Vance said. "This situation would mess with anyone's head. We're all you've got right now, so you're clinging to us and seeing things that aren't there. That's it."

She pressed her lips together, her gaze on the table instead of us. Would she cry?

It wouldn't be the first time I'd made a girl cry, but I had a feel it might just be the only time I gave a damn. A part of me wanted to take it all back, but I couldn't. This was a small pain now to stop a larger one later.

I recalled after Isla died, the hole I found myself in. I'd been so lost in that darkness, with no idea how to get out of it. The pain had been unbearable, and the last thing I wanted was for Kenz to feel that after this ended.

This was to save her real pain later.

Kenz inhaled deeply, then pulled her shoulders back. Seeing her like that reminded me of her real past, of the truth of her parentage. This wasn't a nobody, but rather the product of two of the most dangerous, feared and respected families in the country. She'd grown up like that, came from that stock, and when she sat there like that? I saw it.

"Don't you dare try to tell me how I feel. You can control what I do, you can lock me up and keep me trapped and overpower me. What I will never allow you to do is tell me that I don't feel what I know I do. You can't belittle me and treat me like a child. My feelings are my own, and, to be fair, I never intended to tell you. I knew you wouldn't accept it let alone return it, so I never planned to let you see it. If you want to tell me that you don't feel the same—fine. That's your right. However, don't you *dare* act like I don't know my own mind or my own heart." She met my gaze head on, as if daring me to argue with her.

She was right, though. Even if I didn't think what she felt was really love, I couldn't convince her of it. The best I could do was make her give up on it, to realize it was pointless, that it wouldn't go anywhere.

So I forced myself to pull on another mask, that of a man who saw her as nothing but a nuisance. I stared back at her, not giving her an inch of space to doubt my words. "Fair enough. If you want to hold on to unrequited love, that's your choice, I guess. Understand that I don't feel the same, and that I won't ever."

She swallowed hard, then turned her gaze toward Vance.

He sighed, looking far less sure even as he spoke. "This isn't going anywhere, love. You're sweet and you're fun, but that's all there is to it."

Hayden rubbed his hands over his face, and when he pulled them away, the misery was obvious. "You're still a kid. You're *way* too young for anything serious, and I don't play around with kids."

She blinked quickly, darting her gaze to Tor for a moment. He said nothing, didn't reach for his phone, but whatever she saw in his gaze must have told her what she needed to know.

I expected her to break down, to start sobbing, to call us all names.

We'd fucking deserve that and worse. Hell, if she wanted to slap me across the face, I'd take it. I wouldn't move away, wouldn't try to lessen it. If that made her feel better, fair enough.

She didn't, though. She used her napkin to wipe her mouth, then set it on the table and stood, her chair scraping against the floor quietly. "Thank you for dinner — it was delicious. I think I'm going to call it an early night."

Hayden opened his mouth, but before anything escaped, he shut it again.

Nothing any of us said right now would make this any better.

She kept her chin held high, as if her pride was all she had left, and walked out of the room. *Talk about regal.* Somehow, she didn't look like she was fleeing, but instead like she'd had enough of our shit and made the choice to walk away.

That was what we'd wanted, wasn't it? We'd wanted to drive her away, to make her understand there was no chance with us, to make everything hurt her less later on.

So why the fuck did getting exactly what I wanted hurt so damned much?

Chapter Three

Vance

Avoiding Kenz turned out to be harder than I'd expected. After the unpleasantness the night before, I'd stayed in my room as much as possible.

I'd dealt with plenty of angry women over my life. I didn't do long-term relationships, and even though I said it upfront, women tended to decide they would be the one to tame me. They liked to get close, to pretend to be fine with temporary, then lost their minds when I moved on.

I never lied to them, never promised them anything other than what I gave them, yet they'd act like *I* was the bad guy.

Yet somehow, avoiding Kenz didn't feel that great. The quiet didn't help at all, making me feel guilty instead of relieved.

It meant that when it hit three in the afternoon without me catching sight of the dark-haired imp, I'd grown antsy.

My knuckles stung when I knocked on her door, and after she called out for me to enter, I did so.

Even that, the way she left her door unlocked, the way she welcomed in whoever had knocked, reminded me of just how vulnerable she really was. Here she was, living in a house with four men she barely knew, with men willing to kill to get what they wanted, and she *loved* us?

She really is a fool.

And yet, where that normally annoyed me, I found it almost charming with her.

She turned toward me and froze, a paintbrush in her hand, her eyes holding a whole damned lot of hesitation.

Was it because she was painting? Did she think seeing her do art would bother me?

She's too damned sweet.

I offered her a smile, trying to ease her mind, then held up the plate of cheese and crackers, already placed into little piles and ready to eat. "You've been holed up in here for a while. I figured you had to be hungry." I set the food on the desk beside her easel. "You can't work on an empty stomach."

"Thank you." She set her brush in the cup of water on the easel tray.

I peered at her painting, surprised by it. Why it surprised me, I had no idea. Maybe because I hadn't seen many of her paintings. I'd seen just rough sketches and quick character studies. Her brush work was phenomenal, really. She'd done the work in acrylics, layering thin washes of color to achieve the shade she wanted. It gave her work a softness that felt so at odds with the hard black lines on the edges, done with a thicker brush.

"Who is that?" I asked.

"My sister." Her voice caught as she said it, as if just admitting it caused a rush of feelings in her. Not just good ones, either. They seemed complicated and mixed up.

Perhaps no family was perfect.

And I'd bet any family with as much dirt as hers would be rather far from perfect. *Fuck knows mine is the same.*

I thought about my mother, who I hadn't seen in nearly a year. She called, and I picked up only as often as I needed to so she didn't send anyone to find me. I could usually get about three weeks before I had to worry, which meant it would be time soon to face that demon.

I guess I could understand the complicated feelings when it came to family.

"She's pretty," I said.

Kenz nodded, her smile weak. "Yeah, she is. It's funny, because naturally her hair is the same color as mine, but now I can't picture her with anything but the red. It suits her."

"From what I heard, she's like fire, that one."

Kenz pulled the chair from the wall over, nodding at it for me, then sat on the foot of her bed and crossed her legs. "She's like that for a reason."

"What reason is that?"

"My father tried to kill her. He sent killers to remove my mother and Nem because he was afraid they'd challenge his hold on power. He thought that the Hester name was hurting him more than helping him anymore, so he wanted to get rid of them both. The killers thought Nem was dead, but as they burned the house down around her, after they'd put a couple bullets through her, she dragged herself out of that house. The Fox, her real father, saved her, but my father thought she was dead. I thought she was dead, too, for ten years."

"But she didn't stay dead?"

Kenz shook her head. "She came back pretending to be someone else. She wanted to get rid of the people who had attacked her and our mother, and to save me. In the end, she even gave my father the chance to run away. She offered him his life if he just left us alone." Kenz sighed, bowing forward as if exhausted. "He said that he wanted to put the bullet where it would hurt the most, so he fired at me. Nem killed him, but the damage was done. It's funny, but until that moment, I still thought he loved me. Even after finding out he'd killed my mom, that he'd attacked Nem, I still couldn't imagine him caring so little about me. Maybe I'm just as stupid as everyone says."

My chest ached at her words, at the way they came out so softly, so drenched in pain. "The sad fact is that people aren't always what they should be, what we want them to be. You wanting to believe in people doesn't make you stupid."

"You sure about that? Because I recall you all making it *very* clear to me last night what you thought about me seeing people like I want to."

Ouch. Hard to argue, because she wasn't wrong. "That's different. Your father is someone who's supposed to care about you, supposed to look out for you. The fact that yours didn't says something terrible about him, not about you."

"Maybe," she whispered, her tone making it clear she didn't quite agree. "Maybe it's me that's the problem."

"How could that be you?"

She pursed her lips and blew out a long stream of air, the action jostling a strand of her dark hair that hung in her face. "Do you know the sort of people I've lived my life around? My mother, my father, my sister, the Quad. I've had so many people around me who are geniuses of all sorts. My mother was tough and smart, and my father might have been heartless, but he was an amazing tactician. Nem is like fire, able to survive and destroy anything in her way. Rune is so tough that few people could win in a fight against him, and Colton could take a shot from so far away it is amazing, and Dane could get anything out of anyone and there isn't any computer system Bray couldn't hack into. I feel like everyone moves around me like superheroes and here I am…normal."

I stared at her, able to watch her because she looked down instead of at me. How could she not understand how amazing she was? How could she doubt herself so much?

"Maybe you are stupid."

She jerked her gaze up, my words clearly startling her. Then again, statements like hers were usually met with platitudes, with reassurance. Her confused expression made me smirk. *I love throwing her off balance.*

"If you don't see how special you are, then hell, you must be stupid."

Kenz snorted, as if not amused by my statement. "You don't understand. How could you? You're Vance Moore."

"And you're Mackenzie Williams," I pointed out. "Seems like we both grew up in the shadows of names we're supposed to live up to."

"Last I checked, you're a famous artist. Seems you lived up to it just fine."

"Then you don't know much. My father's a well-known politician and my older brother followed suit. It was expected that I'd follow that trend. In fact, my father liked to point out that with a face like mine, I could win votes easily. Instead of getting an angelic politician like he wanted, he got a man whore who doesn't even produce any art anymore. Trust me, I'm not the golden child in my family, either." Even as I admitted that, as I laughed as though it was funny, it sure as fuck didn't *feel* funny.

Instead, I felt that cold look from my father, the way each time I'd come to dinner, he'd ask if I'd finally gotten over my little rebellious stage and was willing to come back into the fold. I recalled all the times I went to shows without family there.

Ah, disappointing parents seemed like my favorite pastime.

Or maybe it was just what I'd grown used to. I didn't love it, but it was all I knew.

I moved my gaze from her painting to find her staring at me. How could she stare at me like that? Like I meant something?

Not like women usually did, the ones who only saw dollar signs above my head. Those women had looked at me as if they already saw a future, like I was a trophy for them to mount on the wall. They'd never given a damn about my feelings, about who I was at all. They'd catered to me, given me whatever I wanted, just because they'd thought it would get them something. Mainly, a future with me.

Kenz, however, didn't see me that way. Instead, she saw parts of me that I'd shown no other person—or the parts that were missing, as it were.

"Well, if your father can't see how amazing *you* are, that's his loss," she said.

"Yeah, right. He's really lucky to have a useless man whore for a son."

Kenz laughed, even though I didn't think anything I said was all that funny. "Well, I can't deny you're a man whore, but that aside, he *is* lucky. You're kinder than you realize, and you've created work that people love. You've created art that will stay around long after any of us are gone. I bet you anything that your name will be remembered well after his is forgotten, so yeah, he's lucky."

Her words took me so by surprise that I struggled to know how to answer. I'd expected her to say something stupid, to tell me I was a good person, that I was nice, that people cared about me. I would have rolled my eyes and written any of that off.

What did those things matter?

However, she'd hit the one spot that mattered to me, and the one that hurt the most. My art. The thing I had loved more than anything else, the thing I'd lost.

I stared down at my damaged hand, surprised when it wavered. I blinked rapidly, refusing to turn into some pussy who cried over something so stupid.

"Yeah, well, that's all over, isn't it?" I ran the fingers of my left hand over my right, feeling the difference between my skin and the firmness of the prosthesis.

Another hand touched mine, making me jump, only to find Kenz had reached out and grasped my damaged hand. She didn't retreat, didn't touch me as though it bothered her. How couldn't it, though? The unnatural stiffness of the false fingers, the memory of the gnarled skin? It turned my stomach and I had to live with it. "Have you tried to learn with your other hand? Or what about other types of prostheses that give you more control?"

I forced a smile I didn't feel. "I tried, especially at first. My left hand just can't do the detail work, and the nerves were damaged in my right hand so badly that I don't have full control even over the fingers I still have."

She frowned for a moment. "The canvas in your room…"

"You think we could just pretend you didn't see that? Not my best moment, that night. I try sometimes, because I'll get this idea in my head. I'll see something and want so badly to paint it. I can see each detail in my mind, like it's right there in front of me, but my hands can't create it. It's frustrating to know what I want to create but be physically unable to."

Before I could think better of it, I used my left hand to cup her cheek, then ran my thumb beneath her eye. "That night I saw your face. It was right there, so clear, every detail, every line, every shadow. I wanted to immortalize that, to create something beautiful that I could keep, but I couldn't even sketch the shape of your eye. It was so bad, it felt like it was mocking us both."

She squeezed my right hand tightly, the pressure uneven as it went between my real hand and the prosthesis. "What if—"

I shook my head and pulled away, unwilling to continue this conversation. "I'm past what ifs, Kenz. I've dealt with this for five years. I know what's possible and what isn't. I've gone to specialists, spent millions on private care, on every crackpot practitioner who told me they could do something to help, and you know what I've learned? It's impossible. Sometimes we lose things, and we can't get them back. I've given up on it, so please, don't tell me how if I just do some random thing, it'll be okay. It won't be, and I've accepted that."

I turned my gaze to her art, trying to change the subject. "The contrast between the soft coloring and hard lines looks good. It helps mirror the different sides of Nem, to show the rough outer edge versus the softer interior that stays hidden."

Kenz swallowed hard, the sound suggesting she hadn't quite finished our previous conversation but knew better than to bring it up again. Instead, she turned her attention to the painting as well. The seriousness in her expression charmed me more than the sexiest of clothing or most sensual come-hither.

Too many artists ignored good advice. They decided they were perfect, that they didn't need to change anything, that their art was flawless merely by existing. Kenz, on the other side, eagerly accepted all lessons.

It was what had drawn me to her the first time I'd met her. The way she'd heard my suggestion about her art, and she'd accepted it openly. Someone who cared more about improving than they did about their own ego was rare in my world, and as it turned out, I liked it.

Kenz nodded, her gaze locked on the painting. "I was afraid the black would stand out too much for outlines."

"I think black is the right choice. However, you kept the eyes soft."

"I thought that would show how she sees the world, that she's kinder than she seems."

"That's how *you* see the world, not her. From what I've heard, Nem sees it differently. The old saying is that the eyes are the windows to the soul, and like this, they fade into the background."

"So should I do the edges in black?"

I shook my head. "That doesn't feel right, either." I tapped my finger against my chin, then it came to me. "Give me a moment."

I went back to my own room, digging through the large chest that held all my art supplies. I had no idea why I'd kept it with me, why I had these things even when I knew I couldn't use them. At least it proved useful this time. I grabbed what I needed then returned to Kenz.

When I entered, I found her leaning forward, her face a breath from the canvas, her eyes locked on Nem's as if she could figure out the problem if she only got a little closer.

It made me smile, especially with how she bit down on her bottom lip, chewing anxiously.

"Try this." I handed what I'd found to Kenz.

She took it without hesitation, reminding me again just how trusting she really was. She stared down at the pen. "What's this?"

"It's a special pen. The ink is made with crushed pearl that sparkles in the light. This one will come out a dark brown that isn't quite black, but when the light hits it, it'll shimmer. It should draw attention to the eyes without giving them the same hard line as the rest of the painting."

Kenz stared down at the pen, her hair falling forward so I couldn't even see her expression. She closed her hand around the pen as though it were precious. "You know," she said, her voice soft. "You might not be able to paint anymore, but don't ever think you're useless. You aren't."

The conversation went quiet, because honestly, I had no idea what to say back to that. How was I supposed to respond to a statement like that?

You sure don't play fair.

"Make sure you eat," I said instead. "I know you want to work, but you aren't going to be much use if you end up with your glucose going crazy."

Kenz flashed me a smile that made my heart race, and what the fuck was up with that? I'd had models spread their thighs for me countless times and none had *ever* made me feel like this.

I'd told Kenz she couldn't possibly love us, but I was starting to fear I'd already fallen for her.

* * * *

Kenz

I stared down at my cell phone, the one Tor had given me so long ago. They'd removed the restrictions on it, which gave me the chance to call whoever I wanted. I'd still bet they kept an eye on it, but it gave me a little more freedom. In addition, they'd sworn that they'd turned off the bug in my glucose monitor.

Not that I believed them. I kept the thing wrapped in a sock to muffle anything, just in case. They could track it with GPS, but I didn't like the idea of them listening in.

Of course, with that freedom came unpleasantness, as I spotted the icon on the front screen that would connect me with Lorien.

They'd explained the reasoning to me, but that didn't mean I liked it one bit. I didn't want to talk to him anymore, to get any closer to him, but I understood the plan. Besides, this was my problem at the end of the day. Lorien wanted *me*. I couldn't sit back and do nothing while the men fixed it for me, could I?

Hayden had offered to stay, but I'd said no. I could do this on my own, right? Besides, it would only feel that much more awkward if anyone watched me while speaking with Lorien.

I've put it off long enough, right?

I forced myself to press the button on the screen labeled only as *Call*. It would route the call through the phone Bradley had left us and dial the one he'd given to Lorien. In short? It would allow us to speak without risking either of us.

"Hello?" The answer came so fast that it didn't have time to ring. Had he been waiting? The thought of him sitting there, phone in hand, was *almost* charming. At least, it might have been if I didn't already know what a horrible person he was. His voice was altered as it had been before.

"Hello." My greeting came out as a whisper.

"I'm glad you called, Kenz. I'd started to worry you might not."

"I was nervous. Can you blame me?"

"No, I can't. Anyone in your position would be cautious about such a discussion. We haven't had a great introduction, after all, and I'm sure you've gotten stories about me. I think I would be more disappointed if you put yourself in danger by rushing into a foolish situation without consideration." He sounded strange because of the voice changer, but he also sounded far more relaxed than the last time.

Perhaps because this was supposed to be a conversation? Maybe he didn't feel as guarded when it was just us?

I thought about what would have happened if I'd arrived at that hotel, if I'd gotten handed over to him instead of the men finding me and bringing me back?

Would he speak to me this nicely? Or was this just a game to him, a way to get me to do what he wanted until I no longer had a choice to obey?

"How are you feeling?" Lorien asked.

"Good."

"You sound tired."

"Everyone tells me that," I admitted.

"Then it is probably true." His words held a teasing tone which felt completely at odds with the man I'd heard about. "Do you struggle with sleep?"

"Sometimes."

"Nightmares?" When I didn't answer, he sighed softly. "Probably from when Kyler shot you."

"How do you know about that?" I asked so quickly that it surprised even me. Then again, almost no one knew about me, so the idea that he had so much information unnerved me.

"I have a very good network of information, Kenz. You should simply assume that I know everything about you."

"Why, though? Why do you care about me at all? A man in your position could have any woman he wants, so why me?"

"Because I want you. Isn't that obvious by now? We're meant to be. I knew it the first time I saw you, the first time I spoke to you."

"And when exactly was that?"

He laughed softly. "Don't worry about that right now. Just trust that I want what's best for you."

"Why do it like *this* then?"

"Because I'm not a man who leaves anything to chance. I don't like to risk not getting what I want, so I ensure things go my way. That's true of my professional life and my personal one. When I found out where you were, it only made sense to make sure you were mine."

"And you thought buying me at an auction was the way to do that?"

"Perhaps not the normal way, but when I spoke to the auction house, I made it perfectly clear that any harm to you would be unacceptable. By going through them, I ensured a safe handover. It also allowed me to stay far enough away that I would take no blame for your disappearance."

"And you planned to just abduct me? Take me away from my old life?"

"I'd hoped you would see reason eventually and choose to stay with me on your own."

"That's a pretty far-fetched hope."

"Is it? You seem taken with the men who did buy you. Stress does strange things to people, creates bonds stronger than most people realize. It speeds along connections and can cause people who would never give each other a chance to fall in love. It wasn't so crazy an idea when you consider how you cling to your captors. I'd hoped after some time with me, you'd see that I loved you, that I cared about you, that you'd grow to feel that way in return."

I wanted to argue with him but…he wasn't wrong. I thought about how I relied on Hayden, how Vance's smile made me happy, how I enjoyed sitting quietly with Tor, how Char's sharp tongue was normal to me now.

I'd accepted them all, and I wasn't sure that would have happened in any other situation.

It made my stomach clench uncomfortably, as I considered what might have happened if the auction had gone Lorien's way, if he'd taken me from the start. Would I have fallen for him?

What if I'd never met my men…?

The idea made me sick. I hated it, wanted to reassure myself that wasn't possible, that I wasn't so fickle as to fall for someone like Lorien. "I wouldn't do that," I whispered.

"No?" His tone encouraged me to talk back, which struck me as strange. Normally, men in Lorien's position preferred their women silent and obedient.

"No. I know the things you've done, so how could I just accept all that?"

"But I'm not the only one. You know Tor is a hired killer who has murdered more people than I could hope to track down. Hayden was a soldier before he worked security, and he has killed just because of orders from superiors. Vance might not be a killer, but he's hurt so many women, some who never really recovered. Char has bilked millions out of people, ruining them financially. They are far from the innocent people you like to pretend. They are not so different from me, except I am more successful."

I tightened my fingers around the phone, not sure how to respond, how to argue with facts that were true. It terrified me, the idea that if I'd met Lorien first, he might have twisted my mind, might have had me thinking the same about him.

He sighed softly, as though having grown tired as well. "Sleep, Kenz. We will speak again tomorrow. Goodnight, my dear."

With that, he hung up, leaving me in the silence of the room alone.

The things he said rang in my head, and I knew sleep wouldn't come easily tonight. Instead, I traced the steps I'd taken since the auction, trying to see if I'd made mistakes, if I'd missed things I should have seen.

I hated that out of everyone in my life, I knew that I could trust myself the least...

Chapter Four

Kenz

I rubbed my eyes as I curled into the smallest ball possible on the couch. Being a woman really sucked a lot of the time. I had to deal with men who didn't respect me, I'd had to dance to their tune my whole damn life, and once a month my uterus decided to tear itself apart like one of those surprise renovation shows.

It was that third one that plagued me right now.

The TV played, a show I hadn't even tried paying attention to. It was some reality cooking show, and the food didn't even make me hungry. My cramps hurt far too much for food to sound appetizing.

Char was home, working in his room, so I'd hardly seen him. Everyone else had things to do, which was why I'd settled myself in the living room instead of my own room. I had no classes, and I'd taken today off from painting.

A long hot bath later and an early bedtime were the best I could do to try to relax. My periods weren't fun, but at least they tended to be on the short side, only lasting about three days. I considered that a small miracle.

My eyes drifted closed, and I figured sleeping was better than hurting. My rest was light, the type where I wasn't sure I actually slept at all. I must have, though, because the soft murmur of voices roused me later.

"She's been sleeping all day?"

"Yeah, so? We know she doesn't sleep well. She probably needed to catch up."

"What if she's sick?" Hayden's worried voice pulled me fully from my sleep.

I opened my eyes, surprised to find the windows dark. *I guess I napped the rest of the day…*

My head rested on something warm, and I frowned for a moment. Had someone given me a pillow?

"Morning, Sleeping Beauty."

I looked up to find Vance smiling down at me, the position strange for a long moment until my brain made sense of it. *My head is in his lap.*

I bolted upright, my cheeks burning. Had I done that by accident? Had I cuddled up to him in my sleep?

How mortifying!

Vance only released an amused chuckle.

Hayden caught our exchange, because he came right over and crouched in front of me. He set his palm on my forehead. It made me feel like a kid again, with someone taking my temperature. "Are you feeling alright?"

I nodded but didn't push him away. His touch felt nice. It wasn't physical, but just the sensation of someone being there beside me was *exactly* what I needed.

He pulled back, making me miss his tough. "No fever."

"I'm not sick," I assured him, then went to get up, to grab some water to help wake me up. The grogginess from napping so long made my head fuzzy and my body heavy.

However, as soon as I got mostly to my feet, my uterus decided to act like an armadillo rolling up on itself, and I gasped a sharp breath before giving up on the whole standing idea. Instead, I sat back down and curled forward as if protecting a wound instead of a poorly planned-out reproductive system.

Hayden was on the spot, catching my chin and lifting my gaze to his. He searched my face, checking my eyes, then placed his fingers on my pulse. His motions were surprisingly frantic, something rare from the normally calm man.

I'd seen him face off against attackers with weapons with less concern than he treated this. *There's nothing for him to fight right now.*

Or perhaps it was better to say there was nothing to take a hit for, no bullet to jump in front of.

"She isn't sick," Vance said with a soft laugh. He sounded like a teenager who enjoyed picking on a kid that didn't know Santa wasn't real.

"What's wrong, then?"

Poor, stupid man.

Hayden was sweet, but he really didn't know much about women, did he?

Vance sat back, a smirk across his perfect face. "She might seem like a kid, but she *is* a woman. Don't you know about that special time of the month for women?"

Hayden's tan skin flushed, the color not so obvious as if Char or Vance had done it, but still visible. He yanked backward as if embarrassed. "Oh," he said.

"I'm not contagious, you jerk," I muttered.

"I didn't mean it like that," Hayden rushed out.

I gave him a glare, not all that mad, but pain tended to make people meaner than they would be any other time.

"What can I do?" Hayden asked.

"Nothing." I brought my knees up, enjoying my soft pajamas that rested loose on my waist. "I'm fine. I just have to take it easy today. By tomorrow, I'll be fine."

Hayden pressed his lips together, then rushed out of the room.

How can he be so responsible in some ways and such a kid in others?

"So that's why you've been sleeping?" Char asked. "I thought you were just lazy."

Vance breathed in loudly, wincing. "Bad choice, buddy."

"What? I can't remember the last time I napped all afternoon. Must be nice."

Vance shook his head, muttering softly under his breath. "I know you're smarter than this. You can't tell me you've never dealt with a woman in this state? If you think they're dangerous normally, it's *nothing* compared to when they're continuously bleeding for five days. They get understandably testy at those times."

Char rolled his eyes, then dropped his gaze back to his phone as though bored with our conversation.

Good. Nothing was coming of it.

Hayden came back in, a box in his hands. He held it out to me, and I took it out of habit.

My gaze went to the present, which made no fucking sense.

"What is this?"

52

"You need them, right? I went to the store last week." He looked so damned proud that I just kept moving my gaze between the box and the idiot in front of me.

"We picked up tampons when we were at the store already," I reminded him.

"I thought more might be better," he said, hesitation in his tone implying he might have caught on that it wasn't the best idea.

"Do you think they're flowers or something? What's next, you're going to put them into a bouquet?"

Sure, I *knew* he'd been trying to help, but the absolute idiocy of him took me by surprise enough that all I could think about was how stupid he really was. How was it that he'd managed to be so successful if he was this horrible with women?

Then again, it must be nice not to have to worry about such things. It was easy for him not to know about things like periods or walking at night alone or any of the bullshit I had to think about. How unfair was that?

A hand wrapped around my wrist, and I cut a glare in that direction, expecting it to be Hayden trying to apologize. What was next? He'd gift me with birth control like they were mints?

Except, golden eyes met mine. Tor tugged softly until I got to my feet. He took the tampons and shoved the box at Hayden's chest, then pulled me from the living room.

I had no idea what he was doing, yet I wasn't sure I cared. I hurt and I was still tired and feeling like I had to take care of Hayden annoyed me. Tor guided me down the hallway, but he passed my room and took me to his. We passed by his bed, which reminded me of the first night I'd slept here, when I'd spent the night right there, in those blankets.

He'd been so scary back then, an unknown I didn't trust. *How things have changed.*

We went into the bathroom, and Tor released me to place the stopper in the tub, then turned on the water. He felt the temperature, fiddling with the handles until he seemed to find it perfect.

After that, he opened the cabinet beneath the vanity and pulled out a wicker box filled with bath items. He took a round purple bath bomb, tore open the plastic and tossed it into the water. It fizzed as it dissolved, the water turning a soft purple while the scent of lavender filled the room.

He gestured at the bathtub, then walked out, closing the door behind him.

Was that it?

He was always quiet, but that unnerved even me. Obviously, he wanted me to get in, but was that really okay? In his bath? My heart raced at the implications of getting naked in his space, and at least it helped me not think about the pain at all.

Instead of fighting it—what was the point for that?—I did as he wanted and stripped down. I set the pile of clothing on the counter, then stepped into the water. It was only about a quarter filled, and the heat soaked into my skin immediately.

I eased down, having to acclimate to the temperature, and by the time I finished, the bath was about halfway full.

Steam filled the room as the water ran, and I had to admit, the baths here were nice. I'd mostly taken quick showers, especially because I hardly got enough time to myself to even hope for something relaxing like a bath. Instead, I'd jump into the water to wash off before *someone* needed me.

Despite the fact I felt safe with these men, I didn't really feel all that relaxed.

My eyes fluttered closed as I leaned back, the water just high enough to cover my breasts now. The bath bomb had changed the color enough to obscure me, which made me feel more at ease.

A tapping next to me made me jump, and when I twisted, I found Tor crouched beside the bathtub.

I wrapped my arms around my chest, especially since sitting up had meant the water no longer covered them. "What the hell!?" I asked.

He turned his head slightly, as if to show he wasn't looking at me, then tapped against the tub ledge again to bring my attention there. A small plate with pieces of chocolate sat there along with a cup of something warm.

"Is that regular chocolate?"

He pulled a wrapper from his pocket and held it up, pointing to the place where it said 'sugar-free.' The fact he thought about such things warmed me more than the hot water, honestly.

"Thanks," I said before I picked up a piece and took a small bite from the corner. It melted almost instantly, and the taste was rich and fantastic. It was a darker chocolate, which was great because that normally had less sugar anyway. It meant it was easier to hide the sugar substitute after taste that often came with such treats. "It's good."

Tor nodded, then reached across the tub and turned off the faucet, the water having reached near the top edge.

He rose, his stance telling me he was going to leave. Before I knew what I was doing, I reached out and caught his pant leg.

He frowned, staring down at where I held him, the line between his eyebrows adorable.

Embarrassment overcame my wants. What was I doing? Wet spots remained on his pants when I released him, reminding me of how stupid I was acting. "Sorry," I whispered, sinking back into the water. "It's fine."

Tor let out a long sigh before walking out. His absence hit me hard, the room incredibly silent without even the water running.

Just as I considered getting out—it didn't feel nearly as relaxing anymore—the door opened again and Tor walked back in. He held a cushion in his hand, which he tossed on the floor beside the tub. He huffed softly as he sat, the action making it almost feel as though we were in the bath together.

Was this what that would feel like?

My mind went off on its own, aided by the atmosphere and heat and Tor's closeness. I pictured candles all over the room, the flickering light romantic. I pictured Tor not on the floor, but in the water, his dark skin bare to me. I'd seen him shirtless, when we sparred, but what would it be like to see all of him?

There was no question that he was strong, but he was lean. When I'd touched him, when we'd worked out together, I'd felt just how firm his body was.

"You're sure better at this than they are," I said. "It surprised me. You're so quiet, I figured you'd have no idea how to deal with women. Why is that?" As soon as I asked, I regretted my choice.

I didn't have my phone, which meant he had no way of answering. It was like asking someone in a wheelchair to follow you up the stairs.

"Sorry," I whispered, embarrassed by the mistake.

Tor snorted softly, then leaned over to where the box still was. He took out a set of crayons.

"Is it arts and crafts time?"

He offered me a look that said he got the joke but wasn't all that impressed before opening the set of five colors. He shifted the pillow toward the other side of the tub, then took the blue crayon and wrote on the white tile that made up the surround of the large tub. *Bath crayons.*

I smiled when the words appeared on the tile. "Did you get those expecting to get into the bath with me?" I lifted my eyebrow to mock Tor about it.

He pressed his lips together, then wrote more. *I might have considered that…*

And just like that, he'd turned the tables. Instead of me teasing him, he'd managed to embarrass me. It always seemed that no matter how hard I tried, I couldn't keep the upper hand with these men for long before they took it right back.

"Not funny," I whispered. "It's rude to tease me like that after rejecting me, you know?"

He took a washcloth and dipped it into the water. My body reacted, as if thinking he were reaching for me, my breath catching in my lungs and my hopes rising. However, he only used the now wet cloth to clear away the words from the tile before adding more.

I'm not teasing. Just being honest.

And just like that, it was impossible to be mad at him. He was just too honest.

So instead, I went back to my previous question. "So how is it you know how to take care of girls on their periods? Are you secretly a playboy and I just don't know it?"

My sister.

"You have a sister?" Him telling me about himself, about his life, had me sitting up before remembering about the entire naked thing and sinking back into the water to hide.

He chuckled and nodded. *She's four years younger. Our mother worked a lot, so it was mostly just the two of us. I took care of her.*

I thought about that, surprised by how normal that seemed.

At first, when I'd met Tor, I'd thought him closed off. He was so silent that it felt like he didn't give a damn about anyone else.

He was a far cry from Hayden, who hovered over others constantly.

However, the longer I spent time with Tor, the more I saw his soft side, the one so easy to miss due to his silence. He'd gotten me sugar-free treats to ensure I could safely enjoy them. He'd run me this bath, gotten these items to make me comfortable.

He was kind in a way that showed he cared for others, which meant the idea of him taking care of a younger sister didn't seem so far-fetched anymore.

"What's she like?"

He sighed, his shoulders drooping. It took him so long to move, I suspected he wouldn't respond. When he did, he wrote his response smaller. Did he expect to write a lot, or did he just want to make the words as little as possible, like that made them less painful? *She's dead. When she was twenty, she was in the wrong place at the wrong time. There was a drive-by, and she just happened to be in the way.*

The letters were less neat than they'd been before. In fact, they were shaky, as though his hand had trembled as he'd written them.

I sat up, not caring about the water level, and set my hand over his where he'd frozen, the crayon still against the tile. "I'm sorry," I told him, wishing I had something more to say than that.

I remembered after my mom had died, how many people had told me they were sorry. They'd filed in to give their condolences to my father and me, but they'd all been empty. The people didn't *do* anything but say pointless words that had changed nothing.

Which was why that sorry tasted like ash on my tongue.

He pulled his hand away and grabbed the rag again, clearing the writing. I didn't lean back again as he wrote.

It's why I'm so against collateral damage. Losing someone is terrible, but pointless death bothers me. There is this emptiness when someone dies for no reason at all.

"And that's why you're after Lorien."

He nodded. *He killed and maimed so many people, and for what? All those deaths were for no reason at all. It is unforgivable.* He sighed, appearing more worn out than I'd seen before. *I know doing this won't clear my debt when it comes to the blood on my hands, but it will even some of that score.*

I'd known what Tor did, that he killed, that he'd taken countless lives, but I'd rarely heard that from him. It was strange, because I'd never seen such hesitation with Colton. He killed for a living as well, but he'd never seen himself as bad because of it.

It made me wonder how Tor had gotten into that line of work. He seemed far too kind.

However, I got the sense that question wouldn't get answered, that it would only sour our conversation, so I let it go.

He cleared his throat, the sound awkward and drawing my attention to him. He stared, and when I dropped my gaze, I realized why.

I'd sat up again, which meant the water no longer covered my breasts. The air in the room wasn't cold, but compared to the hot water, my nipples had reacted and tightened to stiff points.

Or maybe that's because he's staring.

My heart pounded against my rib cage, so loud I worried he'd hear it, that he'd know just how he affected me, just how much I wanted to cross that line.

With so much against us...who knew how much time I had left? Whether that ended with success or failure or death or capture, no future I'd envisioned included a happily ever after with him. It meant that I wanted to feel...whatever this was, whatever it could be.

Tor jerked his gaze away, his breathing rougher than it had been before. At least that proved he was interested in my breasts, if nothing else. It also showed that a bit of ogling was all he'd offer me.

Instead of complaining—what was the point in that?—I leaned back and closed my eyes, letting the heat do its job and relax me. Before I knew it, I'd fallen asleep.

Tor

She's way too vulnerable. The thought had struck me so many times since meeting Kenz.

She wasn't stupid, not in the least. In fact, each time I learned more about her, I recognized just how smart she truly was. She didn't leave herself open because she didn't know the dangers, but because she was brave enough to trust those around her.

It struck me as strange, and each time I witnessed it, an unease inside me grew.

Did she just not view me as a man with needs? That happened, at times, because of my inability to speak. People treated me like a child, as though a lack of speech made me less of an adult.

Was that why she felt comfortable enough around me to fall asleep while completely naked?

What if I were someone else? My hand clenched at the idea of what another man might do in this situation. A picture in my head showed some faceless figure touching her, using the advantage to take what they wanted.

I let out a tortured sigh as I pushed away the thought. Nothing good would come of thinking about things that hadn't happened.

Her breathing had evened out, and when she started to slide into the water, I caught her arm. Sure, touching her when she was naked wasn't my first choice, but I couldn't let her drown.

Perhaps I should have woken her, but she slept so rarely and so fitfully, I just couldn't bring myself to do so. I slid my arm behind her, hooking my fingers around her side beneath her opposite arm, careful not to let my touch wander to anything less innocent. This kept her upright enough so she didn't drown.

It also meant that sometimes, as she breathed deeply, her breasts rose out of the water and into view.

And damn, did her pink nipples tempt me. They seemed to tease me, just begging for attention, like two flowers floating on top of the water.

Stop it, you pervert! No matter how much I scolded myself or tried to look away, however, I couldn't stop the way my brain stayed locked in that cycle.

Finally, when I feared my self-control wasn't *nearly* as good as I would have liked, I gave in.

I shook her arm, but she barely woke at all. Was she really that tired?

Giving up, I grabbed my robe and used it when I hauled her out of the tub. I didn't bother to get her arms into the sleeves, using the robe instead like a large towel. Her hair was dry since she hadn't taken a full shower, and the terrycloth robe soaked up most of the water on her skin.

The idea of taking her back to her room hit me, but then I thought about running into anyone else. She was naked and vulnerable, and I found myself reluctant to let anyone else see her this way.

Which was silly.

Silly or not, though, I couldn't seem to let go of that. Instead, I tucked her into my bed. She'd slept here that first night, and since then, the room had felt far too quiet, far too lonely.

Which was strange, since I'd never thought of my life in those terms before. Being alone had been normal to me, comfortable, so why did solitude bother me now?

I sat on the edge of the bed, staring at her. Her hair was braided back, as she often left it when at home, but strands had escaped from the rest and fallen into her face. She looked even younger when asleep, even more innocent of the world around her. How could she sleep so comfortably with me around like this?

Why wasn't she awake? Watching me to ensure I didn't harm her?

Because she is a fool. And it sure lured me in…

I sighed, then went to rise, to leave her be. A good night's sleep would help her feel better in the morning, and there was no good reason for me to remain.

Before I could stand, however, Kenz shifted, wrapping an arm around me as though I were a stuffed animal, and she didn't plan to let go.

Any resolve I might have had fled at that, at the way even in her sleep she seemed to instinctually crave contact and affection. It made me wonder just how starved for such things she really was.

So I did the dumbest thing I could have—I turned and stretched out beside her. I pulled the blanket over her—no need to tempt myself more than I already was—but stayed on top of it myself.

She scooted closer, nuzzling against my chest as if there were no better place in the world for her.

And me? I was the idiot who wrapped an arm around her and closed my eyes, savoring the chance to feel warm and comfortable, no matter how short that time would be.

Chapter Five

Kenz

I reached above me and stretched, the tight muscles in my back loosening. The sun beat down, but somehow, it felt nice. Maybe it was because I'd spent far too much time inside, so now I welcomed even this heat.

After spending all morning sketching with no notable progress, I'd decided a little time outside was exactly what I needed. I had my headphones on, music playing, as I weeded the small plot of flowers in the backyard.

I'd never seen any of the men out here, which made me suspect they hired a service. Of course, given how overrun with weeds it had gotten, the service hadn't come in a while.

They probably stopped it when I came to live here.

Yet another way my presence was interrupting other people's lives. Instead of letting that get to me, I pulled another weed out then added it to the bucket I'd set beside the raised bed.

One of the things I'd learned over the years was that just plugging along wasn't the best way to deal with something. Too often we ended up focused on what needed to get done, and the ways to do it would escape us. The fact was that when I hit a wall, the best way to keep going wasn't to keep slamming my head against it.

So instead of sitting there, staring at bad sketch after bad sketch, I'd taken myself outside.

The sensation of people looking at me let me know one of the men kept an eye on me. It wasn't a surprise, and while it would have annoyed me any other time, I found myself smiling at the familiar feeling. Even if I looked up, I doubted I'd spot whoever it was.

They wanted me to feel like I had time alone even if I didn't.

Which brought me back to this morning, to when I'd woken naked in Tor's bed.

No, not *just* naked, but beside the man himself. Seeing him like that had startled me, the way his hair seemed messier, the relaxed muscles of his face. I still couldn't tell what he was thinking, of course, but his expression didn't have the same forced blankness I normally saw.

Unable to face him, I'd slipped from the bed. A part of me thought he'd woken—I couldn't really believe I could get out of his bed without him noticing. His fingers had tightened for a moment around me, as if to hold me there, before loosening again and letting me escape.

Later, when he came to get a cup of coffee, he hadn't mentioned the night before.

Was that for his comfort or mine?

Did it even matter?

Not really.

My cheeks burned as I remembered how he'd looked at me, and that had *nothing* to do with the hot sun.

My fingers itched, as though to pick up a pencil. Wait…did I want to draw that?

That lust in his golden eyes, the pressing of his fingers into my skin, the heartbeat long seconds where we had both rested on the precipice between what we wanted and what we couldn't have.

Grisham's words hit me again, about art that made people feel. An image like that would make them feel for sure…

However, the last thing I wanted was a lecture about how foolish I was, how I didn't want what I wanted. I'd had enough rejection already—I didn't need to court any more.

The idea took me back to my last piece of Nem. Grisham said I needed to put myself out there, to tear off my skin to expose the nerves. Could I do that?

And if I could, how?

My mind wandered as I worked at the weeds. What mattered most to me? What moved me?

I thought back about growing up. I remembered so little of it, at least before my mother died. I had a few memories of her, but not many. I recalled the painting I did of her, one based on pictures, but that was just her.

What if I painted us all? The four of us who made up that family. My mother, my father, Nem and me. Could I show the cracks between us? The pain? The distance? The blood?

Before I considered it, I took out my phone and dialed Colton's number. I turned off my headphones and hit the speaker button to make it easier to listen.

He answered with a voice I rarely heard from him, one colder and darker than I knew. "What?"

"Answering the phone like that won't make you any friends."

I could almost *hear* his smile across the line, as though the dropping of his guard made an audible noise. "I don't recognize this number, Kenz."

"That's because it's new. You should be grateful you have it, now."

"Oh, trust me, I am." He chuckled, then the sound of muffled shouting came through from his end. A grunt, then the tearing of tape, and finally silence. "You don't normally call me. Is everything okay?"

I decided to tactfully ignore the fact that he clearly had someone tied up. Sometimes relationships required some willful ignorance, after all. He pretended not to notice that I used to feed my vegetables to the family dog, and I pretended not to know that he killed people for a living.

Maybe our family is more normal than I thought.

"I have an end-of-year exhibit coming up."

"It's in eight weeks, right?"

Normal people might have wondered how he knew something I'd never told him, but I had long ago stopped worrying about such things. If I called and he didn't know something, that might have concerned me. "That's right. It'll determine my placement for next year. The thing is, I'm having trouble coming up with work that's good enough."

"You're too hard on yourself, Kenz. You're a fantastic artist. I'm sure you'll do great."

His praise made me laugh. It was sweet, of course, and I appreciated it, but I also knew better than to trust him. I could have smeared dirt on a page and Colton would have killed anyone who dared say a bad word about it.

"I'm not calling you for reassurance, Colton. I need a favor."

"Anything," he said without hesitation.

"I need you to get some pictures for me. Ones of the family, of all of us together."

And there was the hesitation. He wouldn't have paused at all had I needed him to kill, kidnap or torture anyone, but I asked for a few photos and he acted like it was a crazy idea.

"Are you sure you want to do that?" he asked, his words slow and cautious.

"I know that having anything that connects me back to my real life is dangerous, but if I can't get this exhibit right, what's the point of the last year?"

"And how will painting something like that help?"

"Because art is supposed to make people *feel* something. I was reminded of that recently, that it isn't about making pretty things that don't matter. If I'm going to think about things that matter, that are important to me, what better way is there than family? Than my past?"

His sigh was long and drawn out, a sure sign he didn't agree with my conclusion. "Your father had most of that packed away, you know?"

"I know, but that's why I'm asking you. You would know exactly where he kept that sort of thing, and you won't pry as much as the others would."

"I don't know about this," he muttered.

"It's a risk, but it's important to me. I promise I'll be careful with them, that I won't let anyone else see them, so no one finds out who I am."

"I don't care about that," he snapped.

His sharp tone caught me so off guard I didn't respond right away. Colton rarely spoke to me like that, always careful not to frighten me.

"Sorry," he whispered, his voice the same I was used to, as though he'd calmed himself down on purpose. "But it isn't about anyone finding out who you are. If you wanted to tell everyone exactly who you are, it wouldn't bother me. We'd hire security and make sure you were safe, but I never was a fan of you hiding in the first place."

"So why do you care if I see pictures?"

"Because those were ugly days, Kenz. They were times when you were alone, frightened, used. You were raised under a contact microscope, forced to endure the death of your mother and sister, then torn away from what little stability you had left. If I had it my way, I'd be happy if everything before you going to Florida was wiped from you mind, if you could forget all the pain from those days. You are out there, on your own, and now you want to open those wounds?"

His words took me by surprise. Colton hadn't ever been a real-feelings sort of man.

Hell, no one had been in my past. My mother had been smart but reserved, expecting us to live up to our bloodline. My father hadn't given a damn about anything except me doing as I was told. My sister had been my soft place, before she'd disappeared, and after she came back? She didn't enjoy talking about emotions at all, as though by ignoring them she could pretend she had none. The Quad had been no different, all of them quick to take care of me but having no understanding of how I really felt.

It meant him not only being aware of such a thing but voicing his opinion showed just how far he'd come, how much he'd changed in the year since rekindling his relationship with Nem.

It warmed me. He deserved happiness — they all did. It might not be the same sort of happiness most people found, but it was their own.

"I understand your point. I'm not going to pretend that going through that is going to be all fun and games, but that doesn't mean I shouldn't do it. I want to give this exhibit my all, to show what I'm capable of, and that means looking deep inside myself. Please, Colton, I need your help."

The silence crackled, and I could imagine his expression. His dark eyes narrowed, a worry line between his brows. He really was easy to read for someone like me, someone who knew him so well.

"I have a family album," he admitted softly. "Your mother started it when pregnant with Nem, and she kept it up until her death. I added pictures after that, but I didn't have the same skills she did. I'll overnight it to the school since you apparently don't go to your apartment anymore." The censure in his tone made me laugh, especially because he must know better than to directly ask me about that.

It seemed Nem had him on a tight leash when it came to me.

"Thank you."

"Not so fast," he interrupted. "You know how this world works. Nothing comes for free."

"You're charging me for a favor?"

"That's right. You want to be an adult, right? Well, this is the real world. You want a favor from me, then you have to offer one in return."

I felt like I was a kid again, outmaneuvered by Colton when I'd thought I was being *so* smart. "Fine.

What do you want?"

"Tell me who you're living with."

And just like that, he slips his leash.

I almost burst out laughing at how quickly he'd done whatever he wanted.

He quickly added on, "I'm not asking for names or addresses or anything. I know you want your space, and even if I hate it, I'll give you that. I just can't comfortably sleep at night unless I hear directly from you that everything is okay. That you're safe. That you're living with people who care about you and will look out for you." He paused, then softened his voice more. "My job is very dangerous, you know? If I can't sleep properly, it might affect my performance."

I rolled my eyes, wishing he could see that over the phone. "What, are you taking lessons from Dane, now? Guilt tripping is beneath you."

"I'm a man who uses whatever weapon at my disposal works the best. You're one of the few who is sweet enough that guilt works."

Even after he told me that, I couldn't exactly refuse. Even if he were joking about it affecting his work, I had no doubt he really was worried. If reassuring him that I was okay helped ease his burden a little, well, I owed him far more than that.

"The people I'm staying with are taking good care of me," I assured him. "They haven't done anything to hurt me, and I don't believe that they would."

"They? When Jarrod told me you were staying with four men, I really thought he'd lost his mind. I figured he'd gotten old and senile and we'd get to put him out of his misery."

"You mean 'have' to put him out of his misery, right?"

"No, I meant exactly what I said." The prickly way the Quad interacted with Jarrod never failed to amuse me, and his comment was no exception. "I never figured our sweet, innocent little Kenz would be shacking up with four men."

"I'm only innocent because *you* all always scared off my boyfriends," I pointed out.

"Of course we did. What sort of useless bodyguard would let their charge around boys with less than pure intentions?"

I didn't bother to hide my laugh that time, amused by the way he pouted over the line. Still, I kept us on track. "Yeah, well, these aren't boys."

"*Wonderful.* That makes me feel better."

"Stop frowning—you'll give yourself wrinkles. Don't worry, they aren't interested in me at all."

"They aren't? Then they're idiots who don't have two brain cells to rub together and I should kill them for that."

"And if they had wanted me?"

"Then I'd kill them for that."

"So they need to die either way?"

"I don't make the rules, Kenz, I only enforce them."

I smiled, enjoying the easy back and forth. Sure, I was keeping things from him, and he was keeping them from me, but our long, shared history made me feel like I was home again.

I'd missed this. Even though they annoyed me, they were my family.

"I really am okay," I promised him. "You have enough problems of your own without taking on imaginary issues with me."

"Fine. I won't kill anyone—*yet.* Just promise me that if things go wrong, no matter how small the problem seems, that you'll reach out to us. We care about you, Kenz, and we've got your back."

"I know you do. I probably haven't every really thanked you for it, but I know I wouldn't be here if it wasn't for you all."

"Don't thank me yet," Colton muttered. "I might still come and put a bullet through one of those men's skulls as a warning."

"Since when is a headshot a warning?"

"It's a warning to the other three." He said that without any laughter in his voice, which had me choosing to pretend it was a joke.

I said goodbye and hung up afterward, ready to end the conversation.

"Charming guy."

Char's voice made me jump, and when I looked over, I realized he'd taken a seat beside me at some point during my conversation.

"Hayden said I could call people," I rushed out.

"I know."

"So why do you look so annoyed?"

"I always look like this."

"Not always." I thought back to his smile, to how damn nice he'd seemed at first.

He sighed and bent one leg, then set his arm on that knee. "You know, one of these days you're going to realize that nice isn't always best."

"I'm not asking you to be fake nice. It would just be great if you didn't act like you hate me."

"I don't hate you." His words came out so soft that I turned toward him, unsure I'd heard him right.

"Could have fooled me."

"I pretend to be nice because it greases wheels and smooths things over. It makes life easier when you give people what they want. You're different."

"Lucky me. I just don't have anything you need enough to pretend, huh?"

He shook his head but didn't look my way. "Why haven't you told your sister and the Quad about us? About what's really going on? If you did, they'd come out and help."

"If I did, they'd kill you all."

"Like they'd be the first people to try. That can't be the whole reason."

I sat there for a moment, the sun making me sweat, my brain working through everything before I offered him an answer. "I've lost most of the people in my life that mattered to me. I lost my mom, my father, my sister, the bodyguards. Even if I've gotten some of them back, in some way, I still went through losing them. If I told Nem what was going on, if I told her about Lorien, she'd rush out here. Whether it was safe or not, what the dangers were, those things wouldn't even occur to her. She'd show up here ready to destroy Lorien."

"And? Last I checked, she seems more than capable of doing that."

"In California she is, where all her power is. Here, though? She'd be at a disadvantage, especially because Lorien knows about her. He knows who I am, so he'd see her coming. I can't lose anyone else, especially not because they were protecting me." I thought back to that night, to when my father had pointed that gun at me. "When my father shot me, Nem had been ready to take the bullet. If she could have, she'd have thrown herself in front of me without thinking about it. Too many people value my life above their own, even though I'm nothing special."

"Nothing special, huh?" He snorted as he asked that, his tone that sarcastic mocking that he so often used.

"I'm really not. I grew up around people smarter and tougher than I was. Nem came from *nothing* when she came back for me, nothing but her skills and her backbone and she toppled the strongest crime family on the West Coast. Everyone around me has always been amazing, and me? Even when Hayden and I were attacked, and I had the gun, I couldn't pull the trigger."

I blew out a long breath full of frustration. "I'm weak, and other people always end up paying the price for that. So, no, I'm not going to call my sister and have her risk herself *again* for me. I can't handle anyone else getting hurt for me, not ever again."

Char said nothing, staring up at the house along with me. I'd expected him to tell me I was wrong—that was the usual response.

Char never did the expected thing, though. Instead, when he spoke, his voice came out incredibly soft. "Do you know why I started pretending to be other people? It was when I turned seven. I was getting shuffled from foster family to foster family, usually because people said my attitude was hard to deal with. I watched other kids get picked and settle down, and you know what? They were all sweet. They smiled and they said the right things and they never got angry. Me, though? No one wanted me. So on my seventh birthday, when I was sitting alone at a café with a candle I'd stolen from a supermarket stuck in a cupcake that I'd saved up to buy, I finally realized that the world doesn't want real. I became what others wanted, then. I smiled and became the perfect little angel. The next year, on my birthday, I sat at the table with my new family, with the cake they'd made for me, and it proved everything I thought. The world didn't want the real me."

His words burned, made me think about all the times when I'd chastised him for not being nicer, when I'd wanted the him he'd shown me that first day. I'd done the same thing, basically, had proven to him that the real him wasn't good enough.

So I leaned to the side until my arm pressed against his. "I won't deny that it'd be nice if you liked me — even a little — but I don't want you to be anyone other than who you are." I let my head rest against his shoulder. "Because this guy right here? He's not so bad."

Neither of us spoke again, letting the sun and the scent of the flower and soil fill the space instead.

These little moments between disasters made it all worth it.

* * * *

Hayden

My head pounded. I loved my work as a bodyguard, but there were days when the less fun parts of it got to me.

Funny enough, most people would think I meant the part where I had to put myself in danger for someone else. They figured the worst part of the job was taking a bullet or blade meant for a client.

That wasn't it, though. I was fine with those, wore the scars I'd collected with pride.

Instead, it was the administrative crap I loathed. The way to break a man wasn't through torture or pain, but through tax forms and bureaucracy. To that end, I'd spent most of the day dealing with such problems.

I'd handed over the majority of the work to a business manager, Laurie, but given the delicate nature of our work, some things still fell to me. We had clients who required strict nondisclosures, who refused to deal with anyone except me. We had clients we'd worked with for years who hated change, who felt as if I were their personal beck-and-call boy for any little problem they had. The business manager did his job well, but I'd built this company from nothing, so some things only I really understood.

"Administrative day?" Vance handed me a large can of sweet tea.

"How can you tell?" I nodded in thanks and pulled the tab to open the drink.

"About once every two months or so you get that same look on your face. It's your 'I had to kiss ass and do paperwork' face."

"And here I thought I hid it so well." I tipped the can back and took three large swigs of the drink. I avoided sugar best I could — I knew it wasn't good for me — but days like this called for an exception.

"Not really. You're a lot easier to read than you think."

"Really?" I huffed, annoyed at the idea of me being so bad at anything. "Most people say that when I'm on the job, they can't read me at all."

"Sure, when you're in bodyguard mode, but the rest of the time? Nope. You might as well scream out whatever is on your mind." Vance turned his gaze toward the house, then smirked. "Especially when it comes to *her*."

I wanted to smack my palm against the back of his head like a parent scolding a child pushing their luck too far, but I had a feeling doing that would only prove his point.

So instead, I took another drink of the tea.

"I really hate the administrative stuff," I admitted, "but I keep thinking about how this might be the last time I do it."

He didn't respond by telling me I was wrong—he knew better than that.

We'd gone into this knowing it would be the end. No one could touch a man like Lorien and expect to come out the other side unscathed. Instead, we were all prepared to throw away our futures to make our past right.

"Do you know what my last painting was?" Vance's voice was soft, and he didn't wait for my answer. "Two days before I went to that hotel, I painted this large picture of wildflowers. There were so many of them and my hand ached so bad by the end of the night after sketching them all. I'd worked for hours, my back sore, my neck tight, and even still, I'd only gotten maybe a third of them colored in. I remember so clearly outlining each one, picking the color, seeing the canvas come alive. I was thinking yesterday about how it'll never get finished. That's the last piece of work to my name and it'll always be half done like that."

I stared up at the sky, wishing that instead of the tea we had a couple beers. It seemed that sort of night, when alcohol could loosen tongues and the tightness in a man's chest from things they couldn't control.

"I have to go home tomorrow," Vance said.

"That time already?" I fought the desire to laugh at Vance's voice, as though he were getting sent to the gallows rather than a family dinner at the sort of home called an estate.

"No, normally I'd get another few months, but it seems my parents saw the interview."

"You had to know that might happen."

"Sure, but I'd hoped this would be over before I had to pay the piper." He flashed me a smile that reminded me of just how young he actually was. Hell, there were times I realized they were *all* so much younger than me. Sometimes I felt more like a babysitter than a colleague.

"You can't put it off just a bit longer?"

"I would if I could, but I've learned my lesson. I can get away with refusing exactly three invites before my parents start getting antsy. When that happens, well, Taylor shows up."

"*Taylor.*" Even I shuddered as I recalled the last time the Moore family guard dog had shown up to escort the '*young master*' back after Vance had ignored too many calls. The last thing I wanted was him in our space ever again. He was too smart, too shrewd. "Yeah, I'd appreciate it if you could keep him from stopping by again. I don't think Kenz would be thrilled with his questions, either."

I thought about Kenz facing off against Taylor, but the moment I did, I couldn't stop my chuckle. Kenz would have to look up and into the tall, stern man's face, but I had a feeling she wouldn't wilt at all. The more time I spent with her, the more I understood just how special she really was. She'd have easily faced off against him without any fear.

And hell, I'd bet Taylor would end up smitten, just like she won over every other person around her.

"So how are you going to get out of the questions?" I asked.

"No idea. Mom told me to bring '*that girl,*' but I can't put her through that. Bringing people to meet my parents is what I do to people I hate, after all."

"But if they don't meet her, they aren't going to leave you alone, right? Won't that just make this all more complicated? We don't want Taylor or anyone else in our business as we get closer to our goal."

"Yeah, I know, but…" His voice trailed off, but I didn't need him to explain, did I?

He didn't want Kenz any more involved with us than she had to be. He didn't want her to deal with the problems of our lives, with the stresses, and Vance had more than his fair share of them. The tabloids were one thing—they grew bored easily and moved on. His parents were another.

"I'll go."

Vance and I both jerked our gazes to the side to find Kenz there, in the darkness, having managed to come up on us without either of us noticing.

Sneaky girl…

"You really don't want to," Vance explained.

"Yeah, I'm *sure* I don't want to, but not everything is about what we want. They're bothering you because of the interview, because of the news, so they aren't going to let this go if they don't meet me, right?"

Vance didn't respond at first, darting his gaze back and forth as if trying to figure out any other options. Finally, he sighed. "Yeah, you're right."

"So it's fine. It's not the first time I've had to dress up and put on a fake smile and meet people. I grew up doing it for my father all the time. If I can handle gangsters and mob bosses and assassins, I'm sure I can handle a few aristocratic parents. Plus, you did that interview as a way to keep me safe, so I sort of owe you."

Having met Vance's parents one time before, I knew she was severely underestimating the couple. I'd rather face a loaded gun than those two...

However, Kenz wasn't the sort of woman to back down when she felt like she was protecting someone.

"You sure? Once we go, you can't really get out of it anymore," Vance said, offering one last chance to back away.

Kenz nodded. "Yep, I'm sure. I can do this for you."

A sharp pain in my chest said I didn't care for her smiling at Vance that way, and the petty, jealous part of me wanted to intervene. I wanted to grasp her chin and make her look at *me* that way, wanted to separate them, to keep whatever was between them to stop growing.

However, that wasn't fair, so I dropped my drink and pretended it didn't bother me.

Just a little longer.

Chapter Six

Vance

The huge house in front of me made my head hurt. Just seeing it, just heading up the driveway set my nerves on edge.

Had this place *ever* felt like home? Despite having grown up in it, having played in these gardens and these hallways until I'd gotten shipped off to boarding school, it never held that nostalgia that others spoke of their childhood homes with.

"How many girls have you brought here before?" Kenz asked from the passenger side of my car. My mother had wanted to send Taylor to pick me up — probably because she didn't trust that I'd actually make it here — but I'd refused.

Kenz was about to be subjected to enough without having me pile on more.

"Not many," I admitted. "Maybe five?"

"That's more than I figured. Meeting the parents is a big step, and you don't strike me as the sort who would want to do that much."

"Trust me, they weren't because I cared about the woman. Usually it was because I fucked around with the wrong girl, with someone who had family in an important enough place to pressure me into a meeting."

Kenz shook her head, the disappointment clear on her face. "You shouldn't play with people like that."

"I don't play with people. Everyone who deals with me knows exactly what they're in for. If someone hopes for more, that's on them. I'm always clear."

The gate slid open before I had to even speak to the guard. Of course it did, though. Every person who worked at this estate knew me, knew my car, and probably expected us.

Yet the opening gate caused that tension inside of me to crank even tighter. *Just breathe through it.* I scolded myself for being so foolish. I never cared what people thought about me, refused to let anyone else dictate my life, had long since given up such worries.

That was what I said, at least. Why then was it that when my parents looked at me with those looks full of disappointment, it always caused this splintering pain inside me?

I drove the car forward, parking it in the empty spot near the front where I'd always parked. My father had yelled at me time and time again about how he didn't like having flashy cars like this one out front, and hell, maybe that was why I ignored him and did as I pleased.

Kenz got out of the car as I did, not waiting for me to open her door. I'd noticed that she waited for

Hayden to do it, but maybe that was because he was the sort to lecture her about security.

There's no safer place than here, though.

Still, something that felt suspiciously like jealousy didn't care for it at all.

She looked up at the house, but she didn't seem nearly as impressed as most of the girls I brought were. *Then again, she grew up in places like this too, didn't she?*

She sure looked at home here. She'd put on the dress I'd bought for her without complaint, and it had fit her just the way I knew it would. Her dark hair and pale skin looked fantastic against the maroon dress, and her silver jewelry shone in the lights from the house.

She was beyond lovely. It was one of the things that surprised me about her again and again. She fit everywhere.

She'd looked comfortable and amazing at the fancy restaurant I'd taken her to, appeared to fit in here at the estate, yet she looked just as good when dressed down at a café or the school cafeteria.

Somehow, she could go anywhere, dress in any way, and it never dimmed her in the least. Perhaps that was just part of her personality and charm.

I held my arm out slightly, and Kenz slid hers through the open space in a practiced motion that showed she'd done this before.

She walked in the heels without issue, even resting against me when she stepped on the slightly uneven cobblestone of the walkway to the front door.

We didn't have to knock — they were expecting us, after all. The moment we stepped onto the front porch, the large front door opened like magic.

Not magic, just Taylor.

"Young Master," he said and bowed slightly, his voice as familiar as my parents'. In many ways, he was the parent they'd never been, the one to watch me, to go to those boarding schools with me. In fact, it was only in the last five years that we'd spent so little time together. "Welcome home."

"This isn't home," I reminded him.

His lips quirked up on one side as though amused by the same exchange we often had. "This will always be your home. And you must be Miss Fox?" He held his hand out, and when Kenz offered her own, he lifted her hand and placed a kiss on her knuckles. The gesture was old-school, and the flush on her cheeks said even she hadn't expected it. "Welcome. It is our pleasure to make your acquaintance and have you here."

I knocked Taylor's hand away and pulled Kenz tighter against my side, annoyance eating at me over him touching her. Which was strange, seeing as he'd introduced himself to all the other women in the same way. Why did it bother me so much this time?

Because Kenz is the first girl I've liked…

That was far too embarrassing, though, so I pushed the thought down before the observant bastard could see it.

However, when his smile widened, it suggested he knew. "Right this way, please. The master and mistress are already in the dining room." He waited for us to enter, then closed the door behind us.

It took me back, seeing this entryway. I still recalled when I was ten and tried to open the door myself, the way the butler had all but had a heart attack over me doing it for myself, how I'd gotten lectured about proper behavior for a *young master*.

Taylor spoke as we walked, giving small tidbits of information about the architecture and history of the house. He'd always enjoyed doing that, showing off the things as though they somehow made him look better.

And it never failed to annoy me.

Kenz paused, and it took Taylor a moment before he noticed, turning back to see what had delayed us.

He smiled and gestured at the large painting on the wall. "That was the young master's favorite. He saw it in an exhibit when he was five. He sat in the gallery until they closed, just staring at it. I had to force him to leave then, to bring him home, crying the whole way."

The image before us was smaller than I remembered it being, but I had been much smaller when we'd gotten it. It was all bright colors that bordered on neon and filled all the way to the edges. It had little negative space, something my father had always complained about, that it was far too busy. I'd loved it, though, the image of the northern lights, even the snow and trees done in fantastic hues that didn't appear natural at all.

"So you put it up here?" Kenz asked.

"It was my choice. I oversee all the people who work in the estate, including the decorator. When I saw how much the young master cherished this, I knew we had to purchase it and put it in a place of honor."

"That was foolish," I muttered, unable to ignore the way my cheeks flushed. "This is hardly art. I was a kid who didn't know what real art was back then."

Kenz pulled away from me and stepped closer to the piece, staring at it in the appraising way only an artist could. "The use of color is amazing. Someone who didn't know anything would think it was random, but it isn't. See, the artist used warm colors on the snow and trees, to show the life of nature, but cooler shades in the sky to show how far away that is, how vast. It all makes you feel safe but also free, two things that aren't always easy to show together like this."

I blinked slowly, taken aback by her statement. It was honest, yet she'd managed to hit the core of what I'd liked about it. I'd never said that out loud, never dared to voice my true feelings. In fact, I'd never even directly told Taylor I'd liked her. He'd simply worked it out from how I'd stared. To have Kenz understand me like that astounded me.

Taylor stared not at the piece but at Kenz, his expression thoughtful. "You are quite astounding, aren't you?" He said that so softly I wasn't sure Kenz heard.

She turned, her eyebrows furrowed to tell me I was right. "What?"

Taylor shook his head and smiled. "Nothing. I was just noting that you have a very good eye. Come along, though, the master and the mistress do not like to be kept waiting."

With that, Kenz offered an apologetic smile and slipped her arm through the crook of mine again. I tried to ignore the warmth in my chest at her words, at the comfort I felt around her.

We entered the large dining room, and I immediately cringed. How many times, when growing up, had I invited friends over only to have them hate the large room, the coldness? I'd wanted to have what I'd seen in all the movies, where friends came over and ate pizza on the floor while they watched some stupid TV show. Instead, I'd gotten five-star meals of ingredients no one recognized in this auditorium of a dining room at a table that could seat twenty-five.

I'd learned my lesson after the first few and had stopped inviting people over.

At least, people I cared about.

Which was why the thought of showing this to Kenz chafed.

"Vance," my mother said, her voice warm. Most people remembered their mothers' voices from when they were sick, when she would stroke their hair and reassure them that they'd be fine.

Not me, though. Taylor had done those things. And my mother? I recalled her voice only when she praised me for good grades.

Still, her voice melted some cold part of me, the part that craved a mother's love no matter how insufficient the version offered to me.

"You're late," my father said gruffly.

"I'm late because I didn't want to come at all," I said without the least bit of shame, rewarded with Kenz pinching my side to scold me.

My mother ignored me and rose from her seat, crossing the short distance to Kenz and me. She reached out to shake Kenz's hand, her smile strange, probably due to a recent injection to paralyze her face. "My name is Bethany Moore, and this is my husband, Harold Moore."

"My name is Mackenzie Fox. Thank you so much for inviting me. Your home is lovely."

"Thank you," my mother said, clearly charmed by Kenz's good manners. "Please, sit. Is there anything you can't eat? Anything we should let the chef know about?"

Kenz shook her head—always the polite one—but I spoke up in her stead. "She's diabetic, so please ask the chef to keep that in mind for her food."

My mother looked toward Taylor, who nodded, then excused himself to the back.

Kenz shot me a sharp look, no doubt telling me not to cause problems for her sake.

Too bad. Like I'd risk her just so she didn't bother a chef whose entire job was to cook what we wanted.

My father had taken the chair at the head of the table, and my mother sat to his side. Kenz sat to his other side — across the table from my mother — and I sat beside her. The wide, empty table ran from there, making the room feel vast.

An uncomfortable tension rested inside me, as though I were exposing Kenz to danger.

Which was hilarious given all I'd done to her thus far... I could have helped her escape right from the start, but instead I kept shoving her into situations that could harm her, things that could take her life, yet I was worried about her meeting my parents?

Talk about fucked-up priorities.

"So how long have you been dating?" my mother asked.

Kenz glanced at me, as though telling me to take point.

"Not long — just a month or so."

"And yet you're already serious enough to go on TV and air your dirty laundry?" my father asked.

So much for a nice conversation.

"It's not dirty laundry." I flashed a forced smile that I knew lacked warmth or humor. "And what was I supposed to do? We got caught on camera, and I was being hounded by reporters. By doing an interview, it made the story less fun."

"It would be better if you behaved yourself so you didn't end up in the tabloids in the first place. I honestly do not understand how you can cause us so many problems? Your brother *never* does this sort of thing."

Right. The precious golden child who always did the right thing, who never made a mistake. Erik Moore, the child my parents had always wanted, and me? Just the spare, the fuck-up, the one who never lived up to expectations.

I sighed because having this fight was the last thing I wanted. I didn't enjoy them in general, but I sure didn't want Kenz to witness it.

"And what do you do?" my mother asked Kenz, in that same tone she used when trying to calm things down between my father and me. She always was the peacemaker, huh? Still, the way she could just move on and pretend nothing had happened was so indicative of how our family ran.

"I'm a student," Kenz said, her tone light and cheerful. It told me all I needed to know — she'd grown up in the *exact* same sort of household and knew how to play that game.

"Oh really? What are you studying?"

"Fine arts with an emphasis in painting," Kenz said, a light in her eyes that showed how much she loved art.

I missed that feeling...

My father snorted softly, the dismissive sound making me draw my hand into a fist to keep myself quiet. He could put me down all he wanted, but I sure wouldn't stand for him doing it to Kenz.

"Are you at the local university?" my mother asked.

Kenz shook her head. "I'm going to the Art Institute."

This time my father at least paused. "That is a difficult school to gain entrance to."

"It was, but I was lucky enough to manage it. I took a lot of extra credits before I got in and had to get so many reference letters. Still, it was worth it."

"But you're so young," my mother said. "You barely look old enough to drink."

Her cheeks flushed, and I knew the reason. In reality, she *wasn't* old enough to drink, at only nineteen, but she couldn't say that. Watching her walk the line between truth and lie was always amusing, though. "I know I look young, but I'm actually twenty-one. I went to boarding schools, and I knew what I wanted to do, so I made sure to be ready."

"That is surprisingly studious," my father said, sitting back as someone served the plates of food to us. "Most of the woman my son runs around with are nothing more than pretty faces. I have to wonder what you're doing around him."

And there it was, the disappointment I was so used to with my father.

Of course, I had to wonder the same thing. The way Kenz had admitted to loving us, it had thrown me for a loop, and I still couldn't quite get a handle on it. There was no doubt—the girl was so far outside of my league it wasn't even funny.

"You realize that any spouse of this family will have a prenup, correct? So if you're hoping for a payout, that won't happen."

Kenz didn't flinch under the harsh look from my father. Her smile never faltered. "I'm not worried about that. My father passed away about a year ago and left me more than enough to live off comfortably in a trust, even after funding my education, so I have absolutely no designs on his money. I'd be happy to sign a contract to that effect right now."

My father blinked slowly, a look I'd never seen on his face. Not much shut my father up. He'd spent his life in the world of politics, used to dealing with rich and entitled people. I'd watched him force the ugliest and most arrogant of men to back up, where his stern expression and sharp words had caused them to submit.

Yet here he was, silenced by the spit of a girl beside him.

Pretending I didn't love her was stupid, wasn't it? Even if I couldn't do anything about it, even if I couldn't give in to it, there wasn't a point or reason for me to lie to myself. Each time I saw her, each time we spoke, each time I saw another side of her, I fell more hopelessly in love with her.

"Sorry I'm late," came a voice that made my shoulders tighten.

I turned to see my brother there, dressed in a black suit that made him look so much like our father. I'd taken more after our mother, but Erik? He was Father's miniature in every fucking way. "If I'd known you were coming, I would have skipped."

"And miss out on some brotherly time? You wound me." Erik slapped his hand against my back, harder than he needed to, as if making a point. Then again, big brothers were all the same, weren't they?

"Hello, Vance." Amy, Erik's wife, came in on his heels, her sweet smile annoying me as it always did. She was far too nice for him, for this family, and it bothered me each time I saw her. It felt like a reminder of Erik getting everything he wanted in life, as if the universe just wanted to make it clear he was that much better than me.

Still, being mean to her would be like kicking a kid, so I played along. "Hi, Amy. It's been a long time."

"Far too long. You should come by sometime—Hailey's been asking about you."

I did the math in my head as I recalled the sweet little blonde girl who had always grabbed my hand the moment I'd gotten to their house. "She's seven now, right?"

Amy sat beside my mother, a huge smile on her face the moment we started to talk about her child. "That's right. She's been practicing with the paints you sent her, and she wants to show you how far she's come."

Guilt hit me at how little I'd seen her, how much of my life I'd devoted to my revenge. Then again, getting any closer to someone that young, knowing how little time I had left was selfish.

Not that I could say that. "I'll come by soon," I lied.

Erik spoke to one of the servers, whispering to him before taking his seat beside Amy. It put us all together like one big, fake, unhappy family.

Talk about a baptism by fire for Kenz…

"I'm Amy."

"Mackenzie," Kenz said, then smiled in a way that could disarm anyone. "But everyone calls me Kenz."

"And what exactly is a girl as young and pretty as you doing with my brother?" Erik asked. "I mean, he *used* to be an artist, but he hasn't done any work in years, which means he's basically unemployed. He doesn't have any plans for the future, and he's slept with so many women it would take a mathematician to figure out an exact number. You could do better."

I pressed my lips together, unable to argue with anything he said. This was exactly why I hadn't wanted to bring Kenz, to subject her to scrutiny or have her hear what my family had to say about me.

"Stop it," Amy scolded her husband, her gaze sharp.

"Sorry." Even if he said the words, Erik's expression said he didn't regret the words at all. "But you *know* what he's like."

"That doesn't mean you have to bring it up to embarrass him," Amy responded.

"This isn't the place for this conversation," my mother interrupted, the words so similar to what I'd heard growing up that it felt like a family motto.

They all spoke over each other, the same way most family get-togethers went around here.

"He's brilliant," Kenz said, her voice so soft that at first, no one noticed. She took a deep breath, then sat up straighter, lifting her chin as I'd seen her do from time to time when fed up. "Vance is brilliant."

This time, she said it loud enough to draw everyone to a stop. They turned and stared at her as though her words made no sense.

Kenz kept going, her voice stronger. "His artwork is amazing. Whether or not he ever does another piece doesn't change the work he's done and what he's contributed to the art world. His name will be in books for decades, probably centuries. His talent is absolutely amazing. Beyond that, I've seen him help others, teach others. He's taken his time to look at my work and tell me where I can improve it, how to grow as an artist."

"But his romantic history—" Erik started to say.

Kenz cut him off, her tone sharp despite the smile she still wore. "So what? I know better than most just how many women he's been involved with, but why does it matter? The women consented. He never tricks anyone or forces anyone into anything."

"It looks bad," my father said.

"Living up to our parents' expectations is an impossible task," Kenz said. "I should know — I spent a long time doing just that. I tried so hard to do what my father wanted, to be the person he wanted me to be, and you know what I found out? It's impossible. He had a fantasy, an idea of some mindless doll who could fulfill a role, but that isn't me. So instead of forcing others to be something they're not, it's better to look at who they really are."

"Trust me, I know *exactly* who and what my son is," my father spat, none of his false politeness from before.

"I don't think you do," she responded without flinching. "You know what you wanted and how he doesn't fit that, but I don't think you really know *him*. If you knew Vance, you'd know how talented he is. You'd know that he treats people well, looking out for them. You'd know that no matter how tired he is, he always does what he can when people ask for help. You'd know that he can't hold his alcohol well and that when he does overdo it, he turns into a little kid who wants cuddles and to be spoiled. Maybe you'd appreciate him a little more if you took the time to really get to know *him* instead of only looking at how he isn't who you wish he was." She shook her head, as though frustrated with the conversation. "I remember once, when I'd so badly wanted a kitten, and I was given one. I hated that cat at first, because it wouldn't come to me the way dogs did. Finally, someone reminded me that a cat isn't a dog. I'd never like the thing if I kept expecting it to act like a dog. Once I gave that up, I was able to get along with the cat because I saw it was a cat, and I cared about it for that. Stop seeing Vance for what he isn't and see him for what he *is*."

No one spoke at first, but I didn't miss the slight smile on Amy's face. My mother's was less obvious but a spark of delight in her blue eyes said Kenz had made yet another fan.

"How dare you speak to me like that," my father said, tripping over the words a bit. Then again, how often did he have to deal with some upstart girl from nowhere lecturing him? "You, some two-bit—"

I rose and slammed my palms on the table hard enough to silence him. "I let you say what you want about me—I'm used to it. I am going to recommend you be *very* careful about making the mistake of speaking as you please about Kenz. Do not mistake my willingness to accept your vile abuse for weakness, however, because I will not tolerate you talking about her that way."

My father's mouth hung open, his dark eyes wide. Then again, had I *ever* spoken to him like that? *Nope, never.* I'd always hoped somewhere in my head that he'd learn to accept me, that he'd stop hating me for everything I wasn't, that he'd see *me*, so I never wanted to push things to a point we couldn't come back from.

Yet the moment he'd been ready to throw an insult her way, my protective instincts had reared up, unwilling to let that pass. The reality was that I wasn't a kid anymore. I wasn't the mindless teenager he still wanted to view me as.

Especially over the past five years, I'd learned my own strength, that I had skills, that I didn't need to just accept everything. It seemed it had only taken this to make me willing to show him.

"Thank you for the invite," I said before holding my hand out to Kenz. "But I refuse to expose Kenz to this sort of behavior. Mother, if you wish to visit again, I'd be happy to do so without Father. Erik, fuck you, and Amy, you look lovely as ever. Goodnight." I didn't wait for a response before pulling Kenz after me to the shocked faces behind us.

"Should we just leave like that?" Kenz asked but didn't pull away from me, allowing me to lead her.

"It's fine," I assured her. "My father wouldn't have been happy no matter how the night ended."

I swung the front door open myself instead of waiting for anyone to do it for me, the small act of rebellion feeling so damned good.

At least, it did until I nearly ran right into Taylor, who stood on the porch, in our way. That bastard was always one step ahead of me. How many times had he pulled this little move when I'd been a teenager sneaking out?

"I'm leaving," I told him, tucking Kenz behind me. I wouldn't expose her to any more ugliness, not on my account.

"Of course, Young Master." Taylor inclined his head in a small nod. "You know, your father won't soon forget this."

"Good. Maybe he won't force me to visit for a while then."

Taylor shifted as though to look behind me, to catch eyes with Kenz. "And you, Miss? You have just soiled your chances at his approval."

Kenz shifted her hand, and I thought she'd pull away. Instead, she moved her hand to hold my other one, my right one, squeezing like she wanted to tell me she had my back no matter what. "If getting his approval meant letting him talk to Vance like that, then I don't want it."

"And you are fine with that? He may cut Vance out of his will. He might cause problems for you, since you did humiliate him, and he doesn't experience that often."

Kenz shifted from behind me, making it clear she neither expected nor needed me to shield her from the consequences of her own choices. "Trust me, some arrogant politician coming after me is the least of my worries. I have far larger enemies than that. If he doesn't like what I said, I'd suggest he look at himself instead of trying to lash out against the person who said it."

I expected Taylor to respond by telling her to be more careful, to warn us both about the dangers my parents could pose, to behave ourselves as we should. Hadn't he said that often enough to me? I could almost repeat it word by word.

Instead, Taylor smiled, the expression softer than I was used to. "Finally, a woman who deserves to stand by your side."

I blinked slowly, so thrown that I couldn't even formulate a response.

Taylor bowed deeply, then stepped aside. "Go on and enjoy your evening. I placed meals in your car already as I suspected you would not get to eat. Please, Young Master, ensure she eats. It is especially important for people with diabetes."

I nodded, whispering out a weak thank you before pulling Kenz along with me.

"Oh, and Miss Fox?" Taylor's voice drew us short, and he leaned in to whisper something into her ear.

Kenz's cheeks flushed, the reaction sparking the jealousy inside me again, so I tugged her to my side then down the stairs, away from Taylor, from this cursed house, from the people inside.

If only I could get control of the feelings inside me that I couldn't even hope to understand or control.

Kenz

I pulled my seat belt on, my heart racing. Vance put the car into reverse, whipping around the driveway in a way that said he'd done this plenty of times, that he knew the exact dimensions and how to work around them. He spun the tires as he raced down the long path.

The gate was already open when we reached the street, as if the house was just as happy to get rid of us as we were to leave. He pulled the car onto the road and gunned it, the engine loud, as though to remind me he drove one hell of a sports car.

"I'm sorry," I said, unable to stop myself.

His left hand was tight on the wheel, his right on the shifter. "For what?"

"I probably made things worse between you with your family. I came to try and help you, but I ended up causing you problems."

"Why did you say all that?"

His question took me by surprise. It was obvious, wasn't it? "I didn't like what they were saying about you. I know *you* don't care what people say about you, but as it turns out, I do."

"But why? What did it matter if they wanted to put me down?"

I shifted in my seat, my fingers wrapped around my seatbelt as he sped along the dark road. "They don't know you at all, but they were putting you down. I just couldn't listen to it anymore, especially because you weren't going to stand up for yourself."

The streetlights poured into the car through the windshield, illuminating his face for brief flashes, but that didn't tell me anything about how he felt. His gaze was locked on the road, and despite how fast we drove, he maneuvered the car easily, clearly used to driving this beast. "You might have made your own life more difficult, just like Taylor said. My father isn't the sort of man to let things go."

"I don't care what he does to me, but I'm sorry if I made things harder on you. Taylor said he might take you out of his will..."

Vance snorted loudly. "I don't care about that. I've made more than enough off my art to not have to worry about money. Hell, my own personal fortune probably rivals the family funds now. They don't know that, of course, since I keep such things private, but I don't give a damn if he writes me out of the will. I've expected him to disown me for a long time, now, so stop apologizing."

The sound of the engine filled the rest of the drive, and it again surprised me just how close Vance's house was to the place we all lived. They only sat a ten-minute drive apart. It was strange, because most families would visit more given that closeness.

Then again, after meeting his family, I understood why that wasn't the case.

Vance pulled the car up to the house, parking a bit farther away than usual, so the security lights from the outside didn't brighten the interior of the car. The engine died when he twisted the key, leaving us there in the darkness and quiet, and I had no idea what to say.

"What did Taylor say to you? At the end?" Vance asked, his gaze locked outside the car instead of on me.

I recalled the older man whispering into my ear, the odd kindness in his voice. "He asked me to take care of you."

Vance laughed softly, the sound bitter. "I hate him some of the time, because he feels like another arm of my father. So many times he lectured me and told me what I needed to do and sounded just like my father. But…" He sighed, then rested his arm over the top of the steering wheel and leaned forward, placing his chin on top of his arm. "I'm older now, and I realize he walked the line between what he had to do for my father and what he wanted to do for me. If I think about who supported me, who came to my shows, who attended my graduations, who I called when I was in trouble, it was always Taylor. He's probably the only real family I had."

"I know what you mean. That was the Quad for me. Maybe it's a weird family, maybe it isn't what people see when they think about family, but it's still a family."

He nodded, but even though his voice was so soft, I couldn't ignore the tension in him. "I've never had anyone stand up for me before. Even Taylor never could go against my father, couldn't do anything about the things he said, the things he did. No one else was in a position to say anything. Even my mother, even when I could tell she didn't like it, she was stuck. You're the first person who ever thought it was worth it to defend me, to face off against him. I don't understand why you'd do this. We aren't even actually dating…"

I turned toward him, setting my hand on his cheek, urging him to look at me even though it seemed like he was trying hard not to do just that. "You're a good person. You don't see it, but you are, and I couldn't stand sitting there and saying nothing while they put you down. I know you see me as some foolish little girl, and maybe I am, but I'm in your corner. I have your back no matter what."

One tense moment passed, where the beating of my heart felt so loud and so fast that it seemed there was no way he could missed it.

"Look at me," I whispered.

He shook his head once. "I can't. If I look at you, I'll do something we both regret."

Does he mean what I think he means?

"I don't care. I don't like when you avoid me."

"Then don't blame me later for this." His words came out only a breath before he was on me.

I expected to feel the press of his lips to mine, craved it, to remember from the last time. However, that didn't happen. His lips touched my cheek, then my jawline. Wet heat danced down my throat, along my pulse, as he placed his left hand on the other side of throat and used his thumb to tip my head back. It gave him more access, and he sure took advantage of that, kissing along the vulnerable front of my throat.

I couldn't hope to hold back my voice, and a moan that sounded *nothing* like me escaped, growing over the noisy kisses he left against my defenseless skin.

"I won't kiss you on the lips," he whispered, his voice having a sensual quality that melted me. Before he had teased, his words holding a fun promise, but they'd never been like *this*. "I already stole your first kiss, so I won't force that on you again."

A begging plea rose from my chest, a desire to do anything to have more of this, to lose myself to his passion and desire. I wanted to feel those talented lips against mine, especially since the last time I'd been so surprised that I hadn't gotten to enjoy it. I was ready this time, so I wanted to experience it again when I wouldn't miss a moment of it.

But when I curled my fingers into the front of his shirt, when I shifted to capture his lips, he turned away and shook his head once in a hard jerk before sliding the strap of my dress down, baring my entire shoulder. Only the snug bodice kept the fabric up and me covered.

"You smell sweet." He whispered the words between his kisses, then dipped his tongue into the line of cleavage right at the neckline of the gown. "You're like a dessert that I've wanted forever, one I'm starving for, but one I know I shouldn't have." He tugged down the neckline, the fabric sliding away to bare me to the chilled air inside the cab of the car.

My breath caught when this all suddenly felt more real. This was the first time a man had seen me like this, in a moment like this. Even if others had seen me nude, it had never been in a passionate moment, never when we were heading toward something more, something I wanted *so* badly.

It all clouded my head so I couldn't think about anything other than the needs of my body. I felt like an animal, lost to desire, desperate for things I'd never experienced, never tasted before.

Vance pulled back enough to look at my bare chest, the moonlight making his blue eyes impossibly bright even in the dim interior. He groaned, the sound low enough to send a shiver through me. He glanced up, meeting my eyes, just as he reached out and cupped one breast in his left hand.

His hand was cool against my heated skin, and for a moment I wanted to hide. I worried whether my body was good enough. Was it to his liking? He'd had enough experience to judge me against famous actresses and models and women whose entire existence was looking good.

How could I live up to that?

A gentle brush against my nipple had me sucking in a harsh breath, the sensation so overwhelming that my back arched of its own accord, like a reflex I couldn't control.

"Don't think about anything else," he said. "I'm not with anyone else, not thinking about anyone else, so don't you dare do it. Focus on me, just for a little while."

Talk about a devil's whisper. His words felt like a deal offered to me, as if he were reaching up from hell. All I needed to do was obey and he'd pull me down with him.

And right now, I *wanted* to go with him. I wanted to give myself over to him, to whatever he wanted, to feel what I knew he could give me.

"Good girl," he whispered and leaned in, his lips going to my neglected breast, to the one he didn't tease with his thumb. He pressed soft kisses, first to the top of my breast, then along the full curve, but avoided the nipple. Despite that, the peak had drawn into a tight point. When he finally turned his head and dragged the flat of his tongue across that swollen point, fireworks lit up the darkness inside me, sparking those feelings to life, electrifying my entire body.

I suddenly found myself angry at the Quad, at Nem, at my father, at everyone who had sheltered me so I'd missed out on this for so long. I moved my arms to wrap around him, leaning toward him, wanting more — *needing* more.

I pushed him backward and crawled into his lap, too lust-drunk to think about how I might make a fool of myself. The fabric of my gown pooled around us, and my body cast him in a shadow as I blocked out the moonlight.

I reached between us, terrified something would steal this moment away. How many times in my life had I thought, for just a moment, that things would work out? That I could have what I wanted? Only to have those things slip away from me?

This was too important. I wanted it too much to risk that. It made me reckless and eager as I slid my hand down his chest, over the hard muscles of his stomach, to the fastener of his slacks. All I had to do was undo this, shift a bit of fabric, and he could slide into me.

I'd worn a thong to prevent any lines in the dress, which meant we could tug that aside. I'd *finally* know what this felt like.

He caught my wrists, holding them in one of his large hands before I could undo his pants. He leaned forward, but his lips didn't touch me again. Instead, he rested his face against my neck, his breath rough and hot against my skin.

I couldn't stand him stopping me, him keeping anything from me, so without thinking about it I rocked my hips. I ground against his hard cock — at least that meant he was interested, right? — but it wasn't enough.

Or rather, it wasn't enough at first. If I kept going, I'd bet it would be eventually. My pride had disappeared, and if I had to rut against him like this to get off, *fine.*

I rolled my hips again, arching my back and leaning back so his erection stroked right against my clit. My lips parted on their own and I cried out softly, not caring how far it carried, who heard, nothing.

"Kenz," he said on a groan, the sound masculine and sexy and sure to fill my filthy dreams from now on. Yet, an edge of it held hesitation, as though he were moments from waking up before I did, ready to stop this.

Please, don't.

I let him hold my wrists still, not bothering to try to take them back. If it made him think he had control of this, I didn't care. My thighs would burn come tomorrow, unused to this movement, but it was worth it. I didn't slow, altering how I grounded against him only to chase my own pleasure, the sensations that made the muscles in my body tighten in waves as I neared my own release.

I leaned back again, the space between my shoulder blades touching something, and a loud noise made me jump.

It took me a moment to realize I'd leaned against the horn.

And just like that, Vance blinked slowly, the moment broken.

At least, it was for him. "Please, don't stop," I begged, not caring how pathetic I sounded.

He swallowed hard and released my wrists. My hope soared only to crash when he grasped the neckline of my gown and pulled it up, then slid the shoulder straps back on.

"*Kenz,*" he said, the lust gone from his voice as if it hadn't been there at all.

Rejected again…

He opened his mouth, and I could see the excuses tumbling around in there. He was getting ready to tell me no, to explain why I was foolish for wanting this, why it was a bad idea. After the evening where I'd felt like I'd finally seen the real him, where I understood him, where we'd gotten closer, he now seemed farther away than ever.

Worse, I still panted hard, breathless, my body having gone haywire in a way that frightened me. I'd been so close, and *he'd* done this to me. He'd touched me, he'd woke this inside me — *again* — and just like before, he tore it away.

I grasped blindly for the door, needing to escape.

"Wait, Kenz," he said, reaching for me, trying to stop me.

"Don't touch me," I snapped, wetness tracking down my cheeks, shame filling me.

"Just let me talk to you."

I shook my head, refusing to look at him. How we'd changed positions, huh? Earlier I'd begged him not to shut me out but now I was the one who couldn't meet his gaze. "Let me go."

"You need to listen to me —"

"No! You don't get to turn me down like this *again* and sit there to tell me how I should be grateful for it."

"It's not like that," he said, his hand tight around my arm.

The clatter made me glance over my shoulder to find Hayden standing on the porch, peering into the darkness toward us. Vance released my arm — he probably didn't want to get caught like this — and I took the chance to flee from the car, from Vance, from all the things my body still craved that I couldn't have.

When I tried to rush past Hayden, he reached out to catch me. I avoided his touch, terrified that I'd shatter if I felt the warmth of someone else, the thing I wanted so badly but couldn't have.

He didn't try again, lifting his hand as though to prove he wouldn't grab me. I turned away, afraid to open my mouth. I had no idea what I'd say if I did that.

Instead, I went past him and rushed up the stairs, for the safety of my room, leaving that mess behind.

Yet again, I'd made a fool of myself, hadn't been good enough, hadn't been enough for someone else.

No matter how much I grew, how far I came, I was never good enough, was I?

Chapter Seven

Kenz

My head ached, but it was nothing a little ibuprofen couldn't handle. Between that and water, I felt mostly human.

Mostly.

I couldn't erase the night before from my mind, and without even meaning for it to happen, flashes of the events would come back to me. My cheeks would heat, my heart race and my body tingle. It was like the ghost of a memory teased me, as though I could feel Vance's lips on me even twelve hours later.

Worse? It kept this simmering heat inside me, one I couldn't rid myself of. I'd thought about trying to take care of myself the night before, but pride had stopped me. It had felt far too pathetic to get turned down then get myself off on the memory of it.

No thank you!

So instead, I pretended to be fine as I cleaned up the living room. They still had a housekeeper stopping by—always when I was gone—but cleaning relaxed me. However, since they had a professional, there hadn't been much to do.

It meant I was on my hands and knees wiping down the baseboards in the corner, since that was the only dust I could find anywhere.

"You don't have to do that." Char's voice had me sitting back on my heels to glance over my shoulder at him. He sat on the edge of the coffee table, watching me as though I was a very stupid dog digging in the yard.

"I know I don't have to."

"So why are you, then?"

Telling him it because I was sexually frustrated was probably not the best answer, so I jerked my gaze away as I answered. "I'm just feeling wound up, and I needed something to do. Cleaning feels like putting the world to rights again."

"Next time, feel free to clean up my room. I don't do it nearly enough and I don't let the cleaners in there."

"Why not?"

"I don't like strange people in my space."

"But you'll let me?" I lifted an eyebrow as I looked back over at him, making sure to keep a teasing tone in my voice. "Does that mean you like me at least a little?"

"Not really," he said, not taking my bait in the least. "But if you do anything that pisses me off, I can just hand you over to Lorien." His smile was cold, and while the words would have freaked me out weeks ago, now I only laughed in response. I knew better than to believe him.

Hayden came into the living room, a plastic caddy in his hands. "We don't have any of that wood spray, but this is what I found." He set the caddy down beside me, filled with cleaning supplies of every type. He hadn't wanted me to clean either, but I guessed he was good at realizing when people needed an outlet for the thoughts and feelings they wanted to ignore.

Some people ate mindlessly when stressed, others drank too much, but for me? I liked to clean.

"Thanks." I grabbed the lemon-scented cleaner and squeezed the trigger so it sprayed on the microfiber cloth. I knew that those chemicals weren't great for me, but the thought of them killing all the bad germs never failed to make me smile.

The front door opened, and for a moment, I thought it was Vance. I hadn't seen him since the night before — I wasn't even sure he'd come in at all. Maybe he'd gone somewhere else for the night? Or maybe he'd drunk himself into a stupor yet again.

Maybe the asshole choked on his own vomit last night.

The moment that thought hit me, a wave of guilt arrived on its heels. I didn't want that, of course.

Instead of Vance, however, Tor walked in with a box in his hands. His gaze found me, and he nodded to indicate it was for me.

"Were you expecting something?" Hayden intercepted the box, taking it from Tor and peering at the labels. "It went to the school, and it says it's from Colton Horhiser?"

"Oh, give here!" I set down the cloth and cleaners and hopped to my feet, then rushed over.

Hayden narrowed his eyes but kept it out of reach. "What is it?"

"Booze and dirty magazines," I said with a sweet smile. "Now, can I have it?"

He sighed but handed the box over, clearly realizing that I knew about it. I slipped my finger beneath the edge on one side and pulled, tearing the tape that kept it closed. After opening the top, I set it on the table.

A letter sat on bubble wrap, and I picked it up first. It was short and sweet — at least half of that fitting the man who had written it.

Kenz,
Be careful and never forget where you come from.

I smiled and set the note on the table, not caring whether the men saw it. That was the nice thing about all my secrets having come out — I didn't have to worry about hiding things anymore.

The bubble wrap came off easily, and in my hands rested a black leather photo album as thick as any dictionary. He hadn't been kidding when he'd said it was big.

"What's that?" Char asked.

"I asked Colton to send me some old photos, so he said he'd send me a scrapbook my mother started." I gave a chiding smile to Hayden. "And I had him send it to the school so he wouldn't have this address."

Though I bet he already does, the nosy bastard.

I sat on the couch, right in the middle, and put the book in my lap.

No one else moved at first, a tension like they weren't sure they were welcome. It made me laugh, and I patted the spot beside me. "Come on, sit down. You can all ohh and ahh over my baby pictures then laugh at the awkward stage I went through when I thought wearing cat ears all the time was a good idea."

To my surprise, Tor sat first. He took the spot to my left, and Hayden sat to my right, both of them close enough to press against me. Then again, we were all looking at the same book — we had to be close.

Char went around, behind the couch, and rested his hip on back. It let him peer over my shoulder. It also truly pinned me in between them all, which was something I hadn't felt in a while.

I'd grown so used to dealing with these men that at times I forgot just how large they were, how intimidating they could be.

And there my body goes again. Clearly I couldn't keep ignoring the lust inside me, especially around them. If they caught sight of it — and they would — they'd just lecture me again.

I opened the cover, trying to ignore any of those thoughts, distracting me with the photos.

"This was my mother, Caroline." I went through the first pictures, pointing out my mother and my father. No one spoke as I did so, as I smiled and stroked my fingers over the baby pictures of Nem. "She went by the name Kelsey Williams back then."

I'd never seen this album before, and what shocked me the most was the attention to detail in each photo. My mother had selected pictures that mattered to her, had placed them so lovingly in the scrapbook, along with paper that matched the tone and color scheme.

It wasn't cutesy like they often were, but rather fit the aesthetic that she'd always had — regal and powerful. It made me feel like a little kid again, the way I often felt around other people. It always felt a bit like everyone else around me had their shit together, were full-fledged adults and I was still rushing around, shoes untied, tripping over my own feet.

I turned page after page, seeing Nem grow up before my eyes. How had I never seen this before? Her precocious smile, the mischief she always seemed to be in. "It's weird seeing her like this," I admitted.

"What do you mean?" Hayden asked.

"I don't remember a lot about her before she disappeared, so I mostly know her as she is now. *Now* she doesn't smile like this, doesn't look so happy or free."

Because she came back for me.

A hand on my back made me raise my head to find Tor staring at me, concern in his golden eyes.

I forced a smile and turned another page. "Sorry, it's just that it's hard to see her like that. It makes it more obvious how much she's changed, how much she went through—for me." I shook my head, flipping pages until we moved forward to a picture of my mother heavily pregnant again.

"She looks so happy." I dragged my fingers over the plastic that covered the entire page.

"Aren't most mothers-to-be happy?" Char asked. "For some reason, women seem to like their offspring."

"She never seemed all that happy as a mom," I admitted. "She was always busy, always doing what was required of 'a woman of her position,' as she'd say to me. I don't know that she ever really wanted kids so much as it was expected of her."

"Even if she wasn't the warmest, I'm sure she loved you," Hayden said. "I mean, you can see it in her face right there, you can see it in every picture where she looks at your sister."

I didn't know if I believed him, but his words still warmed me. I flipped through pictures of me as a baby, surprised to find how normal I looked.

I didn't seem like some 'Mafia princess,' in them. Instead, I appeared like any normal child, crying or laughing or making a mess. I wished I could remember those times, because they seemed so average that I wanted to know how that felt.

"The Quad?" Hayden asked when a picture of Nem, the Quad and I together appeared.

I smiled at the familiar expressions of the men and nodded. "It figures only Dane is smiling. He's always smiling, even when he really shouldn't be."

"They adore you, don't they?"

"I guess." I tapped the photo. "They were the only solid thing in my life for a long time, the only thing I could rely on. I know how the rest of the world sees them, but I see them differently because I *know* them. There's no one I would trust more. They would stay up late with me when I was sick or take me to my doctors' appointments or come to the parent-teacher conferences. They were a bigger part of my childhood than either of my parents ever were."

I took a deep breath, then whispered the next part after I turned the page to find a single image without all the fancy styling. It showed me in a black dress, my arms wrapped around Rune's neck as he held me in a graveyard. "This was the funeral of my mother and my sister."

"Where's your father?"

"He was there, shaking hands and greeting others. At the time, I thought it was just the way things were done. You never were supposed to let others see your weakness, so it didn't seem strange to me that he could do that. Of course, I didn't realize at the time that he'd been the one to kill them."

Just like that, the air in the room thinned to the point that I struggled to draw it in.

Char spoke, his voice softer than I expected, making me suspect he was trying hard to sound almost gentle. "I'm sorry you had to go through that."

"You don't understand. Do you know why it happened? Because the Quad went with me to a specialist appointment. I had a lot of doctor appointments, and instead of having them there to protect my mom and my sister, they went with me. It gave my father a chance to attack them, a chance he wouldn't have gotten if they hadn't been with me." I forced myself to say the last part. "It's my fault it happened."

"It isn't your fault," Hayden said and set his hand on top of mine. It took his touch for me to realize I'd curled my fingers in, gripping the corner of the unadorned page to the point that it wrinkled. His warmth let me ease those fingers before I damaged anything. He kept speaking. "It wasn't a child's fault because their father decided to kill two people. Your father made that choice, and the blame is his—not yours."

The words felt like cool water on a burn. I'd never dared to utter that truth before, that I felt responsible for it all, that I'd carried that burden for so many years.

I'd trodden the water of my life, with that weight always pushing me down, forcing me to suck water into my lungs, because I couldn't let it go, couldn't put it down. I didn't know if I believed him, but just *hearing* the words helped so much.

A droplet of water struck the plastic that sat over the photo, and I had no idea what it was from at first. Tor cupped my cheek, then wiped away another drop. *Oh, I'm crying.*

I blinked to clear them away, then smiled, the expression perhaps not entirely real but easier than before.

Tor sighed and grabbed his phone, typing a message so quickly that he could impress a teenager. When he finished, he turned the screen toward me.

You don't have to pretend to be okay.

"I'm not."

Yeah, you are. You always do that, smile when you don't feel like it, act like you're okay when you aren't. You don't need to do that, not here.

"I guess I just don't like people worrying about me. I never feel like I'm pulling my own weight, like I live up to others, so the last thing I want is to give the people around me anything else to worry about. I don't want to cause more problems than I have." The sight of the men, all dressed up at the funeral, felt so bittersweet. "I was raised by the best of the best, came from the best bloodlines anywhere, had all the ingredients to make another astounding person, but I always fall short. I feel like an imperfect clone, someone who resembles the original but just can't quite live up to it."

I expected Hayden to reassure me, to tell me I was young and all young people didn't think enough of themselves. I even expected Tor to show me his screen, to tell me I was too hard on myself, that I didn't see myself right.

What I didn't expect was for Char to respond, though what *wasn't* a surprise was how the awkward and surly man chose to do it. A sting in my scalp made me turn my head to look up and behind me, to where he still rested against the back of the couch.

"Did you just pull my hair?"

"I sure did. You were thinking stupid things and that's the price."

"That's pretty rude."

"Yeah, well, we both know I'm rude. Don't think stupid things and I won't have to yank on your hair." The smile he flashed me was almost blinding, almost enough to make my thoughts go hazy. I'd seen his fake smile, knew how charming he could be, but this was different. The smile had an edge to it, a sadness, a sarcasm, but those made it more beautiful. They made it real.

"Thank you," I whispered, not just to Char but to them all. It was for so much, so many things that I couldn't even specify them all. It was for how they listened to me, how they *saw* me, how they gave me the first chance in so long to feel steady.

They weren't the Quad, but they'd given me a similar feel of security, of a foundation that I'd missed since I'd discovered that my past, my family wasn't what I'd thought. The day my father shot me, the day my life had gotten torn apart, I'd never thought I'd find myself again, that I'd ever put it back together.

This life was messy, and it was clumsy, and it was patched together from so many broken, sharp pieces, but what I'd found and hobbled together in this house, with these men, was more than I thought I'd ever have again.

* * * *

Kenz

"Isn't it strange how quickly this has become normal?" Lorien's voice floated through the line, already familiar, even though I knew it wasn't his real voice.

"How so?"

"I've never had a person I spoke to daily before, yet I find myself looking forward to the evening, to hearing your voice. I fear that I would not sleep well if I didn't get the chance to speak to you." His words were sweet, as they often were, but I knew better than to trust that.

I'd grown up seeing Dane play similar games, had witnessed how easily Char could manipulate others with a smile and a few charming words. Still, it was hard not to let it affect me at all.

I really am starving for praise, aren't I? I tried to ignore how pathetic it was.

"Are you done for the day?"

"Yes," I told him. "I worked on some paintings earlier."

"Yes, you have an exhibit coming up, don't you?"

I shifted, not caring for him knowing that. Then again, there was no doubt he'd done his research on me. Lying served no purpose, so I tried to remind myself of the purpose of these calls. "Yeah, I do."

"How is it going?"

"Honestly? A bit rough. I went over some old photos, though, to try and find some inspiration. It was suggested to me to go back to the start, to my core, to what made me who I am."

"Did that help?"

"I think so. I'm not quite there yet, but I feel like for the first time, I see the end."

"What do you want to do after you graduate?"

"Assuming I get to graduate?"

His laugh was soft, though the voice changer made it strange, slightly unnatural. "If you want to, of course.

I know what people say about me, but I'm not a monster. I have no desire to lock you away and dictate your entire life. In fact, I would hope you will continue your education—painting not only makes you happy, but you have a talent for it."

His words surprised me. I recalled when I'd nearly married that man my father had chosen. He'd planned on me giving up the chance at school, giving up art, all to become the perfect little housewife for him. The idea that I might have my own wants or desires played no part in his plans.

"Does that really surprise you so much?" Lorien asked.

"A bit," I admitted. "In my experience, when people want to force a woman into a relationship, they don't give her a whole lot of freedom."

"And if I just wanted to force you, I could have at any time. Do you really think I couldn't? That I don't know where you are? That I don't have access to enough manpower to just take you now, consequences be damned? Instead, I'm here trying to convince you, to win you. What is the point of any of it if I make you unhappy?"

My heart beat faster, and I wasn't sure why. It wasn't love—it wasn't even a crush. Instead, it felt like a warning in my head, as though his words were a dangerous lure that I should know better than to chase.

"Are you sleeping well? You sound tired."

"I don't sleep well much," I admitted. "It's just hard to get my mind to stop, and even when I sleep, I wake up a lot."

"That happens with people who don't feel confident in their world. They feel as though they need to stay on alert at all times, that they need to be on guard. Is that how you feel, Kenz? Unsettled?"

I opened my mouth to tell him no, but nothing came out. When had my sleep gotten really bad?

After my father tried to kill me.

The world I'd gotten used to before that, it hadn't been happy, but I'd understood it. After that, though, when Nem had come back, when my father had turned out to be a piece of shit, that had all changed. Suddenly, no matter how heavy my lids got, I couldn't seem to relax. I couldn't set down all those worries, that fear of tomorrow, and just rest.

When I didn't answer, Lorien's voice dropped lower, until it sounded like a whisper into my ear instead of across the line. "Lie down, Kenz."

"What?"

"You're done for today, so turn off the lights and lie down." He chuckled. "And do not think to lie to me— I'll know."

I wanted to argue, but I couldn't deny the exhaustion. I'd almost wanted to skip this call and just go to bed early, to get ready for tomorrow, but I'd had to do the things I needed.

So I sighed and leaned over, flipping the light off on the nightstand, plunging the room into darkness. The curtains were open, but the moon wasn't on the side of the house, so little light came into the room.

"Good girl. Now, under the covers."

I *really* wanted to tell him no. Something about him telling me what to do chafed, made me want to rebel, but I knew better. This was the game, right? Play along, get him comfortable, then make my move once I had him where I needed him.

So I scooted under the light blanket, the sheets cool against my skin.

"A good night's sleep will make tomorrow easier," Lorien said. It was strange, but between the darkness and me lying down, this conversation felt so much more intimate. It felt like lovers talking in bed before sleep, and I had no idea what I thought about that.

It reminded me of all the times the others, the men I actually wanted, had pushed me away. What would it feel like to have this? To feel a masculine voice whispering to me in the darkness?

My lids grew heavier, and I kept them closed for longer intervals between blinks.

"That's right." His voice was so far away, and it lulled me deeper into rest. "Just let go, Kenz. Get some sleep. We'll talk tomorrow."

Sleep took me, because I had no way to resist, no idea how to make sense of the conflicting feelings inside me. After the long day, the uncertainty, the waiting, I finally had a moment where I could set it down and just rest.

Is this what life could be like for me? Or am I just kidding myself?

Chapter Eight

Kenz

Is this what men call blue balls?

I was fairly certain I didn't actually have balls — my sex-ed had been at least that good — but I had to guess this was the same exact feeling.

My body felt strange, like I didn't fully control it. My cheeks heated when I caught sight of the men, and I struggled to meet their gazes directly. Everything felt... *tense.*

My skin seemed to have shrunk until it was too tight, until a brush of anything against it made me shiver in want. While I'd managed sleep, I'd wake up drench in sweat and not because of nightmares.

Instead, it was because of filthy dreams, and the worst part? Because of my inexperience, it wasn't like I could come up with any amazingly detailed scenarios. Plus, it was never enough, and when I woke, my shame got the better of me and I'd just roll over to try to sleep as I ignored the aching between my legs.

I stretched out on the porch outside, wearing a pair of shorts and a bralette, letting the sun soak into me as though it could sear away the desire inside me.

It never did, but I could pretend, right?

"Call me if that changes." Hayden's voice had me looking to my left to find him coming around the corner, his phone to his ear. He had the tone he used when talking about work.

However, the moment I saw him, I knew that not even bathing in lava would take care of the lust inside me. He wore no shirt and had a sheen of sweat over his tan skin.

He wasn't as young as the rest of them, but it was hard to remember when I saw him like this. His body was the sort they put pictures of in pin-up calendars, and I could see him fitting perfectly in a summer month, maybe dressed up as a firefighter with no shirt. His chest was broad and his dark nipples drew my gaze. The dark hair that ran in a small line from just beneath his navel to the button of his low-slung jeans stole my breath and what few coherent thoughts I had left.

I pictured myself on my knees in front of him, peering up that perfect body of his to find his dark eyes locked on me. He'd praise me, reassure me, tell me how good I was doing. I knew I'd be able to let go of all those worries inside of me because he'd take care of me.

"You look amazing." His words made me smile, the lust in them. Some part of me knew they weren't real, that he wouldn't say that, but I wanted to hear it so badly, I let myself pretend.

"Kenz?" His real voice shook away the fantasy, especially when it seemed more annoyed than pleased.

"What?" I asked, sitting up and placing my hands behind me, to rest my weight on.

"I said that you shouldn't just lay out dressed like that."

"Like what?" I peered down at me, my brows furrowed. My shorts weren't *that* short, and the bralette didn't show much cleavage and reached a good inch below my bustline. "It's not like I'm walking around in a thong."

He went into a coughing fit, hitting his hand against his chest. Had he just choked on his own saliva because of my comment?

Times like this made me laugh, remembering that despite the age difference, he could be just that awkward around me. *And he calls me innocent.*

"Don't talk like that!" he said once he caught his breath.

"Like what? I said thong, not dildo."

He sighed and sat beside me, the action always making me smile. He looked funny seated on the ground, and he always groaned when forced to get up and off the floor, complaining about being too old for that. "You should be a lot more careful."

"I think I've been pretty careful," I argued. "I never go anywhere without you all, I'm always watching for people stalking me, I never call anyone I don't need to."

"I don't mean like that." He cast me a side-eye, but a flush to his cheeks suggested he was trying to not look at me. "You *do* realize you're a girl, right?"

I patted down my body, then widened my eyes when I reached my chest. "Is *that* why I have these?"

"Very funny," he deadpanned. "You're a young girl living with four adult men. You should be more aware of your surroundings."

I waved him off. "I'm sorry, but I'm not going to do that. I'm going to dress how I want and I'm not going to worry about what anyone else thinks about it. It's not *my* job to dress for *your* comfort."

Hayden huffed softly. "You're too trusting. It terrifies me that when I'm not around to keep an eye on you, you'll end up hurt. I mean, you seem to completely forget you're living with men, that you're so vulnerable. You fall asleep wherever you want, you leave yourself so exposed to danger, you sunbathe in next to nothing, and through it all, it doesn't even *occur* to you that anything bad might happen."

"Yeah, well, I might be worried if it wasn't for the fact that *none* of you are interested in me. Let's be real — I could sunbathe naked out here and I'd just get a lecture about how that isn't ladylike." I closed my eyes as I pictured that exact thing, smirking at the way they'd try to explain to me my mistake.

"That's because we want what's best for you, but you shouldn't push it. Men do have a point where their self-control snaps, Kenz. We have a place where our instincts overwhelm our good sense."

That heat inside me grew again as I wondered how Hayden would look if he got to that point, if I pushed him over that line. Would he be rough? Would he hold me still, his aggressive lips against mine, his seeking hands stripping me down? I wouldn't fight him, of course. Nope, I'd welcome it, begging him to keep going, but I had to admit, the thought of such a clear-headed man not thinking straight drew me in.

Or maybe it was better to say that I liked the idea of him losing his control because of *me*.

My cheeks felt warmer than before, and it wasn't because of the sun at all. It was the fantasy in my mind. When I opened my eyes again, however, it didn't help.

Instead, I found Hayden there, somehow looking even better than before. His bare skin, his dark eyes, his body close enough I could so easily reach out and touch him. My fingers itched, moving as though to grasp him already. My hand shifted, just a bit, miles ahead of my brain.

I stopped myself—somehow—and sat up quickly. I didn't need *another* rejection. They hurt too much, and my pride had taken enough of a beating already.

"Are you okay?" Hayden pressed his palm to my forehead. "Your face is flushed. Are you sick?"

I bit my bottom lip to stop a moan from escaping, frustration eating away at me. He wanted to talk about *me* needing to be careful? About *me* not understanding men's desires, but he was the one who didn't seem to get it!

He kept touching me, even after knowing how I felt, after rejecting me. It suddenly felt overwhelming and unfair, the chaos in my body impossible to ignore.

"I'm not sick." I slapped his hand away then got to my feet, embarrassed by my overreaction, by him not getting it. "I'm just overheated," I lied. "I'm going to go shower and cool down."

I didn't wait for him to say anything before escaping the yard and his *far* too tempting body.

Talk about someone who needs to stop walking around wearing so little...

All I knew for sure was that I'd need to deal with this need inside me before I did something stupid—again—and made a fool of myself.

* * * *

Kenz

It wasn't even dark yet, but as it turned out, my libido didn't care about pesky details like that. I'd showered the sweat from sitting in the sun off, but even cold water hadn't cooled the heat inside me at all.

When I got out, wrapped in a towel, I realized I couldn't keep going on like this. That want inside me just kept getting worse, and I saw no way it would change in the near future. I wasn't magically going to end up with a partner, especially with how my life was going currently.

Sometimes a girl has to take care of things herself.

The mattress gave as I sat on the end of the bed. I dragged my fingers over my lips, the softness giving beneath the touch, as I imagined the warmth and press of someone else.

I pictured my fingers were someone else's as I moved them down my throat. I shivered, my skin electrified from both the shower and from seeing Hayden shirtless.

Really, who could blame me? I lived with four men who were *far* more attractive than was fair. Every day I was surrounded by a feast but here I was, starving.

When I reached the line where the towel wrapped around me, I tugged the terrycloth free. Something about doing this in the sunlight felt so much different than at night. It made me feel sensual and sexy in a way I didn't normally. I could have crawled beneath the blankets, but the heat made me not want to, my skin still damp from the shower.

So instead, I scooted up on the bed, leaving the towel there at the foot. I rested my back against the large, incredibly soft pillows. My eyes slid closed so I could focus on the feelings instead of anything else.

It also let my mind drift. When I was out there, in front of the others, I had to pretend I didn't care about them as much as I knew I did. I had to keep it all to myself or risk another lecture and rejection. Here, though?

Alone in the room, with my eyes closed and my fantasies playing out in my mind, I didn't have to force or fake anything.

My nipple tightened beneath my gentle coaxing as I moved one hand to my breast. I thought back to how skillfully Vance had touched me, trying to replicate what he'd done.

I parted my lips and let a soft moan escape, trying to keep it quiet but unable to silence it entirely. I teased my nipple, shifted between light brushes over the tip before dragging my nail against the hardened point. Meanwhile, I slid my other hand down my front, over my damp skin, passing my stomach, my navel, to the juncture of my thighs.

I hadn't grown up unaware of my own body, or raised to think it was dirty. This was far from the first time I'd enjoyed some private time — though I hadn't since coming here — yet this felt even better than usual.

Maybe it was because I finally had a face in my mind? Before, I'd picture identity-less people. They'd been bodies and hands and lips, but that was it. They'd meant nothing to me, had lacked any connection, anything that made my heart race.

This time, however, they had faces.

I pictured Vance's playful smirk, the way I knew everything would be a fun game with him. I *heard* Char's mocking tone, the way he'd probably tease me during, and the small thrill at how that bite of humiliation would make me want him more. I thought about Hayden's strong hands, the way I always felt safe with him, how even if he was awkward most of the time, he never stopped trying to do what he thought was best for me. Lastly, right as I brushed my pointer finger through my drenched folds, I pictured Tor there, his golden eyes staring up at me from between my thighs as he teased me with his tongue. The fantasy was so powerful, so real, that I would have sworn my finger was his.

Still, it had been so long since I'd done this, and I had no idea when I might again, so I found myself reluctant to get right to the good part. I'd never forgive myself if I *wham-bam-thank-you-ma'am-ed* myself.

So I teased more, slipping along my wet pussy, dancing over the top of my hooded clit without touching it directly. It wasn't enough, and almost of their own accord, my knees parted, spreading wide, giving me more room. I pictured Tor's hands pressing them wide, exposing parts of me that no man had ever seen.

And *fuck,* I wanted to be seen.

I wanted someone to look at me, not like a kid, not like a burden, not like an item to own, but as a woman they wanted because they couldn't wait another second to touch me. I craved that with everything I was, to have a moment where I was the most important thing in the world to someone.

The memory of Hayden outside hit me again, how the light had shown the golden hues in his deeply tan skin. I thought about how hot that skin would be if I touched it, warmed from the heat and the sun. I wanted to drag my tongue over his wide, flat nipple, to sink my teeth into the hard muscles of his chest and leave a mark.

My cunt tightened as I slid along it again, as if begging me for something that I'd never had.

Normally, when I masturbated, I stayed outside. I focused on my clit, using either my fingers or a vibrator to get off. It always worked, and I found it hard to complain. I'd bought a dildo before, of course, had tried, but that felt different.

Impersonal, a bit uncomfortable. Even if I wanted to feel more, to experience more, it hadn't really felt like my sort of thing.

However, as my mind went down so many filthy paths, as I tried desperately to picture the men naked, my pussy fluttered as though just as curious as I was.

I pressed my pointer finger against the opening of my cunt, hesitation in the touch. I thought about the times Hayden had taken my hand in his, about just how large those hands — and thus fingers — were. They were far thicker than my own, which made me gasp when I sank just the tip of one finger into me.

The heat of my cunt surprised me. Why did it suddenly not feel like my own? As if my body had changed and I hardly recognized it at all? Whatever the reason, I didn't let myself dwell.

I sank more of that finger into me, then rubbed the heel of that hand against my clit. It wasn't as direct as if I'd used my fingers, not enough to push me over the edge, which was why my hips moved as though seeking more.

"Yes," I whispered into the darkness of my own mind. Even if the sun filled the room, my thoughts remained dim, clouded by lust of the scent of my own body and the fantasies that held me. "Please," I begged to no one.

I pumped that one finger into me, raising my hips each time, wanting to go deeper. *If Hayden were here, he could reach far deeper.* His fingers were longer and thicker than mine, and he wouldn't have to reach down my body to gain access. If he were there, between my legs, he could sink so far into me, to touch places that I'd never even dared with a toy.

It played like a movie in my mind, the sensation of his lips on my thighs as he plunged those fingers into me, using the hands that had protected me so many times already to bring me pleasure.

The fake him, the one in my mind, didn't look at me like I was a kid. It didn't reject me or push me away. Instead, it gave me everything while whispering that he had me, that he wouldn't let me go, that he'd stay with me no matter what.

And I believed that false him because I wanted it so badly.

"Please, let me come, Hayden," I whispered, my voice breathless and strange to my own ears. I'd *never* sounded like that before, hadn't ever spoken while pleasuring myself before. Then again, I'd never been this into it, either.

It seemed absence made the heart grow fonder, or at least rejection made the libido grow more shameless.

My body started to crest over that edge, the point of no return when this shivering, tingling sensation ran over my spine and through the muscles of my thighs.

Just as I gave in, prepared to drown in that wonderful, mindless pleasure, a loud crash stopped me.

My eyes popped open, and standing there at the door was the very man I fantasized about, his dark eyes wide and locked on me, a shattered cup on the ground.

Talk about a way to ruin a perfectly good orgasm…

Hayden

What the hell are you doing, you dirty old man?

The thought hit me so hard, it could have left a bruise. Not that it mattered, because as it turned out, the sight of Kenz could shut down my entire brain.

She was on top of the covers of her bed, the light pouring in through the window so not a bit of her was obscured. A forgotten towel rested at the foot of the bed and the familiar scent of her shampoo filled the room. She'd stretched out, her head on the pillow, her wet dark hair pulled up into a messy bun on the top of her head, making her appear disheveled.

And the rest of her? Well, it was *very* naked. She had one hand on her breast, cupping the bottom while she stroked over the nipple. Her other hand was between her spread thighs, with one finger deep inside her as she rubbed her palm against her clit. Her hand was in the way of seeing the top of her pussy, but I easily saw where she had sunk one finger into her pretty cunt.

I should have turned around and walked out. I should apologize and tell her I was so sorry, that I'd knocked but hadn't gotten a response, but none of that came to mind.

Especially because after I'd managed to drop the glass, she'd opened those dark eyes of hers and frozen, locking us in some strange, sexually charged standoff.

A footstep behind me woke me up, especially when from down the hall, Vance called, "Did something break? Everything okay?"

The idea of anyone else seeing her like this was unacceptable, so I quickly twisted to call back. "Yeah, it's fine. I just dropped something. Not a problem." I slammed the door shut, frantic to create some privacy for Kenz before she got walked in on by *everyone*.

Especially because just keeping myself under control felt insurmountable. The last thing I wanted was to have to deal with anyone else going through it.

Of course, after twisting the lock, something else occurred to me. I rested my forehead on the wood, wishing it was cool steel instead to help calm my racing heart. "I meant to be on the outside of this door when I closed it," I said softly.

The bed creaked, and the fluttering of fabric came a moment before her shy voice. "I'm decent."

Maybe in person, but nothing could scrape that memory out of my mind.

I turned but kept my gaze on the floor, then rubbed my hand over the back of my neck. I needed to clean up the shattered glass, right? That seemed a safe enough line of thought. Anything other than her lovely pale skin, than the soft pink of her cunt, than the way her nipples had been a rose color I wanted so badly to taste.

No, bad man! She's a kid!

She was *nineteen*. My brain refused to even do the gymnastics to work out how much older than her I was, to acknowledge just how inappropriate my thoughts were. She might think she was interested, but she'd get over that nonsense soon enough.

The last thing I needed was to touch her, to leave her with a memory she'd only come to regret eventually.

"I'm sorry," she said, her tone uneasy.

Stop being an asshole.

I took a deep breath to calm myself. I needed to be the adult here, right? "You didn't do anything wrong." I rubbed the back of my neck with one hand, trying to keep my voice wrong. "That's a totally natural thing to do. Kids your age—"

"*Kids my age?*"

Ouch, that tone of hers said I'd picked the exact wrong thing to say, didn't it?

Then again, that was far from uncommon for me.

"I just mean, you're young, so self-exploration, that's totally natural. It's normal, you know?"

The silence that filled the room was so thick I could have choked on it. Worse? I swore I could smell her, that some wonderful, feminine scent wafted through the room. I wanted to grasp her wrist and lick her finger clean, to—

No!

Kenz laughed. It sounded like the sort of laugh a person let out when they reached the end of their rope, when nothing was funny but they either laughed or lost their shit entirely.

It made me finally lift my gaze to see her, that towel wrapped loosely around her as she sat on her knees on the mattress. Her hands held the edges of the towel together, her knuckles white from how tightly she gripped it.

She wiped away a tear as she laughed with her other hand. "You really are clueless, aren't you?"

"Yeah, well, I can't deny that. I've got a lot of skills, was given plenty of blessings, but being good with women has never been one of them."

"Oh, I can tell. I mean, I'm *sure* you heard what I said, right?"

I jerked my gaze to the side and nodded, unable to answer out loud. She meant when she'd called *my* name, telling me in no uncertain terms exactly what her fantasy had been about. Even if the sight of her naked and doing *that* weren't enough to burn into my memories, the sound of her voice as she'd called out to me for more?

That would never shake free.

"And yet you still start giving me some sort of 'your body is changing' lecture like a middle school science teacher?" She shook her head and let out a long sigh.

"Sorry," I muttered, unsure what else to say.

"I know I'm not sexy," she said, her voice so quiet I had to strain to hear it. "I'm not unaware of what I am and what I'm not. I'm not one of those women who is super sensual, some femme fatale that men fall over themselves to be with, but am I really *so* unattractive that you see me like that and all you can think of is talking about girls my age?"

My chest ached at the tone of her voice, the doubt there. It had me sighing, because I'd *never* been any good at standing by while others suffered. So even if this ruined my image, I couldn't let her just think that.

"That's not it," I admitted. "I'm not saying you're not attractive."

"I don't need pity compliments."

"It's not pity, Kenz. Look, you're *so* young compared to me. Seeing you that way feels wrong, like I'm taking advantage of you, especially because of the position you're in—at least in part because of me."

"Last I checked, men didn't worry too deeply about things like that, not if they actually want a girl."

"And that's the difference, that's my point. *Boys* don't, but men damned well better. Even the *idea* of touching you, of seeing you like that, makes me feel like some old pervert lusting after someone I've got not business with. So when I walked in and saw that, when I heard you, I froze. I didn't want to make you feel bad, like you'd done something wrong, and I had no idea what else to say."

She hesitated for so long that I risked looking at her. *Bad choice.* She looked so innocent there, kneeling on the bed, wrapped in a white towel, a flush still on her cheeks. Just looking at her reminded me of the soft curves of her body, of how wet her finger had looked as she'd pumped it into herself. What made it worse—or hell, maybe better?—was that vulnerability she had, the way she stared at me with so much trust.

"So you're telling me you *are* attracted to me?" Her question made her look vulnerable, and it was because of that honesty of hers. She wasn't fishing for compliments, but rather asking because she couldn't quite believe it.

"Only an idiot wouldn't be," I answered.

"So why do you keep turning me down?"

"I already explained that to you. You're—"

"Don't call me young again!" Her voice rose that time, as though she'd had more than enough of my bull.

I can't blame her for that, can I? Still, the spark of temper made me fight a smile. It probably wouldn't go well to tell her I found her adorable when she was angry, right? Even I wasn't stupid enough around women to do something like that.

Instead of saying anything back — I had a feeling that no matter what I tried, I'd get it wrong — I stayed quiet to give her the space to voice her feelings.

"You know my past now, know what I've gone through. I am not some kid who was so sheltered I don't know anything about life. I don't need you to make choices for me because you don't think I can make them myself."

"I know you're smart, Kenz, and that you're tough."

"Then trust that I know my own mind. Stop treating me like I can't run my own life, the way *everyone* treats me."

"You're just confused."

"I'm not confused — I'm horny!"

And just like that, any argument I had went straight out of my head. I thought back to the women I'd slept with over the years, mostly casual relationships that never got serious, and *none* of them would have dared say something so honest. No, even if they wanted to seduce me, they played coy, they teased, they liked the chase.

So Kenz managed to completely disarm me by coming right out and telling me the truth, no matter how embarrassing it must have been.

Judging from the red on her cheeks, she found it *very* embarrassing.

But she wasn't done yet, because she kept going. "I'm an adult whether you want to recognize it or not. I have the same exact biological urges as any other adult, the same wants, the same needs. Stop looking at me like I'm an innocent kid, because I'm not. I'm a woman, and you all have jerked me around for weeks now. You tell me to be careful about what *I* wear but what about you? You walk around without a shirt not giving a damn about how I feel! So you know what, yes, I realized you — *none of you* — were going to man up and do anything so I had to take care of myself."

She finished her tirade with a frustrated huff, as though she were so over me.

Her words, though, they stuck with me. I'd worked so hard at ignoring her, at trying not to see her that way, that I hadn't ever really thought she'd see *me* that way.

Sure, she'd said she loved us, but I'd taken that as some innocent schoolgirl crush. I figured she had some idea in her head about a white dress and a picket fence and a life that I couldn't give her — that none of us could.

Never in my wildest imagination would I have thought that she'd want me in a more carnal way. It should have concerned me, but instead?

I wanted to stand taller, to puff my chest out like an idiot. The idea that this girl who could have about anyone thinking of me like that? Whatever hope I'd had of staying detached disappeared.

She swallowed hard, and a fire in her eyes said she'd noticed that I hadn't spoken or left yet. "I know how dangerous all this is. I know better than most how quickly life can change, how fast everything can get snatched away. I'm not sitting here looking for forever — I know none of us can promise that."

"So what are you asking for?"

"Just be honest and trust that I'm honest, too. If I want something, don't assume I don't understand. If you don't want me, fine, tell me that, but don't tell me it's all for my own good."

I stepped forward, a shard of glass cracking beneath my boot, forgotten in the heat of the moment. I'd have to clean it up later, but for now? It didn't matter at all. I stopped at the foot of the bed, then caught her chin and lifted her face until she looked at me.

Staring down at her like this made my heart beat recklessly fast, made me feel dizzy and powerful and out of control all at once. Her eyes were dark and large and so trusting.

"You scare the hell out of me, Kenz. You feel like a trap, like everything I want all at once, but at the worst possible time. I keep thinking you have to be a test for me, some divine punishment where the universe puts what I want most in front of me knowing I can't possibly have it. When I opened that door and saw you? When I heard you say my name? It was like the universe was laughing at me."

The pink of her tongue flashed as she licked her bottom lip, the action even sexier because I knew she didn't do it to tease me. No, Kenz didn't have that in her. "The only reason you think you can't have me is because of what's in your head. I'm not an idiot—I know my age and I know yours and I'm still here, aren't I? Show me the respect I deserve by not thinking you know my mind better than I do."

I bent down and pressed my forehead against hers, her tempting lips so close I could have claimed them in a kiss. She would have let me, too.

But...I couldn't bring myself to cross that line.

I remembered how she'd slapped Vance, how she'd admitted she'd never had a kiss before.

I couldn't take her firsts, not when I knew I couldn't offer her the forever she deserved. I never wanted her to look back on me, on us, and hate us for taking things that weren't ours to have.

But I also couldn't walk out on her.

So I did the next best thing, or at least I told myself that. Sometimes, in my line of work, when a man knew he'd have to do terrible things, all he could do was pick the one that did the least damage.

I released her, then unlaced my boots and left them on the floor before I slid into the bed. I put my back against her pillows, wrapped an arm around her waist and tugged her against my chest. She fit *so* perfectly there, cradled in my arms, seated between my legs, that I knew I was in trouble.

This girl had complete power over me, and I didn't even want to fight it anymore.

Kenz

I froze, surrounded by so much of Hayden that I had no idea how to react. He still wore no shirt, which allowed the warmth of his skin to soak into me, only the towel between us.

"What are you doing?" I asked in a soft whisper.

"You were almost there, right?" His lips teased my shoulder, the touch soft and coaxing. "You're the one who said you were horny, so keep going."

"And what are you going to do?"

"You know what I told you before, don't you? I said I'd always be behind you, that I'd support you, that I'd take care of you. That's what I'm doing." His voice came out dark and low, and his nearness made his whispers electrified my skin.

"So we're going to—"

"No. I hear you, and I'm trying, but I'm not prepared to actually do much with you. I'm still afraid you'll realize it's a bad idea."

"Then just leave," I snapped and went to sit up.

His strong arm wrapped around me and pinned me back to him, the action pulling loose the edge of the towel so it started to open at the front. "No. You need this, right? And I was already here" — he pressed a sweet kiss to my temple — "so keep going just like you were."

A petty part of me wanted to tell him to go to hell. I wasn't some dirty movie for him to watch, after all. It felt unfair for him to put a limit there, to make it clear he wouldn't get too involved while still getting to watch me at such a personal moment.

But the other part, the larger one, didn't give a damn. It would take what it could get, no matter how little.

If this was all he'd offer, I was pathetic enough to happily take it.

So I relaxed, resting fully against him. His heart pounded hard and fast. *Is he as nervous as I am?* It didn't seem possible, but his racing pulse suggested it. Strange as it was, him being nervous made me bolder.

I took a deep breath, then undid the towel the rest of the way, letting it hang fully open. It remained pinned between us, but if he glanced down now, he'd see all of me. Thankfully, with him behind me, I couldn't tell if he did or not, or more important — how he felt about it.

His breath quickened, teasing my ear, my neck. "You really are beautiful," he whispered.

I closed my eyes, letting his voice ease me and my fears. It felt like the world was only the two of us, just in this moment. I cupped my other breast, and the moment I touched my nipple, it reignited the desire from before, sparking it back to life.

It felt like the fire had never gone out, the way the embers burned even after a campfire died, ready to flare up the moment is found any fuel.

I gave up any worries about this, about how I looked, about what he thought. In some ways, I ignored entirely that Hayden was behind me, pressed against my back, because if I thought about that too much, my nerves would get the best of me.

I had him here—I wouldn't risk ruining it early. Instead, I gave in to my own desire and moved my other hand down my body to the juncture of my thighs, to where I needed attention the most. My pussy was just as wet as before, and when I slipped one finger inside, it felt different than it had before.

Why? It still wasn't as good as I suspected it could be, but with Hayden's breath teasing the tiny hairs on my neck, I pictured him even more clearly.

"Just one finger?" His voice made me jump, but as much as it surprised me, it excited me. Real him was *so much* better than fantasy him, even if the real him didn't touch me. "Are you really satisfied with just one?"

"I don't usually…" My words drifted off as I spoke, the answer too telling, too vulgar to utter out loud. I'd already been as brave as I could manage by all but yelling at him that I was horny. Telling him I didn't normally masturbate by fucking myself with anything was too far.

He groaned, the sound deep and masculine and one I'd *never* heard from him before. He kept the one arm wrapped around me, trapping me, but it didn't feel stifling. Instead, it made me feel safe, as though with that arm, he held back all the threats and all the bad things in the world. "You really don't know what saying things like that do to a man, right? Or maybe you don't understand what men want when they hear things like that?"

"Or maybe I want you to do something when I say it," I argued softly.

"You say that because you don't know what monsters men can be, the things we want. When I walked around that corner earlier and saw you dressed in so little, stretched out in the sun?" He didn't finish the thought, but he didn't need to.

I might not have any real experience, but even I knew what someone might think about at a time like that.

Especially because *I'd* thought similar things when I'd seen him shirtless. If he was a pervert, well, so was I.

I shifted, the energy in my body growing until I had to move my hips. The action pressed something hard against my back, and it took only a moment for my lust-riddled brain to make sense of that.

He's hard.

That surprised me, and why was that? Wasn't that exactly what I wanted? Some proof that he found me attractive? Something that made me feel desired, that he couldn't lie about? He might have had reservations, nothing might happen beyond this, but just the fact that his cock had responded to me was enough.

"I'm pathetic," he whispered before he pressed his lips to my neck, the kisses soft and teasing, as though he handled something precious and fragile. "I've *never* let my personal feelings affect a client before, never been unable to resist before, but here I am, hard and pressed against a *teenager*." His tone held so much self-loathing, but it didn't stop the accompanying lust in his voice.

When I slid my finger out, I pinned it with my middle finger and pressed the two into me. The added fullness felt different, though I wouldn't at first say better.

Except it made me think that the two were probably closer to the width of a single one of Hayden's thick fingers. It let me fantasize that he wasn't so hands-off.

He worried about my age, but the truth was that this was all scary. Having him there, having someone I trusted help me, guide me, it reassured me. It made me feel like sex wasn't nearly as terrifying as it had felt before. In fact, his age and experience were undoubtably part of what drew me.

I didn't want him in spite of those things, but they were a part of what I loved about him.

And no matter how annoying his habit of overthinking was, even that made me feel safe. I didn't have to worry because I knew he'd already done so.

I tilted my head, exposing more of my neck to his treacherous kisses. I wanted to wear marks from him, to feel some connection after this fleeting moment ended, to have proof it had happened at all.

I ground my palm against my swollen clit, my movements instinctual, and I lifted my hips each time I sank my fingers in deep.

This time, when my release neared, I chased after it. I rushed toward it, *needing* to feel the snap of all that tension inside me. After all the rejections, all the time in close quarters with men I wanted so badly but who refused to touch me, I feared I'd go mad if I didn't satisfy this lust at least on my own.

The first wave of pleasure crashed over me. It started with a tightening in my cunt, the walls clenching around my fingers, and spread from there. My thighs, the muscles in my back, they all followed suit and contracted. I arched my back, and my hand that had teased my breast flew backward, clutching for something to hold on to to keep me from getting rushed away in the torrent of sensations.

And the thing I found to hold on to? Hayden's arm, still around me. I wrapped my fingers around his thick wrist, clinging to him as though I were on a cliff and he were my only hope of not plummeting to my end.

It *felt* like my end, too. I kept grinding the heel of my hand against my clit, prolonging this feeling, this blissful, mindless pleasure. The feeling of his arm around me, his hard cock against my back, his familiar scent of sandalwood that surrounded me, it all helped me lose myself in that lovely, sensual haze.

The seconds ticked by slowly, but eventually, just when my lungs burned because I couldn't even draw in air, that building pressure inside me fully snapped free and I gasped in a rough breath.

I leaned fully back against Hayden's warm, solid chest, panting hard as I tried to calm my racing heart.

"That was beautiful," he whispered.

His voice, so close, startled me. When I shifted, I realized my fingers were still inside me. That haziness from before, when lust had made things simple, disappeared.

It made me realize I was naked, that Hayden could see every inch of me, and we hadn't even done this in the safety of darkness. I peered down my body to find my chest flushed, my nipples still hard, and between my thighs? *My hand.*

I pulled my hand away, whimpering when even that much stimulation proved how sensitive I remained. I lifted my hand to find my own wetness covering the two fingers I'd had inside me.

I went to sit up, to go wipe off, but Hayden gripped me tighter. "Stay just a little longer."

"I need to wash my hand," I said, the words embarrassing me.

He caught my wrist with his other hand. "I don't want to move. When we do, we'll break this moment and have to go back to real life. Instead, I want to stay in this dream a little longer." He tugged my hand back, and I thought he'd wipe it off on something.

Instead, warmth enveloped the two fingers that had just been inside me. Hayden's tongue moved against me, sliding along the seam between them, capturing every bit of my juices.

The action felt so depraved I had no idea what to say. Worse, it felt like a nudge, telling my body to get ready for round two.

However, after finishing his work, after devouring every trace of wetness from my fingers, Hayden released them with one last teasing lick. He showed no signs of releasing me, of talking, of doing anything.

And no matter how uncomfortable it felt at first, I quickly relaxed in his embrace. The steady beating of his heart, the warmth of his skin, even the place where his still-hard cock nestled against my back, it all eased me.

Before I knew it, my eyes closed and I fell asleep against him, his words echoing in my head.

If this is a dream, I don't want to wake up from it just yet either.

Chapter Nine

Char

Kenz didn't have much of a poker face. Normally, that annoyed me. It felt like looking at an open wound on someone. I could take advantage of it, and often did, but it still set my nerves on edge.

Maybe bringing her along had been a bad decision. Usually, I worked alone. At the rare times when I needed someone else, I'd hire someone expendable or trick a person if they didn't need any real information.

However, with everything going on, I didn't want to risk either of those options. There was far too much in the air—I didn't need any other potential problems by bringing in new people.

Which meant instead of something easy and uncomplicated, I had Kenz at my side, a notebook in her arms as she shifted her weight from foot to foot. She looked nice in the suit—a knee-length black skirt that hugged her curves, paired with a crisp white button-up shirt. No jacket, though, because I didn't want her looking *too* professional.

"Mr. James is ready to see you," the receptionist said, her smile far too suggestive.

She seemed the type who had taken this job to gain access to rich, successful men she could get her claws into. It explained the way the top few buttons on her shirt sat undone, the way she leaned forward when speaking so I could see right down her shirt to the lacy black bra beneath.

I glanced to my side, to Kenz, and had to stifle a laugh at how different she appeared. She didn't play those games, didn't have that come-hither look, didn't draw a man in the same way. The receptionist was a black widow, ready to devour men in whatever way she could. Kenz, though?

She was the kitten I liked to call her. Even when she had a fit, it amounted to little beyond her baring her little teeth and swiping with her tiny claws.

So why was it that I couldn't seem to get her out of my mind?

Instead of worrying about it, I rose and nodded at the receptionist, heading toward the office door just past her. Kenz's heels clicked against the tile as she followed, looking like an uncomfortable shadow behind me.

Which was the exact part she needed to act. I could have picked something difficult for her, but it made more sense to play to her strengths.

"Mr. Ulysses," the man who sat on the other side of the desk said in greeting as we entered the office. A huge window sat behind him, overlooking the city. That showed the advantage of having an office on the upper floor of a huge building like this.

Dirty money sure buys nice things.

Hadn't I seen that, though? It was why people did the things they did, after all.

"Thank you for taking the time to see me, Mr. James." I shook the man's hand, keeping my expression blank.

Then again, sliding into a personality made me feel safe and comfortable. It didn't matter what person I was being.

The friendly, charming best friend? The seductive playboy? The guy women take home to meet their parents? The bad boy with a heart of gold? Or this guy — a hard-ass business exec who would do anything to get what he wanted.

Whatever job I had, I just had to find the right person to become to make it happen. And Mr. James here was the sort to respect power, making this personality the perfect trap for him.

"I'm afraid I've had a very busy week," he said as he gestured for us to sit. "When it rains, it pours, right?"

I sat in the chair closer to the door while Kenz took the other seat. Her fingers clutched the notebook tightly, the telling action making it clear how nervous she was.

It annoyed me, in a way. Did she think I wouldn't be able to keep her safe? Did she worry like this when out with Hayden or Tor?

I'd been underestimated a lot in my life, and used it to my advantage, but I didn't much care for Kenz seeing me that way.

I pushed that away, focusing instead of the plan. "I've heard as much. It is one reason I asked for this meeting. Given the stability issues in your company right now, I'm not sure this is the best time to get into business with you."

Mr. James' face tightened, and his surprise made me want to laugh. Clearly, the man had less of a mind for business than he wanted to believe. Any worthwhile exec would have seen this coming the moment the news stories had broken about the company's problems.

And boy were they problems. Three board members were under investigation, multiple investors had pulled out and rumor had it that Mr. James himself would get looked at soon enough.

All because he liked to make deals that were as lucrative as they were illegal.

And all because I made sure those facts ended up in the right hands.

"I can assure you the problems are nothing to worry about," he rushed out. "They're being handled as we speak. Within two weeks, it'll all have blown over."

I let nothing show on my face, not the amusement at his confidence or the annoyance that he wasn't wrong. He'd greased the right palms, whispered into the right ears. Within those two weeks, the authorities would pin the blame on just one board member and close the case.

Mr. James expected it to be business as usual.

Or not.

"I'm not so sure," I said, then held my hand out to Kenz. She gave me the file tucked into the notebook she held, her hand trembling.

Then again, she didn't understand any of this. I'd given her almost no information, just throwing the outfit at her this morning and telling her she'd help me on a job today.

"Play the part of my secretary," I'd told her.

I pushed the file across the desk without opening it. The moment of him seeing it but not knowing what it might hold, that primed the fear I wanted him to feel. Scared people talked *much* faster and made their choices more rashly.

Mr. James opened the file with hesitation, and his expression tightened with each page he turned.

Then again, I *knew* I had him. I never went into meetings like this without being sure how it would go, that I had everything in order. It was all a basic playbook.

Offer them what they want and make them think they can have it.

Create a problem that they fear will take it all away.

Show them that the only way out is to go along with what you want.

It was so simple, and in the end, it always worked. It all came down to figuring out what a person needed, then making them believe only I could get it for them.

In this case, Mr. James' company had started to flounder, and when he thought he'd fixed it, that hope had raised him up. Now, however, I brought the hammer down and he had to recognize that nothing he did, nothing he could do, would save him anymore.

Nothing but me.

"How did you get this?" he asked.

"It wasn't difficult. I don't make a habit of dealing with others unless I know their vices and weaknesses. You, of course, made that far easier than usual since you have so many. I doubt your wife will be very happy to find out you moved yet another mistress into an apartment that you pay for." I spoke as he moved through the pages, through the evidence I'd compiled.

"That is an issue between a married couple," he muttered. "Besides, affairs aren't a big deal. No one cares about that anymore."

"Are you sure? Because as I understand it, it was your wife's money that was invested into your company, making her the largest shareholder. I wonder how willing she will be to support you if she finds out you are still unable to keep your dick in your pants?"

Mr. James' lips blanched and he darted his gaze around as though looking for some escape, some way to change the course he'd set himself on.

I kept going, wanting to drive home where he was. "Then there is the fact that the love nest you paid for? You've paid for it out of corporate funds. That is embezzlement, and if this were made public, even the authorities you've paid off won't be able to look the other way."

He crumpled one of the pages in his hand as he made a fist, his gaze hard as he stared right at me. Ah, there it was. Back someone into a corner and they all eventually show their teeth.

Mine are bigger, though.

I'd faced off worse than him without blinking. This washed-up cheater wasn't about to be the one to make me flinch.

Never play chicken with someone who has nothing to lose.

"You realize I have some very unsavory friends, don't you? If I press this button, I can have people come in here who ensure you two never walk out of here alive, that you are never found. What then? What does any of this matter if you never get to show it to anyone?" He stood and slammed his palm on the desk, hitting the papers in the open file. "You have aimed far too high here."

I didn't smile, instead staying in my role. "Have I? Do you really think I would come here without a plan? That I would show you this unless I was sure I could walk out of it?" I *tsk'd* softly to show my disappointtment in his short-sighted assessment.

"What I think is that you walked in here with one little girl by your side. You've stepped way too far out on a ledge without a safety line. I'd suggest you think *very* carefully about your future before you consider threatening someone like me again. You are just some rich asshole who thinks that because you've made some money in the stock market, you have power. No, trust me, *I* have real power."

I waited for him to wear himself out in his little tirade, enjoying how he puffed his chest out. When he finished, I waited a long, silent moment before responding. "That is where you're wrong. My name isn't Jake Ulysses. The company I run doesn't exist. You saw what you wanted to see and didn't look any deeper, didn't figure out none of it was real."

"So who are you?"

"That doesn't matter. All that matters is what I want. If you want this to stay quiet, you will transfer this amount into this account by six o'clock tonight." I pulled a card out of the chest pocket of my suit jacket and tossed it onto the desk beside his hand. Even still, I didn't rise from my seat.

No, it was better for me to appear unconcerned about him and his ranting, to make it seem all his threats didn't bother me at all.

And they didn't, to be honest.

He picked up the card, his eyes widening for a moment at the amount. "This..." he said, but pressed his lips together before voicing what no doubt he'd figured out.

"That's right. It is rather simple. Do that, and this information never sees the light of day."

"And what keeps me from calling in those friends I mentioned?"

I gestured at Kenz. "Her."

Mr. James looked over at Kenz, seeming to take real notice of her for the first time. "Forgive me, but I don't see anything about her that would stop me."

"That's because, yet again, you fail to take notice of the most important things. My associate here isn't a secretary. She is, in fact, a journalism student who is interning at a local news station."

Color drained from Mr. James' face, a sure sign he'd recognized how he'd ended up out maneuvered.

"She's left the information at the news station. If anything happens to her, if she doesn't return, that information will already be in the hands of those who can properly spread it. Basically? If you hurt us or try to stop us from leaving, all this and more will come out. Also, our disappearance will sit right at your door for the police to investigate."

Mr. James collapsed into his seat. He looked over at Kenz, his gaze wild, a bad sign. It was *never* good when someone got to that point, when they struggled that last bit, because they could make horrible choices that were harder to predict. "Why don't we make a deal, Miss? If you have the information, then only you need to walk out of here. What if I pay you half this amount, and in exchange, your friend here is mine? You turn over that information to me and I can assure you, I'll make it worth your time. I mean, you're just a pawn to this guy, right? Whatever he promised you—I'll give you more."

I almost chuckled at his attempt. It wasn't a bad move, and the fact he could surprise me was amusing. Rarely did people manage to make a move I hadn't expected, that I hadn't prepared for. It might have even worked if Kenz really were some journalist student who I'd brought along as simple insurance.

I glanced to the side, to Kenz, who sat up straight and stared right back at Mr. James. A moment of worry crossed my mind.

Mr. James had surprised me — could Kenz?

No. She'd never. It wasn't that I thought she wouldn't because she cared about me, but rather because Mr. James couldn't offer her anything worthwhile. She had access to money, so why would she help him?

"I'm just a man in a hard place," Mr. James pressed. "Yes, I have a mistress, but do you know why? My wife sleeps with other men all the time, thinking that because her family has money, she can do what she wants. So, yes, I found someone who loves me, and I paid it out of the corporate money because otherwise, my wife would find out. However, I also didn't accept any yearly bonuses the last five years! That means it works out. Are you really going to let this conman blackmail me like this? I may not be perfect, but is he any better? Using that to extort millions from me?"

The certainty I'd had before was *far* less certain now. The asshole had managed to hit the spot Kenz was weak, to play the victim to a woman who had a heart way too big for her own good.

I fought my own expression, keeping my mask in place perfectly, playing the part to keep myself calm. Had I made a mistake? Had I screwed this up? If so, why? Was it Kenz? Did she throw me off this bad?

Kenz stood, her back straight, looking nothing like the nervous intern she had earlier. How she flipped that switch so perfectly, I had no idea, especially because she did it naturally, not as part of a game. "No, thank you."

"Why not? He's some criminal, and I can tell by the look on your face that you aren't."

I wanted to hear her say that she trusted me, that I wasn't who this man claimed I was—even if I knew he wasn't wrong. I wanted her to stand up for me, to defend me, no matter how pointless that was.

Except, when she spoke, they weren't the words I'd wanted to hear.

"You're right—I'm not a criminal. I'd suggest you do as he asks, because trust me, he'll follow through on his threats." Her words came out strong but flat, as if she knew their truth even if she didn't like it much.

The final snap as Mr. James accepted his place said we'd won, but Kenz's expression didn't make me feel much like a winner.

"I'll have the money transferred by five," he said. "I trust that will end this."

"So long as you give me no reason to return, yes. You'll never see me again."

He nodded, his shoulders slumped. The sight of a broken person rarely did anything for me, but I didn't much mind it from him. I left the room, leaving the papers there for him.

Kenz followed me, neither of us speaking until we got into the car. The questions in my head swirled until I couldn't keep them in anymore.

"Why did you side with me?" I asked as I pulled the car into the street.

"I don't have anywhere else to go," she said, the words quiet.

"You're a terrible liar. You should really stop trying it, especially with me. Why go along with my plan? Why do as I asked? Why tell him no?"

She didn't look at me, her gaze locked outside instead. "He said you were a conman and a criminal, and you know what? He wasn't wrong."

Ouch. The words wounded me in a way I wasn't used to. I knew how people saw me, knew what I was, but somehow hearing it from Kenz hurt in an unexpected way. I pushed that aside, slid on a fake smile to hide how I felt. "That's right. So again, knowing that, why side with me?"

"Because you might be those things, but I'm not. If I betray those around me, how am I any better?"

My hand tightened on the steering wheel until my knuckles ached.

I knew what I was, so why the fuck did I hate it so much when Kenz saw what everyone else did?

* * * *

Kenz

What I really wanted to do was go home.

The strangest part was when I thought that, I didn't think about my apartment. Instead, I saw the house in my head, the open living room, the flowers in the backyard, the room that I'd made my own.

I'd lived in so many places that I hadn't thought any would ever really feel like home, but somehow, so quickly, this one had.

However, that didn't seem likely.

After helping Char with his job, after watching as he'd extorted millions from a man, he didn't seem quite done with me yet. The sour taste of the entire thing lingered in my mouth.

Mr. James was a piece of shit, no doubt about that. He probably deserved some karma for his actions, but how did Char getting rich off it balance the scales at all?

It made Char just another user, just another bad person taking advantage where he could.

Why did that bother me so much? I'd known he was a conman, but somewhere in my mind, I'd foolishly thought he did it for good, that he didn't hurt others, that he wasn't just a scavenger picking the flesh from the bones of other creatures.

I hate being wrong.

We arrived at an unassuming building of a drab gray color. It wasn't a house, but didn't strike me as a business, either. Greenery lined the building, with large dark windows all over the front. At the corner was a small sign with *Oak Hills Senior Living Facility* written on it.

Thinking we must have taken a wrong turn, I frowned and looked over at Char. He didn't look at me even though I'd bet he knew I stared at him. He hadn't said a word since I'd told him how I really felt, after all.

Instead of pulling back out of the lot and into the street, he parked the car near the front.

He said nothing as he got out of the car, so I remained inside for a moment. Did he want me to follow? Or was I just a pet that he'd leave in the car unattended while he did what he wanted.

What if he's here to take advantage of these people, too?

That idea got me leaving the car and rushing after him. While I wasn't about to betray him for a fistful of money, I also wouldn't stand by while he swindled little over ladies out of their retirement funds...

We reached the front door, and when I glanced to the side, I found his mask firmly in place. *Ah, he's being the sweet, charming Char, huh?*

It was strange, but after spending time with him, I recognized each of his personalities, could tell them apart. The memory of the smile he'd given me after I'd told him the truth burned in my memory, the way it had wrapped around him to hide his true feelings. He did that a lot, didn't he?

Who was the real man? Did he even know?

He walked through the front door, and a woman in scrubs stood at the large front desk. Her clearly fake smile turned real when she spotted Char.

"You're back!"

A bad feeling grew inside me. If he'd been here before, was he trying to ingratiate himself to these people? A pit in my stomach gnawed at me.

"Hello, Lucy," Char said, that cheerful, friendly voice the same one I'd heard that first day, that I'd heard directed at others since then but never me. "How have you been?"

"Good—just working, you know? I didn't know you'd be by today."

"Is it a bad time?"

"Of course not, not for you! Go on in—you know the way." She gave him a similar look to the receptionist at the office building we'd been in, as though he could make anyone smitten with him in moments.

It wasn't quite the same way Vance did, where he used his name and position to draw people in. He was who he was no matter whether people liked it or not, and it just worked for him.

Char, on the other hand, got people in his grasp by impressive observation and manipulation. I'd watched him do it enough to see through it, how he took note of every reaction and changed his behavior to better suit his need.

I followed him, staying to his side and just behind him. The home was nicer than I would have expected, though I supposed I had little experience with them in general. I just knew what I'd seen on television before, expecting a dim and dingy place that smelled slightly of death.

Instead, bright light poured in through the large windows and the people we passed all appeared rather happy.

We entered a large room with tables set around, many folks at all the different spots. Puzzles sat on some tables, while others had people playing cards or chess or just talking. The atmosphere was pleasant, relaxing.

"Char!" an aged voice called out, drawing my attention to the table it had come from. An older woman sat in a wheelchair there, her long gray hair braided back and away from her face. Wrinkles showed, many of them around her lips, like a scrapbook of all the times she'd smiled and laughed over her life.

Char waved before heading that way, his expression still the same one he'd used with the receptionist.

No, not *quite* the same, I realized. I spotted just the smallest hint of real affection in this look, one that had been missing with the women before.

"How are you feeling, Claire?" Char asked before leaning in and pressing a kiss to the woman's cheek.

She laughed and slapped his arm. "You're incorrigible, you know that? I didn't know you were going to stop by today. If I'd known, I'd have made some cookies." She paused, then looked past Char to me. "And who is this lovely young lady?"

Despite my unease at being here, my worries about what Char might be up to, I smiled at Claire. "My name is Kenz."

"What a pretty name. I'm Claire. Please, take a seat." She waved toward the other chairs at the table, the large puzzle in front of her.

Char sat, and I took a seat beside him.

"How do you know each other?" Claire asked.

I darted my gaze over to Char, unsure what to say. He'd given me an idea of what to say when dealing with Mr. James, the part I was to play, but he'd said nothing about this stop. While I didn't love the idea of whatever he might be up to here, I didn't want to step on his toes, either. I'd learned from the last job how dangerous these could get.

"She's a friend," Char said with a shrug.

"A friend, hmm?" Claire lifted one of her white eyebrows, then chuckled. "Is that what kids are calling it now? Ah, to be young and in love again."

He sighed, as though the words were unwelcome but not unexpected. "This is *hardly* love. Besides, don't pretend you can't fall in love again. I've heard ninety is the new sixty." His words came out almost playful.

"Love requires a certain level of stupidity that you lose when you reach my age. It's for the foolish, for those who don't know how unwise it is."

"But you're still as feisty as anyone in their twenties," Char pressed.

"Can you believe that they had a makeup artist come in here last week to give us makeovers?" Claire shook her head, though her eyes remained alight with laughter.

"That sounds nice," I said, thinking about how much some of the people here might have enjoyed such attention.

"She told us we could still be sexy at our age."

"And she made it out alive?" Char snorted. "Are you getting docile at your age?"

I glared at Char for the rude comment before looking back at Claire. "Is that bad?"

"Let women in their twenties be sexy, but when does it end? I'm ninety-six, sweetie, and I don't need to be sexy anymore. Let me age and turn into the scary creature in the fog that nature intends me to be, now. I have no need for things like that—I'm so much more than that." She looked at me then, her green eyes bright and sharp. For a moment, she didn't look like a frail old woman, but instead had a strength that astounded me, a mind that one should be wary of.

In fact, she looked like the fog monster she had just wanted to be.

"You're still young enough to not realize just how much you're worth, how much strength you have inside you. The world will tell you to be pretty, to be quiet and biddable and sweet, but you are so much more than that. Don't wait until you're my age to recognize that."

It was strange to speak to her, especially because I hadn't had parental figures in so long—especially a mother. I had no grandparents, didn't have aunts to step in and take that role. Even Nem hadn't been part of my life for most of my years growing up.

Was that what drew me to Claire?

Maybe a person never grows out of wanting a mom, huh?

"Char," called out a man as he walked over, his hand wrapped tightly around a cane.

"Hello, Frank," Char said, and the ease with which he seemed to know everyone's names surprised me. It suggested he spent enough time here to catalog and recall so much. "How's it going?"

"It's going okay."

"You're sweating a lot. Are you not feeling well?" Char was on his feet a moment later, a hand on the man's elbow to steady him.

"I'm okay," Frank assured him, patting the hand gently.

"Are you taking your medicine?" Char asked, his voice low.

Frank sighed, weariness in his expression. "Not much of it," he admitted.

"Why not?"

"You know what bureaucracies are like. Doctor says I need thirty pills a month, but insurance says they'll only cover fifteen." Frank shrugged as though it was no big deal. "So it's fine—I'm just rationing 'em."

Char's eyes darkened, though his smile never faded in the least. "Come on, let me walk you back to your room and I'll take a look at your paperwork, huh?"

Frank tried to say no, to tell Char not to worry, but Char was an expert at getting people do to as he wanted. It only took another minute before the two walked off, with Char keeping the older man steady as they went.

I started to rise, to follow, but Claire's voice stopped me. "Let them go—they'll be fine. Why don't you stay and keep me company?"

I couldn't find a good way or reason to say no, so I lowered myself back into the seat.

"This is the first time Char's brought anyone with him. So, let me guess, you've known Char about…" Claire paused and tapped one of her short nails against her wrinkled lips. "A month?"

"How did you know?"

"I've known Char for quite a few years now, but about a month ago, he came in here with the strangest expression. Since then, he's seemed different. One of the truths I've learned in my life is that nothing unsettles a man's life quite like the appearance of a woman." Claire laughed at her own words, the sound lyrical and open. "And now, after meeting you? You seem like just the sort of girl who could put our Char on the defensive."

"I don't know about that," I muttered. "He's hard to understand."

"Of course he is. That man wears a fake smile the way police wear bulletproof vests. He isn't for the weak or the faint of heart, that's for sure." She spoke about him with the affection usually reserved for one's grandchildren, which made me curious.

"How do you know him?"

Claire shifted, wincing as though even that movement aggravated her joints. Still, she didn't complain, continuing on. "I met him what must have been eight years ago, now, so no, he isn't my grandchild." Her smile suggested she knew what I was asking without me having to say it out loud.

She's far too similar to Char. No wonder they get along so well.

Of course, if they met eight years ago, I struggled to think he was taking advantage of them. That would have meant for a very long con, and I couldn't believe Claire or the others here had enough money to make that worth it.

"So how did you meet, then?"

"He came by here to ask questions about the person who ran this place. I don't know what brought his attention to it, why he set his sights on that, but he started coming in to visit at that time. He got to know me and a few others, and what can I say? I'm a sucker for a brilliant man. I could tell he was smart, but there was this wall there, this darkness in his eyes, and I guess when you get to my age, you want to help those who are going to still be here after you're gone."

"What happened with the person who ran the place?"

"Now that, I'm not sure about. That's the thing with Char — if you want details, you're probably out of luck. He isn't the type to say more than he has to. What I know is that after about a month of him stopping by, the old manager quit without a word. After that, this place got better. The prices for things went down, our fees went down, the food got better. Rumors are that the manager had been skimming money and pocketing the extras."

I frowned as the pieces of information came together. It sure *sounded* like the way Char would work, didn't it? I could almost see him finding the evidence needed to get the manager to leave, working behind the scenes then pretending as though he'd done nothing at all.

But why? What did he get out of it? Maybe he hadn't given a damn about Claire or the other people here, but had done it only because he'd extorted something from the manager at the same time? Perhaps helping the home out was nothing more than a side effect?

Why would he still be visiting, then?

"So he just stops by now?" I asked.

"Yes. Usually once a week or so he'll stop in. He might not be my grandson, but I'm pretty sure he's gained a whole host of grandparents here. I swear, I think a few of us have his picture in our wallets and we show them off to anyone who comes by." Claire's smile showed exactly how fond of Char she was, and the way Frank had spoken to him said she wasn't the only one.

I knew he showed people his best side, gave them what they wanted to make them pliable, but this felt different.

"What if he wasn't what you think he is?" I asked softly. Unable to help it, I went on. "What if what he shows you isn't real? What if he isn't the good person you think he is?"

Claire pressed her lips together then sighed. "Everyone has a darker side. They have parts of themselves they hide because they don't think other people can accept those parts. Char, he has more of those than most. I worry about him, you know? I wonder if he's shown anyone the real him, if he's let down that guard he's got for anyone. Life is long and it is lonely if you can't rely on others. Char hides behind what he thinks people want, and I've found that when people do that, it's because they don't think anyone could love the real them. After eight years, though, I've gotten glimpses. I've *seen* what he does, how he comes here week after week and does what he can. I guarantee you that by next week, Frank will have the medication he needs one way or another. Whether it gets approved by his insurance or the pharmacy claims it's cheaper or the home here starts supplying it—it'll work out. That's the Char I know, the one he doesn't show enough people, the one who does whatever it takes to make things work out and never once asks for anything back, never even takes credit for it."

I thought about the way Char had gotten Mr. James to pay that amount to a random bank account, and I struggled to believe Claire. It all sounded good, but how could I accept it after all I'd seen? Maybe Claire just wanted to see him the easiest way for her.

"I'll help you with the puzzle," I said when I couldn't think of a way to continue our conversation.

"Don't go too fast," Claire said.

"Why not?"

"Because the best way to ensure you've got another day is to leave things undone. Unfinished business will always keep a person going."

"Well, that's fine," I answered. "If we finish this, we'll just start another one today."

Claire smirked, as though thoroughly pleased. "Well, now I'm sure of it. You're a good match for Char, just as long as you both stop pretending to be people you aren't." With that, she picked up a piece and fit it into the puzzle.

I felt like this had been a glimpse into the man I couldn't understand, but I wasn't sure I was any clearer than I'd been before.

He was like trying to put a puzzle together upside down, and I had no idea what the real picture really was.

* * * *

"Kenz?" A hand on my shoulder shook me gently as the familiar voice drew me awake.

Which surprised me as I didn't recall falling asleep.

When I opened my eyes, I found Char's face close to mine, his red hair bright in the sun that cascaded in through the large windows. I had a moment of thinking what it would be like to wake up like this in bed with him. Would he speak to me this sweetly? Wake me with a gentle kiss to my lips?

No, he's more likely to pinch me if no one else is here to see.

And yet, my cheek twitched as a strange fondness filled my chest at the notion of his surly, sleepy voice, the not-so-likable part of him only I got to see.

What is wrong with me that I'd like that?

"You should know that you're supposed to wake Sleeping Beauty with a kiss," Claire said.

My cheeks heated as I realized we had an audience, and that I'd fallen asleep at the table.

Char reached for me, and I closed my eyes, that still-groggy part of my brain wondering if he'd kiss me. Instead, his fingers brushed my forehead, and a strange sensation made me frown.

I opened my eyes to find that Char had plucked a puzzle piece that had evidently stuck to my head when I'd fallen asleep at the table. He snorted, giving me a chiding look only I saw before he turned and fit the piece into the puzzle without even a moment of hesitation.

Show off.

"I'm so sorry," I rushed out to Claire. "I can't believe I fell asleep."

Claire waved off my concern. "Don't be. You looked tired, and if you were tired enough to fall asleep here, you needed it. Besides, I've seen how Char gets carried away with whatever he's doing. It's hard to blame you when you're left just sitting here." Her words were clearly scolding Char.

He pressed his lips together, a crack in that mask of his, before affixing his smile back on his face and turning. "I'd better get Sleeping Beauty back. It was good to see you, Claire. Make sure you give me a call if you need anything."

"We're having a dinner here next month. It's for family."

"Last I checked, I'm not family."

"Maybe not by blood, but that's never mattered. The truth is that most the blood relatives don't come to these things. It'd be nice if you came and brought Kenz with you."

Char's gaze darted to me, but he neither agreed nor declined. Instead, he bypassed the question. "I'll have to take a look at my schedule."

He said his goodbyes to Claire, and on our way out, he stopped at a number of others to chat. Each one treated him like Claire had, as though they couldn't be happier to see him. He asked them about their health, the recent issues, all the questions showing he not only knew about them but had committed those facts to memory.

The more I saw, the less I thought he was doing this for personal gain.

"Is she ready?" Char asked the receptionist before we left.

She nodded. "Yeah, she's waiting for you. You know the way."

Char tucked his hands into his pockets and headed the opposite way from the receptionist desk than we'd gone before, passing the front door, until we reached an office with the door open. Char poked his head in, and when the woman behind the desk spotted him, she flashed the same happy smile I'd seen from every person here.

"Sorry it took so long," she apologized as stood and came around her desk. "I was on a call with distributors for our needles. They want to raise the price and they're being very difficult because they know they're the only game in town." She let out a long sigh, exhaustion suggesting that the calls had taken a lot out of her.

Char's eyes sparkled with that same intelligence Claire had mentioned, as though he were already working through that problem to find a solution.

"You stop that," the woman said. "Let me handle this one, okay? You've done more than enough, and you'll drive yourself crazy trying to fix every little problem."

Char shrugged. "I have no idea what you're talking about."

What a crock. It didn't take knowing him well to tell he wasn't innocent, that he knew exactly what she meant.

And the woman's expression said she knew it, too.

"Oh, and that other problem?" the woman said. "It's been handled, too."

"Oh, has it?"

"Yeah, I just got word that the money was redistributed to the accounts of each resident who paid—plus interest. I'm sure they'll be thrilled when they find out."

"Yeah, I bet they will, too. What a strange world. I'm glad it got sorted out. Well, we better get going."

"Thank you," the woman said, her tone having grown serious. "I know you don't want to hear it, that you won't accept it, but thank you."

Char paused by the door. "I have no idea what you're talking about. I'm just glad it worked out." With that, he walked out.

I followed him, feeling like all day I'd been behind him, watching him interact and work without knowing all the details.

We got back into the car. The last time, after dealing with Mr. James, it had been Char to question me, to blurt out his thoughts. This time, it was my turn. "It's after six o'clock. The money you extorted from Mr. James went to these people, didn't it?" Before he could answer, I added on, "And don't lie to me. Consider it payment for my help today—I want the truth this time."

He sighed and kept his gaze locked on the building instead of at me. He didn't smile, didn't wear the costume of someone else. "Mr. James runs a personal finance business. He's made a big chunk of his funds by defrauding the elderly. People end up in homes like these and need help managing their finances, and Mr. James sends people there, promising to help them, only to drain them dry. By the time the people realize there's a problem, it's too late, and they have lawyers good enough to make everything appear legit. I found out about it a couple months ago when the manager here let me know about a few residents who were making large payments to Mr. James' company. I looked into it and figured out he was doing it to a lot of people."

"So you blackmailed him to get the money back?" I paused, then thought about the man's expression when he'd seen the card. "And Mr. James knew it was because of this, didn't he?"

"He should have. The name of the account I had him pay the money into was 'Carrington,' which was the code name he used to talk about the project."

"So it was a warning to him not to do that anymore?"

Char nodded. "I don't like having to deal with the same problem more than once, and a good threat tends to make me not need to."

I stared down at my hands, unable to ignore my guilt. I'd been wrong about him, hadn't I? I'd said cruel words because I hadn't taken the time to try to understand what he'd done or why, labeling him bad just because I'd jumped to conclusions.

"I'm sorry," I said.

"No need to apologize."

"Of course there is. I called you a conman and a criminal."

He turned finally, but when he looked right at me, I wished he hadn't. His gaze was angry and somehow cold at the same time. It chilled me, making me want to move away.

"I *am* both of those things, Kenz. You weren't wrong about me. I con people out of their money, their property, their information, even their lives when it suits me. I break the law to do the things I want to do. I've left plenty of victims in my wake, so don't take one moment where I look good and think that's all of me. You were right, and you should keep that in mind when dealing with me. I will use and discard anything I need to in order to get what I want—that includes you."

With that, he looked away and turned the key in the ignition, the engine roaring to life as though to end the conversation.

He'd meant those words to be a threat, but I struggled to hear it like that, to accept it. Instead, Claire's words ran through my head. *People who keep others away do it because they're afraid.*

Char did things to help others, showed them a false face to create distance, didn't even admit to what he'd done. Just like those times, he'd spat these words at me to push me away, to hide himself behind harsh threats and truths twisted into knots so tight they were hardly recognizable.

Char might have been a conman and a criminal, but I had a feeling he wasn't the bad person he wanted others to think he was.

Chapter Ten

Vance

"What is this?" Kenz peered at me with a look full of so much suspicion that it made me laugh.

Women didn't tend to be all that suspicious of me, at least not at first. Later, sometimes, after they realized they couldn't manipulate me into whatever they wanted, they started to look at me like that. Usually, though, they fell in line the moment I smiled and offered them a few sweet words.

Kenz was far too smart to fall for such things, though, which was why she peered around the space then gave me a look that said she didn't trust me in the least.

"It's a gift," I said. When she didn't soften, I laughed softly then gestured toward the aisle set up in the center of the open space. "You don't have that much time before your exhibit, right? I thought that standing in the room where the work will be displayed might give you some inspiration." I crossed my arms, thinking back to my exhibits in the past, when I'd feel that same rush of deciding what to enter, where to place it, how it would all fit together. "Seeing how the light in the room is, feeling the energy of the space, the way the spots sit, it helps to work out what would work best."

"Did you used to do this?"

I shook my head. "Not usually, no. Most of my exhibits had my manager picking pieces already done. If I did pieces just for a show, they were usually commissioned, so I already knew what I'd do. The last time I got to just paint what I wanted was back before I'd started selling it, I guess." I shuffled my foot against the hardwood floor of the art gallery. "I didn't go to college, so I never really got the chance to work on whatever I wanted. I'm sort of envious of that."

Kenz said nothing, and when the silence became too much to sit through any longer, I turned to find her staring at me. "What is this really all about?"

The laugh I let out was empty because she really was difficult to deal with, wasn't she? "You won't just let me move on, will you?"

"I don't like half measures. If you want to say something, you should say it."

I miss women who fall all over themselves for me.

"Fine. I'm sorry, okay? I called ahead to find out where the exhibit would be held, then asked the gallery if I could rent the space for the evening. I wanted to apologize for what happened last time, and this was the only thing I could think of." Putting it all on the board didn't sit well for me.

Normally, people accepted gifts with smiles, all too willing to move on from whatever had bothered them. I didn't give the gifts because I was sorry, usually, but because it was easier to deal with people who were properly appeased.

Especially women, since in my experience they were experts at screwing up a man's life when pissed off.

This might have been the first time I'd wanted to apologize because I actually felt bad, though, because even after avoiding Kenz for a couple days, I hadn't been able to put her hurt face out of my mind.

And *sure,* I'd also thought about how her skin had tasted, and how I'd wrapped my lips around her tight, pert nipples. However, for once, the gift wasn't just an attempt to see them again.

She blew out a hard breath, the tension she'd had easing out of her. It made me realize just how awkward we'd been since that night, how much space she'd kept between us, how uncertain her gaze had been. "I'm sorry, too."

"For what?"

She tore her gaze away, staring instead at the canvas set on the easel. "I've been avoiding you."

"I can't really blame you for that."

"No? But if it was reversed, if I'd put the brakes on between us, I wouldn't want you to treat me like the bad guy. You're allowed to not want me, to stop things, and I need to not get so hurt by it."

Hurt? She did me in with that word, especially because it brought back up her expression from that night. It had been hurt, really. I shook my head, unwilling to let her take the blame. "It's not your fault. I know I've jerked you around, and that isn't something I do. Normally, I'm upfront and clear about what I want and what I don't. If someone isn't on board with that, I move on. You, though? I can't seem to get my head on straight with you."

"What do you mean?" Kenz didn't seem to ask that as a ploy—she sounded just as confused as I felt.

"I mean that you confuse me. I know this is temporary, that we've got a goal and once that's over, this is done with. Normally, that wouldn't bother me a bit. In fact, an entanglement with an end date makes it all easier."

"So am I just not enough?" Kenz asked. "I mean, I get that. I haven't lived under a rock—I know the sort of women you've dated. Maybe I just don't live up to that? Convenience isn't always enough." If she'd said those things as a way for me to reassure her, I'd have walked out. It wouldn't have sat right at all.

However, one of the things about her that I couldn't ignore was how unfailingly upfront she could be. She honestly thought my back and forth was all about her not being enough?

The girl might be sweet and smart, but she has no real idea of what she is.

"That's not it," I said, even if I knew I should just keep my mouth shut. "Every other woman, I haven't given a damn about. If you'd thrown yourself at me day one, I'd have taken you to bed with a smile. No problem. We'd have both enjoyed the hell out of it. Now, though? I just keep thinking about the women from my past. They're all either still hoping to get a hold of me or they hate me. I don't think I can't stand you ending up like that. I guess I'm a coward—afraid to try anything but unable to resist it sometimes."

She frowned, as though trying to work through it, to decide whether she believed me.

I couldn't stand talking about it anymore, though, so instead I tapped my fingers on the canvas. "Come on, we've only got so long here. So let's focus on the purpose."

She pressed her lips together, no doubt catching on to my attempt to change the subject. Still, she nodded and went over to the easel. "What about you?"

I went to the bench in the corner of the room and sat, leaning my back against the wall. "I'm good here. Don't worry about me."

I thought she might argue, but the lure of the offer proved too great, because Kenz took her bottom lip between her teeth then turned her back to me, facing the canvas and picked up a pencil set in the tray.

And if there was a place where Kenz really shone, this was it. I knew I didn't have a lot of time left, a fact that sometimes made me antsy, made me feel like I had to do more, fill my time better, since it was in short supply. However, I wasn't sure if there was any better way to spend it than watching her paint.

Two hours later, I knew watching her had been the right choice. Something about Kenz with a paintbrush was as lovely as it was painful. She got this look on her face, this concentration that drew me in. It reminded me of what I'd lost, of what I'd never get back.

She sketched for a while, but eventually she moved on to paint, blocking in the basic colors.

The image she'd picked wasn't entirely clear to me, the sketch lines so light that I struggled to make sense of it. There was a lot of white, and she worked hard to add soft shadows to it.

Was it fabric?

My curiosity got the best of me, even though I didn't want to interrupt her process. "What are you working on?"

Her hand paused, lifting the brush off the canvas as though coming out of a trance. Then again, I knew how focus could make the entire world disappear. "A dress." She stepped backward to survey the painting from a different perspective.

I got up and off my bench, wincing slightly at the ache in my hip. While Lorien's attack had only taken the use of my hand, my entire body felt as though it had aged after that. My joints ached more than they had before, but maybe that was just from getting older. I came to stand beside her, finally able to see more of the details.

"That's a wedding dress."

She nodded and set the paintbrush in the water cup. "Yeah, it is."

The image was pulled in tight, showing the bust of a woman, the intricate white fabric, lace details, down to hip area. A gloved hand rested on the front, as though the woman had placed her hands there in surprise or happiness.

It was sweet, but a bit dull. The dress was well done, even with only the basic colors started. It was the sort of image where people would lean in, amazed by the carefully painted details on the dress.

"It surprises me," I said. "I've never seen you do fashion work. Trying something new for the exhibit?"

She opened her mouth to answer, but before she did, a voice I didn't recognize called from behind us, "Well isn't this a surprise?"

I turned, placing myself in front of Kenz, annoyed at the fact that I wasn't nearly as good at sensing danger as Hayden or Tor.

However, the man standing there didn't strike me as someone preparing to hurt Kenz. He was tall and fit, though not nearly as heavily muscled as Hayden. He wore a pair of glasses, rimmed on the top in thick brown, but thin wire on the bottom. He had light brown hair with gray in it, despite not appearing older than forty. He wore a long-sleeved gray shirt and offered Kenz a smile that implied he knew her.

"Grisham," she said and moved out from behind me.

The name let me know who this was. When I'd heard about her student adviser, I'd assumed he'd be some seventy-year-old man who had done this for more years than Kenz had been alive. I sure hadn't thought I'd find him to be young and relatively attractive.

Or that he'd smile at her like that…

"Are you taking a look at the space?"

Kenz nodded, her gaze shifting over to me as though uncomfortable. "Vance rented it out so I could work here. He thought it might help me if I got to see the light and shadow and vibe of the space where the work would be shown."

Grisham looked at me, his gaze far too smart for my liking. "That's a good idea. It's not one many people would think of, so I'm pretty impressed. Of course, what else would I expect from the very talented Vance Moore?" His words held an edge, something that nearly felt like jealousy?

Does he have feelings for Kenz?

I wanted to say that was insane, that he was too old for her, until I recognized that he was probably younger than Hayden and not all that much older than I was.

Talk about a double standard.

Not that I ever cared much about being fair, so long as I got what I wanted.

I gave him my best smile, the one I used when I wanted to warn a person not to push too far. "She seemed like she was having a hard time and I wanted to support her."

"Well, isn't that nice?" Grisham walked closer, and I found myself annoyed when I had to look up slightly into his face. Worse, his gaze moved to the painting, as though I were unimportant.

There hadn't been many times in my life when people had treated me as unimportant.

Well, other than my family, of course.

"The lines on this are good," Grisham said. He leaned closer, studying the piece with what was obviously a trained eye. "Why did you choose to close in like this? Some artists get lazy and do things like this so they don't have to do so many details, but you aren't that type."

Kenz stepped over closer to Grisham and the work, which didn't sit right with me at all. "I did it because that's the area that's important. Unless I did a much larger piece than is allowed, I couldn't get the details I wanted. I wanted to show the lace, the pearl buttons, the shimmer in the fabric of the gloves."

The way she spoke to Grisham set my teeth on edge. I didn't care for this connection between them, the way she listened to him, the way she explained as though she cared about his opinion.

Why, though? Wasn't that his job?

The distance between them, only scant inches, told me *exactly* why. I enjoyed her looking at me like that, hearing me, trusting me. Art was a way we connected, a way we understood one another where others didn't.

It felt like *our* thing, but now here Grisham was, shoving his nose into it.

I crossed my arms, trying to keep my temper in check.

"And how do you think this is going to move people? Remember our last conversation? You have to make them feel *something*. What do you think they'll feel from this?"

A line appeared between Kenz's dark eyebrows as though she didn't care for the criticism. However, being so her, she picked up her paintbrush. "That's because I'm not done yet."

Grisham shifted his weight to one foot, the stance of a man who didn't plan to go anywhere. It gave her permission to keep going.

I expected Kenz to dip the brush back in the white and brown, to block in more shadows of the fabric, but she didn't. Instead, she dipped the end of an angled brush into the red.

Her motions were quick but focused, which told me this addition had been planned from the start. She didn't paint with any hesitation, as though she were making it up on the spot. The red went on the bodice, surrounding the hand. She used white and brown to vary the shades of red and added a thick, dripping line down the painting.

Layering in the shadows and highlights would take a long time more, to finish it all, but when she set the paintbrush down after another twenty minutes, the truth of the painting was obvious.

The horror of it, the pain, it bled just like the wound the woman in the painting carried. Kenz had painted, for the first time I'd seen, herself.

This was her on her wedding day, the day when her father had shot her.

Kenz

My hand shook as I stared at the painting before me. I recalled the shock from that day, the pain, the crushing sense of loss as everything I thought I'd known had slipped away.

I'd never painted myself before. If a class required a 'self-portrait' I'd always managed to get out of it. Somehow, the moment I considered drawing myself, my mind would blank.

Perhaps I didn't really see myself, or maybe I just didn't want to face myself. Even this time, I'd not included my face.

My face didn't matter. What mattered here was that wound, the scar I still carried that sank deeper than the bullet ever had.

I tried to keep my breathing slow, but my heart had already started to race. A phantom pain in my side reminded me of how I'd felt before I'd ever recognized the sound of the gunshot. It all threatened to collapse in on me, to drown me in the reds that now covered the painting.

And along with those reds? The white of the dress felt just as threatening. It took me back to walking down that aisle, to the way the stylist had yanked on the strings at the back to tighten it, the way it had stolen my breath before she'd done up that line of buttons.

Warmth on my back made me jump, as if it were the muzzle of a gun instead of a hand.

"Sorry," Grisham said, pulling his hand away at my reaction.

I blinked slowly to try to center myself. Falling apart in front of Vance would be bad enough, but I didn't want Grisham to see this part of me. He didn't even have the background to understand why I reacted like that—and I didn't want him to.

Another hand wrapped around my hip and pulled me away from Grisham, putting distance between us. I found myself against a familiar solid form, and Vance's scent helped settle my racing mind. He slid his arm around me, keeping me against his side, as though to reassure me that I wasn't back there, wasn't in that dress, wasn't bleeding out.

It let me pull in a shaky breath.

"You did well," Grisham said, his voice drawing my attention. He stared at me, not seeming bothered or surprised at all about Vance's actions. Then again, as far as everyone knew, we were dating. "You captured something good here, something powerful. This is an example of what you're capable of when you dig deep inside yourself, when you use that to pull those things out of others."

He turned his gaze back to the painting, his lips curling into a smile full of pride. "I knew you had this in you, that you understood the depths of pain and could show it to others. Don't forget how you feel right now, because *this* is where your power comes from." He took a step backward. "If you keep this up, the exhibit will be a success, so stay in that same place. I look forward to seeing what you've got the next time we meet."

Grisham took a few steps away, then paused to look at Vance. "And it was nice to meet you, as well. I hope you can continue to support Kenz and help do what's best for her." With that, he left.

After he was gone, my knees stopped doing their job. It was like, without him there, I couldn't keep myself together quite as well.

Maybe I just feel like I can break down with only Vance here to see.

Normally I had to be strong, had to pretend to be okay so I didn't worry people, so they didn't see my weakness. Something about Vance made me not feel as though I had to do that.

Vance took my weight easily, and nowhere in my mind did I fear I'd fall. Despite how Vance could frustrate me, I trusted him to hold on to me.

He shifted me, sliding an arm beneath my knees and lifting me against his chest. I didn't fight it, setting my head against him, following his steady breaths and trying to match mine to his.

He set me down on the bench where he'd sat, then knelt in front of me. He was taller, which meant I barely had to look down to see his familiar blue eyes.

He really is handsome. It was almost annoying how good looking he was. He was talented, rich, popular. Why the hell did he have to be so attractive as well? Fate sure had given him far too many helping hands, hadn't it?

His lips curled up on one side. "This isn't the place to stare at me like that, you know?"

His words, calling me out, made me laugh. It loosened that tightness in my chest, the panic attack that had started.

"Better. You feeling okay, now?"

"Yeah, I am. Thanks—and sorry."

"Nothing to be sorry about. I didn't understand why you were painting that at first—it didn't seem like your style at all." He paused, as though he didn't want to say the next part. It wasn't hard to guess what he wanted to know, given what had happened. Still, he pushed on and said it. "That was from when you were shot, right? That's you?"

I nodded but couldn't bring myself to peer over at the piece itself. If I saw the red, I didn't know how I'd react, and I didn't want to fall headlong into that anxiety again, that dark place. "Yeah. I picked the dress out with my sister. I didn't want to get married. I'd begged my dad not to make me. None of it mattered, though. No matter how much I didn't want to do it, I still put that dress on, still played my part, still walked down that aisle."

"You went that far?" Vance frowned as he ran his left hand up and down my arm in a reassuring gesture.

"Yeah, I did. It turned out the wedding was never intended to go through. My dad planned to have me killed then anyway, to use the event to secure himself more power. If Nem hadn't shown up, he would have gotten exactly what he wanted. When she showed up, when he realized he'd lost control, he tried to kill Nem. The Fox took that bullet for her, and my dad dragged me out to escape. Nem followed us, and it was the three of us in the forest alone."

I let out a thin laugh as I thought back on it. "It's funny because it was almost like a family gathering, the three of us, back together. Even then, even as I saw that my sister was alive, as I realized that my father was at fault for our mother's death, I still didn't think he'd hurt me. I didn't want to think that." I touched my side, where the scar sat beneath my shirt. "He targeted me because he knew it would hurt Nem the most. He didn't really care enough to even want me dead. I was that unimportant to him."

"You don't have to talk about this," Vance said. His comment didn't feel like a shut down, as though he were trying to get me to be quiet, but rather like offering an out.

"I remember a doctor cutting my dress off. I wonder sometimes what happened to it—thrown away, I'm sure. Maybe it's stupid, but I guess I wonder because it was still my wedding dress. It still mattered, in some weird way, and the idea of it getting tossed feels wrong." I sighed when I wasn't sure how to explain that. "Maybe I just want to burn it myself?"

Vance moved his hand from my arm to my cheek. The touch comforted me so much that I couldn't stop myself from nuzzling against his palm, from the warmth and strength there. "You're important to more people than you think."

"Yeah, to people who have to care about me. My sister, the Quad, even the Fox. People who give a damn about me do so because of my family or my blood or my name. Do you know why I paint? Because it's something I can do that isn't about anyone else. It's my skill, and my work, and things like my last name or my parents, those things don't control it."

"I care about you, and I had no idea what your real name was until you'd already wrapped me around your finger."

I jerked my gaze up at his words, at the way I struggled to make sense of them. They were so honest that it surprised me.

He laughed softly. "I'm not the only one, either. Hayden, Tor and even Char—as stubborn and surly as he is—all care."

"Because you need me to get what you want," I pointed out.

"That's why we bought you, sure, but we could have tried to trade you over anytime. We could have used you as bait, but we haven't."

"You're all good people, even if you try to hide it. None of you want to make innocents suffer for your own revenge. That isn't about me."

Vance sat up straighter and leaned in. As he neared me, my heart raced again, but for a very different reason than earlier. Was this it? Would this be my first real kiss? Not the one from last time, when he'd stolen it, when it hadn't been real.

Except, it wasn't. His lips touched my cheek, so close I could have turned just a hair to catch his lips.

When he pulled back, I stared at him, the question in my gaze. Why?

"I screwed this up the first time, and I won't do that again. So if you want a kiss, *you're* going to have to decide. I won't steal anything else from you."

I pressed my lips together, not caring for that *at all*.

Sure, it was sweet, and I knew it was for me, but that didn't mean I liked being put on the spot like that. Being chased felt far safer than having to make the first move — especially since I kept getting rejected.

"Sorry to interrupt," a woman said, waking me from what had felt like a private moment.

I jerked backward, hitting the back of my head on the wall in what was no doubt an overreaction.

"We're going to be locking up in about ten minutes."

Vance chuckled as he stared at me, and that made my cheeks heat. He set his hand on the bench and used it to stand. "Sorry, I lost track of time. We'll pack up here and get going."

"If you need the room again, just let us know," the woman said, her expression the same one I'd seen many times from women looking at Vance — smitten.

Suddenly the idea of kissing him didn't feel so far-fetched. In fact, a part of me wanted to do it right now, in front of this woman, to make a point.

Except, the woman turned and left before the half-baked idea could spur me into anything embarrassing.

Vance didn't move away, and him standing above me while I sat put me at a very distinct disadvantage. He cupped my chin, tipping my face up toward him. He ran his thumb along my bottom lip, as though teasing me when he knew what I really wanted. "You know? I think I like you jealous."

"I wasn't jealous."

"No?" His laugh called me a liar, but he didn't press. Instead, he stroked my bottom lip once more, then turned around to pack up the canvas, paint supplies and easel.

The moment gave me the chance to calm and gather myself. Things had been so uneasy between Vance and myself, I'd somehow forgotten this side of him.

It made sense that women fell for him so easily, and I was ill-equipped if he really wanted to turn that charm on. If he wanted anything from me, I doubted I stood a chance against him.

And I don't think I mind that one bit.

* * * *

Kenz

I wiped the coffee table in the living room while giving Vance a dirty look. No matter how many times

I cleaned the table, I almost swore he dropped a piece of cereal on purpose just to annoy me.

The fact he snacked on dry cereal was weird enough, especially for a guy who'd grown up as rich and pampered as he had. I'd expected people like him to snack on caviar or something equally fancy.

Instead, he liked to buy cheap, sugar-filled cereal, put some in a cup—never a bowl—and eat it like chips.

"I'm not your housekeeper," I muttered.

"I just like to see you bend over to pick the pieces up," he said with his normal, far-too-charming smile.

Thankfully, things had gotten back to normal in the house—at least, as normal as they could be given our situation. Vance had stopped avoiding me and Hayden pretended our little moment together had never happened.

I might not love that, but at least it made things comfortable. I still spoke to Lorien in the evenings, our calls often short—he seemed exceedingly busy—but they always happened. The fact that he made time surprised me.

It helped prove the point that whatever misguided ideas were in his head, he thought he cared about me, that he was serious about making me fall for him.

I couldn't imagine falling for someone who had done the things he had, but at the same time, I couldn't deny a warmth had started to appear each time we spoke. His voice had turned more familiar, especially because I often spoke to him just before I fell asleep. Just hearing him relaxed me, as though my body thought that signaled time for bed.

After I cleaned the table, feeling more at ease after my morning routine, I wiped the sweat from my forehead. It wasn't hard work, and the men were always clear that I didn't need to do it, but it made me feel at ease. It felt like putting things right in my world again.

I tucked the roll of paper towels under my arm and headed into the kitchen to put it back. I had nothing planned for the day, and it seemed the men were the same. They were all here, milling around the house, doing their own things.

Vance read in the living room — probably just so he could harass me. Hayden and Char exercised outside, while Tor seemed to be doing research on his computer at the dining room table. For my part, I'd drawn some earlier, worked on the flowerbeds in the backyard with Hayden's help, then decided to do a little cleaning before lunch.

When I stepped into the kitchen, my brain stuttered to a halt.

It felt like when, as a kid, I'd seen a teacher at a store once. My mind couldn't make sense of seeing someone outside of the role I'd expected from them.

That was the reason I dropped the paper towels when I found Jarrod seated on the kitchen counter as though he lived there as well.

And just like that, everything went to hell.

Chapter Eleven

Kenz

Jarrod was a man who could cause problems for just about anyone, and never had he proven it more than by sitting on the kitchen counter, a pistol in his hand, and drawing the attention of Vance, Char, Hayden and Tor.

He might have been dead if any of them were armed, in fact.

I found myself yanked behind a large body, the action so fast that at first I had no idea who had done it. An inhalation where sandalwood filled my nostrils told me it was Hayden.

Then again, he was usually the quickest to save me, wasn't he?

"Who are you?" Hayden asked, his voice with that chilling edge I rarely heard.

"I suggest you be very careful about yanking Kenz around," Jarrod answered, his voice with the same darkness.

No, not the same, *far* darker. Hayden would do a lot to save someone, but Jarrod had done worse for far less noble reasons.

I hit my fist against Hayden's back to get his attention. "It's okay—I know him."

Even as I tried to move around Hayden, another hand caught my arm and kept me still. I glanced to the side to find Vance flanking me there, keeping me behind Hayden. "Just because you know him doesn't mean we do."

"Sneaking into someone's house isn't very smart," Char said, a smile on his lips, his voice cheery despite the way his words were a very obvious threat.

"Sneaking into someone's house is extremely smart if I don't trust the people enough to ring the doorbell. You can learn a lot about someone by what they keep in their home." Jarrod's voice showed no signs of fear, but I wasn't sure I'd seen that from him before. He'd softened after falling for Sasha, after moving in with her, but that didn't change his core. He was still the man who had helped turn Nem into the killer she was, so no matter how nice he might seem at times, I knew what lurked beneath that exterior.

"Admitting to illegally searching our things isn't the smartest thing," Hayden said. "Especially when you are horribly outnumbered."

"I prefer being outnumbered. It gives me more targets." Most people would have smiled at that threat, but I knew better. Jarrod would utter those words with complete seriousness.

And as for me? The idea of Jarrod searching *my* home went too far. This wasn't a target—it was the place I felt comfortable. I thought of him going through my things, as well, searching through my belongings, going through the personal items of the men. It had me pushing away from Vance and Hayden, twisting out of their grasp, until I could see Jarrod again.

I pointed my finger at him. "How *dare* you search my things!"

He tucked the gun down, by his side, as though he'd just come to his senses and didn't want me to see him with one. It almost made me laugh that he was *still* doing this, just like the Quad did, as though I couldn't handle the harsher aspects of life. "It wasn't like that, Kenz."

"Like hell it wasn't! I don't care if you like what I'm doing or not—don't you ever even think about searching my things again."

"I wanted to make sure you were okay, that these men weren't doing anything to you. It's not like I searched your private home."

"This *is* my home, at least for right now. I swear, if you ever so much as think about stepping over that line again, I will personally make your life a living hell."

Jarrod pressed his lips together, an unhappy expression on his face, before he muttered a soft, "Sorry," just loud enough for me to catch.

Which brought the whole exchange into focus enough for me to recognize how ridiculous it really was. Jarrod was a dangerous killer, and here I was— weaponless, with only the most basic grasp of self-defense—yelling at him. And worse? He actually apologized.

Our back and forth must have thrown the men off, too, because the men stared around as if unsure how to respond. No adult man would seem like quite the same dangerous individual when put in their place by a nineteen-year-old girl.

"You want to introduce us?" Vance said when no one spoke for a long time.

I looked at Jarrod, unwilling to say anything he didn't want me to. He sighed loudly, then leaned forward but didn't leave the counter. "My name is Jarrod. I'm her sister's father."

Char cursed so softly that I doubted anyone but me heard it, and when he spoke, he had that cheery voice on again. "The Fox?"

Jarrod nodded, not even trying to deny it. "That's right, and given that curse you let out" — it seemed Jarrod at least had caught it — "you know about me. That should tell you how cautious you should be right now when you're holding something so precious to me."

His words caught me off guard.

He'd looked out for me, sure. He'd become a sort of father figure to me, one I hadn't expected, one I didn't know how to deal with. I'd never had a real father, so I had nothing to compare it to, no way to measure or understand it.

Jarrod wasn't the type to talk about his feelings, so him saying that — and in front of men he clearly didn't trust — stunned me into silence.

Hayden peered back at me, seeming to search my expression for what I thought. Whatever he found must have allowed him to come to a decision, because he faced back toward Jarrod. "If you're a part of her life, then you're welcome here."

The front door opened, making the men and I turned our heads in confusion. What was today? Enter uninvited day?

Jarrod let out a loud, unhappy sigh, the sort of sound I never expected from him. The meaning and reason became clear, however, when Sasha walked in, a smile on her face, her blonde hair pulled half back to show her bright, happy expression.

"Kenz!" She held her arms out as though she hadn't just walked into a tense situation with guns involved. Did that show that she'd spent enough time around Jarrod to not let such things bother her anymore?

And the welcoming attitude got me moving, because who could ignore an offer from her? I embraced her back, enjoying the way her hugs felt like warmth itself. If Jarrod served as a father, Sasha might have just been like a mother, even if I'd spent less time around her.

She let me go, then set her hands on my cheeks and stared into my eyes, looking over my face, a clinical edge as she no doubt checked for injuries or signs of illness. It seemed nurses never could quite let go of that.

"You were supposed to wait until I contacted you," Jarrod said, his voice a mixture of warmth and censure as he spoke to Sasha. "It could have been dangerous."

Sasha released me and turned toward Jarrod, setting her hands on her hips and facing him down the same way I had. He could make almost any man cower, yet he kept getting run around by the women in his life. It was almost adorable.

"It had been twenty minutes. I know you—if there weren't any gunshots yet, it was fine."

"That's not how this works and you know it."

Sasha offered a dazzling smile, the sort of look that made it clear just how she'd gotten him to fall for her. "I also knew that even if there was something wrong, you'd protect me."

Jarrod narrowed his eyes. "Don't you try to play me like that, Sasha. I don't make exceptions when it comes to your safety." His words had a line of threat in them, a warning.

And Sasha entirely ignored it as she headed over to the fridge and opened it. "Let's see what we have here. Perfect, there's enough for me to make a stir-fry. Kenz, would you start the rice?"

Char, Hayden, Vance and Tor said nothing, looking around as though they weren't sure how we'd gotten here, how the day had changed so much. Instead of a lazy day at home, they now had a stranger making food in their kitchen and a man with a gun on the counter.

Yet they recovered fast when Hayden shrugged. "Seems like we're having lunch together. Vance, can you get extra dishes from the pantry?"

Sasha closed the fridge, veggies in her arms, before she gave one more pointed look at Jarrod. "Go set the table and remember my rule."

"No guns at the table," Jarrod muttered and hopped off the counter as though a child scolded for bad behavior.

Sasha pulled the knife from the block where it had been and pointed the end at my men. "That goes for you all."

Hayden chuckled. "Yes, ma'am."

And just like that, Sasha had managed to disarm a room full of dangerous men. *Talk about impressive.*

An hour later, I sat at the weirdest dinner I'd ever attended.

And that was saying something for me, since I'd eaten with Mafia bosses and famous celebrities and hitmen and politicians. None of those had quite this level of tension, though.

We all sat at the large table, with one empty seat since the table could seat eight. Sasha sat between Jarrod and me — probably because he wouldn't allow her to sit beside men he didn't know. The three of us were on one side of the table, with Hayden at the head of the table to my other side, then Char, Vance and Tor across from us. It left the other head of the table empty.

Keep the one who's the most likely to shoot people away from others.

It felt like putting a reactive dog alone to prevent fights.

I glanced at Jarrod, who ate while never taking his gaze off the men across from him.

"Whatever you're thinking, it's probably rude." He didn't so much as look my way even though I knew he'd intended his words for me. It seemed even if he didn't look at anyone else, he knew what was going on.

"Well, this is incredibly awkward," Sasha said with a laugh. "I'm sorry for Jarrod — he doesn't have much socialization. We're working on it."

Jarrod snorted but didn't argue.

Vance chuckled. "I'm pretty sure I like you. My name is Vance Moore."

Sasha smiled in return. "My name is Sasha. I'm a nurse by trade, but I stopped doing it professionally. Now I work sort of on contract, helping out where I can."

By which she meant that Nem and Jarrod would have her take care of injuries that would raise too many questions at the hospital.

Just like my bullet wound.

Sasha kept going, showing no signs of unease in the situation. "And I know exactly who you are. There was a showing of your work at an exhibit in California and I waited in line for an hour to get in. It was amazing."

A bittersweet look crossed Vance's face. "Thanks."

Sasha seemed to pick up on the hesitation there, moving on, her gaze shifting to Hayden.

He picked up on her point. "My name is Hayden. I have a personal security business and I do bodyguard work as well."

Char offered up his best, fakest smile, turning on the charm that made me wonder why I'd ever fallen for it. "I'm Char. I do a bit of this and that."

Sasha didn't press that one, but after being with Jarrod, she probably understood an answer like that meant the truth was a bit ugly. When her gaze moved to Tor, I piped up.

"Tor can't speak."

Sasha set her fork down, her hands moving quickly.

Tor lifted his eyebrow, then responded, the gestures meaning nothing to me.

"You know sign language?" I asked.

Sasha shrugged. "Not much. I learned a little to help with deaf patients, but I still remember a little. Anything beyond the basics or requests for pain meds and I'm not much help."

"Being able to get drugs feels like the most important ones," Vance said, breaking the tension.

The meal went on like that, with us all dancing around the truth, around the questions they all had, no doubt.

Funnily enough, this feels like the most normal family dinner I've ever had.

* * * *

Kenz

I put the plates in the dishwasher as Sasha and the men remained at the table, drinking coffee that Char had made.

I'd needed a moment away, to escape the anxiety that ran through me as Jarrod stared daggers at the men.

"I don't like them."

I didn't bother to turn toward Jarrod when I heard his voice. He liked sneaking up on people, taking them by surprise, which meant I didn't react to it much anymore. "That's not a surprise. You don't like anyone."

"What is it with women picking terrible men? You, Nem, Caroline—"

"Sasha?"

He snorted. "Yeah, her too. Hell, she probably has the worst taste of all."

I closed the dishwasher and hit the Start button, then turned and leaned against the counter to stare at him. "You're not that bad."

"You just don't see it. It makes me even more worried about these guys, because clearly you don't judge a person well."

"And if you're here, I bet you know everything there is to know about them."

He didn't deny it, and I was so not surprised that he'd have researched them that I couldn't even find it in me to be angry.

"So much for trusting me, huh?"

Jarrod came over and leaned against the counter beside me. We usually had our conversations like this, where we both looked in the same direction instead of at one another. It was easier to speak freely when I didn't have his silver eyes locked on me.

They were the same ones Nem had, and sometimes I wondered if that wasn't part of my connection to him. Seeing those eyes made me feel as if I already knew him.

"If I really didn't trust you, I'd have already handed this over to Nem."

"So why haven't you?"

"Because as much as I don't like it, you've got to make your own choices. It's something I learned from Sasha. I almost lost her, almost got her killed all because I wanted to make decisions for her, because I thought that doing everything for her would keep her safe. Turns out that isn't the way it works."

"Sasha's good for you."

"Yeah, she really is. She's more than I deserve — that's for sure. If it wasn't for her, I'd have already hauled your ass home. I guess she's giving me patience in my golden years." He paused, then sighed softly. "That doesn't change that I really don't like you being here with them. I don't know what exactly they're up to, but they don't have the backgrounds of men you'd meet normally."

I pressed my lips together, unwilling to lie to him.

"And you don't want to tell me, huh? I should have seen that coming. Tell me you know who they really are, though. I need to know that you're in this with your eyes open, at least."

"I know who they are."

"All of it?"

I nodded, shuffling my foot along the kitchen tile. "I know about Vance's less than stellar dating history. Hayden, well, mostly he's just overprotective and horrible with women. Char cons people and lies more than Dane."

"And Tor?" Jarrod asked that last one in a knowing tone.

"Yeah, I know he kills people." Admitting it out loud made my stomach lurch, but I tried not to let that show.

"And you're okay with that?"

"How can I look down on him when Colton does the same thing? When *you've* done the same thing?"

Jarrod made a soft sound as though to admit to my point. "They've gotten serious the last five years, all of them seeming to cut ties with most of their old lives. I don't know what exactly they're after, but I'm sure it's nothing good. Nobody changes their entire life like that unless it's for something big. I'm afraid you're getting into something that's more than you can handle."

He didn't give me time to respond—though what was there to say more than I already had? If he didn't want to trust me, to think I could handle it, then I couldn't say anything else to convince him of it.

"I know I need to not be so worried about you. You're a smart girl, and you're tough, but when I look at you, I see Nem."

"Why? We don't look much alike, and I know I don't live up to her."

"Because I failed her. I thought she'd be okay, that she'd be better off without me, so I stayed away. In the end, it almost killed her. When I saw you bleeding that night, it felt like looking at her again that night when I saved her. You have no idea how it feels to watch the life slip away from your child in your arms, to know you're responsible for it. I brought Nem back, but just barely, and when you were hurt, it felt like going through it all over again."

Jarrod's voice was so soft that it hardly rose above a whisper. I held my breath to keep him talking, afraid the least bit of noise or movement from me would dam up the unexpected flow of information.

"So when I act like this, when I do too much, it isn't because I don't trust you. It's because even if we don't share any blood, I see you as my daughter, too, and I don't want to see my children suffer ever again." He laughed and shook his head. "That's pretty sad, huh? So much for my reputation."

His words burned, ones that were so much more than I could have imagined. It was like he knew how little I trusted myself, how much I worried about where I fit into their life, their family, how isolated and different I felt. Jarrod's words told me I'd gotten that wrong, that he'd accepted me as his own, that he looked after me because he wanted to—not because he was required to.

It took me back to when I'd been recovering—when we'd both been recovering from wounds my father had inflicted on us—and he'd played rom-coms for me, to try to calm me. He'd stayed with me, all night for when the nightmares had come, to make sure I knew I wasn't alone.

He was stubborn and overbearing and dangerous, but he put everything aside to protect me. The fact he wasn't my biological father didn't matter—he'd chosen to take up that role, and I knew I owed a lot of who and what I was now to that and to him.

So I did the thing I knew he'd hate, but too damned bad. I turned and threw my arms around him in a tight hug.

He froze at first. This man who had done unspeakable things, who hadn't blinked when standing against four full-grown men, behaved like a fainting goat from a little hug.

After a long moment, he wrapped his arms around me as well, the action awkward, making me suspect he wasn't used to it. Then again, Nem wasn't the hugging type, so he probably didn't have a clue how to interact with me.

I guess we're both figuring that out.

His awkwardness, the things he did that annoyed the hell out of me, they all made more sense now. They were his pretty terrible and clumsy attempts to take care of me.

"Thank you," I told him, keeping my voice low, hoping he understood that I meant about everything.

He squeezed me tight for a moment, the touch feeling like a lot of fear. Then again, he had to face his own past to let me live my life, something that hadn't really occurred to me before.

When he let go and stepped back, his gaze turned toward the floor as though unsure how to deal with the horror of a hug. He rubbed the back of his neck.

And just like that, he gave me the confidence boost I'd needed, a reminder of what I'd overcome and who I had behind me. If I could survive so much, I could deal with anything that came my way.

Chapter Twelve

Jarrod

My hand clenched around the water bottle as I stood in the backyard, watching how Kenz interacted with Hayden.

I don't like it.

I'd scoped out a wonderful stretch of swampland not too far away, the sort of place where a short boat ride would ensure that bodies were never found.

Of course, with how large these men are, it would take two trips to get them all out there. I'd passed a small Mom and Pop hardware store that sold concrete blocks to weigh down the bodies, and crocodiles would do the rest of the work for me.

"Stop thinking about where to bury them." Sasha wrapped her arm around my side, cuddling in close to me.

"I would never think about burying them."

"Ah, so this time it was the swamp, huh?"

I peered down and into her face, taken aback again by how she could so casually say such a thing. From Nem that would have been normal, but Sasha was so much sweeter, and she hated the thought of anyone hurt.

Sometimes I worried I'd jaded her, that I'd somehow tainted her. However, when she leaned against me, I couldn't bring myself to regret a moment of my time with her.

"What do you think of them?" I asked.

"I think they care about her. You can tell just by the way they look at her. In fact, I'd go so far as to say they love her even if they're fighting it."

"They'd better fight it if they want to keep their hands," I growled out.

Sasha chuckled. "Who would have thought you'd be a dad cleaning his shotgun when his daughter's boyfriend stops by? It's surprisingly charming."

"If only I was dealing with a horny teenage boy instead of four full-grown men. A kid would be a lot easier to scare off, after all." I let out a long sigh, trying to ease the frustration inside me. I'd come when Sasha had pushed me, when I hadn't managed a good night's sleep since seeing Kenz in that alleyway. Instead, my brain had just kept working about what was going on with her, whether she was okay, or if she needed help.

Eventually, Sasha had insisted we visit, and I'd purposely *not* mentioned it to Nem. She didn't need to know about my trip, because it would only make her want to come all the more.

"I don't like this," I admitted.

"I know. We came all this way, though, and don't you think it's a missed opportunity if you walk away now?"

I turned my head to look at her, unsure of her point.

Sasha leaned up on her tiptoes and pressed a soft quick kiss to my lips. "I'm going to go in for a little girl time. Seems like if you want to get to know someone, you need to sit down and actually *talk* to them, don't you think?"

With that, she left, heading inside and reminding me again why I fell for her.

She was far smarter than I was, at the end of the day.

Within a few minutes, the men came outside, one by one, their gazes finding me as if they'd had the same thought.

Which meant I needed to be an adult and deal with reality.

My youngest had fallen in love, and now I had to make it *perfectly* clear to these assholes what I'd do if they dared to break her heart.

Tor

I sure as hell never figured I'd sit down with the Fox like this. Then again, given his reputation, few people who got this close to him survived the encounter.

And if anyone had told me he was some loving father, I'd have thought them crazy. Yet, the more I saw him interact with Kenz, the more obvious that became, and it was the *only* reason I would sit with him like this.

"First, let me say that I'm no fool. I've been in this life a long time, have heard people tell me more lies than you can imagine. If you try to bullshit me, I'll know, so I suggest you don't."

Char went to speak, hiding securely behind his fake smile.

Jarrod held a finger up to him. "How about we start with you and that fake smile? Hard to trust Kenz to someone who can't even show a real expression."

Char paused for a moment, his face not shifting in the least, until he let the smile fall away. "Now I know where she gets that annoying ability to see what a person's really thinking."

"You can thank Dane for that little lesson, not me. I'm not going to bother asking what you all are after, because I have a feeling knowing isn't going to do any of us any good. If I know, I'm going to want to get involved, and Kenz doesn't want that. Instead, I want to know that you all are going to look out for her."

Hayden spoke up this time. "I can assure you that her safety is my top concern. She goes nowhere without a guard and the house is secure."

"Seeing how I broke in, I wouldn't call that secure."

Hayden didn't even flinch. "I've already watched the security videos and saw how you got in. Trust me, no one can attempt that again. Besides, I'm not sure how many people could actually manage to scale a two-story building without holds, bypass a security system as good as ours, and do all of that without drawing any attention. Your reputation is well deserved."

Jarrod didn't respond to that, taking it neither as a compliment or a chastisement. It showed the level of control the man had over his feelings and reactions.

"Are you getting her involved in something dangerous? Because if you have problems, I don't want to see her drawn into it something she has no business in." Jarrod's sharp gaze moved from one of us to the next.

Vance responded to that question. "She was already involved. I can assure you *we* didn't pull her into this mess. In fact, if we weren't here at all, she'd be a lot worse off."

"I notice you didn't say she isn't in danger, only that you didn't cause it."

"You told us not to lie." Vance kept a half smirk on his lips, but at least with him, it was normal.

Jarrod nodded slowly. "I think I know enough for now. I'll go back home, and I'll assure her sister that everything is okay."

"Thank you," Hayden said.

"Not so fast," Jarrod interrupted him. "Because I need to make something perfectly clear. The idea of leaving Kenz in *anyone's* care doesn't sit well with me. My entire life has been about fixing people's problems myself, after all, so relying on anyone to fix her issue isn't something I find comfortable. This matters more to me than those jobs, but I can't intervene."

"You being this hands-off surprises me," Char said.

"I learned my lesson before about trying to micromanage people. They don't tend to react well. If you have a plant that you want to grow strong, you can't crush it—you have to give it room to grow on its own. Kenz is an adult now, and she's got to find her own way, get her own feet under her. She doesn't trust herself, and it's hard to blame her when she's always had others making the choices for her. I may not like it, and it scares the shit out of me, but I've got to let her handle herself. Whatever happens, she's got to take control of her own life."

His words left a bad taste in my mouth, probably because it brought home how many people cared for her, and how much of a risk to her really existed. If we made the wrong move, if we screwed this up, it wasn't just us who would pay the price.

Part of me was grateful for my inability to speak, because I'd already parted my lips as though to tell him the reality of the situation.

Except, if we called Nem, the Quad or Jarrod into this, we could kiss our revenge goodbye. If Lorien caught word of Nem sniffing around, he'd disappear. No, worse, he might take the gloves off and manage to grab Kenz before ending up in the wind.

And the man could do just that. He had the knowledge and resources to make it almost impossible to find him.

Which meant telling Jarrod the truth would only make it all worse.

"You need to understand something important. If anything happens to Kenz, you all will be held personally responsible," Jarrod said as though reading my mind.

"You mean if we do anything to her, don't you?" Vance asked.

"No. See, keeping her safe was *our* job before. If you want to take that over now, then you'll be responsible for *anything* that happens to her. If she gets hurt, I'd suggest you start running right away, because you should know hell will be coming after you."

And just like that, I knew exactly where Kenz had gotten her backbone. People like this didn't produce wallflowers, after all.

Chapter Thirteen

Kenz

I slapped down my cards and smirked at Char. "Read 'em and weep!"

When I reached for the chips, he clicked his tongue. "Not so fast, kitten."

The sinking feeling in my stomach came a moment before he dropped his own cards, proving he'd won. I scrunched my nose up as he gathered the chips, adding to his already large pile.

Not that he was *quite* winning. Tor had held his own, the two seeming to read one another without any problem. So mostly, they played, and I lost.

Still, it was fun.

After Jarrod and Sasha left, Vance and Hayden had headed out for errands. It left Tor, Char and I alone, and Tor had tossed a deck of cards into my lap after my fifth sigh of boredom.

I hadn't expected these two to be quite this much fun, given they weren't usually as charming or talkative as the other two, but I'd been wrong.

I'd had a great time. Also, each time I got down to my last chip, I'd somehow manage to finally win a couple hands to stay in the game. No doubt that was their doing, but they didn't call attention to it so neither did I.

"No more games," Char said. "Let's play for keeps now. Loser has to answer a question honestly."

I groaned. "As the constant loser here, I'm going to say I'm not a fan of this idea. It'll just end up an interrogation of me."

"I thought you were being honest now," Char said, his smirk saying he *knew* he was backing me into a corner.

"Sure, but it feels unfair to do it like that. If we're doing this, we need a better game! Something that I have a hope of winning. I want you all to have to answer things, too." I knew my bottom lip stuck out in a pout, but if it made my point, that was fine by me.

"So what do you suggest?" Char asked.

My phone buzzed, and when I peered over at it, a text from Tor sat there. *Truth or drink. We ask a question and anyone who doesn't answer takes a drink.*

I stared at the screen, as though I could work out what had happened. "Did Vance manage to hack your phone or something, because that idea *can't* have come from you," I argued.

Tor gave me a rare smile, and boy, he should have smiled more often. It softened his features and made him seem like a different person, less closed off, less impossible to get to know.

As if I could have possibly said no after a look like that.

That very poor idea left the three of us in Tor's room, seated on the floor, with a bottle of plum brandy in front of me. The alcohol was surprisingly sweet, which I happily welcomed. I remembered when I'd drunk at the restaurant with Vance, back before I'd realized he was playing me.

At least this time they'd given me alcohol that wasn't nearly as strong as theirs. Judging from the liquor in the other bottles, however, I had a feeling Tor and Char weren't quite hanging in there as well.

I guess the plum brandy is my handicap.

Still, I'd learned more than I expected. Tor had set his phone aside, using a small whiteboard instead, and his handwriting had gotten worse as we'd played. So far, he and Char hadn't declined a single question, even the ones I'd have expected them to pass on.

As for me? I'd passed on a few, especially as they'd drunk even without avoiding the questions.

"When was the last time you took care of yourself?" Char asked, offering up one of those questions that I didn't plan to answer.

Though, I sat on an edge where the alcohol had loosened my lips, and I was afraid if it clouded my head any more, I'd say things I didn't mean to.

I lifted the bottle of rose-colored liquor and took another drink.

"Chicken," Char muttered but didn't touch his drink. "Yesterday for me. Tor, you in or are you tapping out?"

Tor narrowed his golden eyes, the action reminding me of a tiger. He picked up his dry erase marker and wrote, then turned the board around. *A week ago.*

The timeframe brought a heat to my cheeks that wasn't caused by the plum brandy. That would have been when he'd run the bath for me, right? When he'd seen me naked, when he'd carried me back to his bed?

I glanced at him and found him staring right back at me, his expression telling me he knew *exactly* what I was thinking. Unable to hold that gaze, I looked back down at the bottle in my hand.

My heart raced, and I worried they'd notice. They'd see the want in my eyes, the way the liquor hadn't created this need but only made it harder to ignore it. And given our history so far — they'd turn me down over it.

To try to hide that, I took my turn to ask a question. "Tell me about your first date."

Char groaned. "Why do you pick such boring topics? If we're talking firsts, we could talk about me making mud pies with a neighbor girl when I was five. It you want to know about my first official date, then I was sixteen. I scrimped and saved enough to take this pretty girl to the movies. I picked a horror movie because I thought she'd cuddle up close to me. Unfortunately, I'd never watched one like that, and it ended up making me feel so sick that I threw up and ruined the whole thing. Tor?"

I set a hand over my mouth to stifle my laughter, especially since his story didn't seem much like the man I knew now. He cut me a sharp look but said nothing as Tor wrote his own answer.

Twenty-two.

"Weren't you a late bloomer?" Char jabbed.

It's harder to impress girls when you can't talk. Those words might have seemed like an attempt to garner pity, but a slight curl to Tor's lips said he didn't mean it that way.

"I, for one, think men more often than not talk themselves *out* of dates in my experience."

"Don't try to get out of answering." Char pointed his finger at me. "Give it up, kitten."

I blew out a breath, hating having to answer but unwilling to drink anymore. The nice buzz I had going on would tip toward drunk if I pressed it much further. "I can't."

"You know the rules," Char said.

I shook my head. "I don't mean I won't answer, I'm saying I *can't*. I can't tell you about my first date because I haven't really had one."

And just like that, I got the looks I'd wanted to avoid. Char's gaze widened, as though he couldn't believe it, while Tor only cocked up one eyebrow.

"Wait just a minute," Char said. "I get that you're innocent — somehow — and you haven't kissed anyone, but you're really going to tell me that you haven't even been on a *date*? Not even an adorable kid playing doctor with the neighbor boy?"

"Don't look at me like that. You *know* how I grew up now, so you should be able to guess why that is. The Quad weren't about to let me go around dating. Even if there were boys I was interested in, the moment they found out about my family, they ran the other way. Finding someone brave enough to keep trying after meeting my father or the Quad isn't all that easy."

I blew out an unhappy breath. "The closest I've had was the fake date with Vance, I guess. Yet another reason to be mad at him, huh?" To avoid those looks of pity that I just *knew* were pointed at me, I lifted the plum brandy and took another swing, letting the slight burn sear away the question.

"You've been in Florida for a year, haven't you? What about now? Can't think you didn't have chances."

"I was lying about my name, my past, everything. How could I get close to anyone when they couldn't even call me by my real name? When my firsts happen, I want them to happen because I know the person and they know me. I want that closeness, that romance. I don't know if I can have it, but it's what I want." I laughed softly. "Also, I didn't want to be responsible for the Quad or Jarrod threatening some poor college student who wasn't ready for it."

The reality was that those men would have ruined any man dumb enough to even give me a try. If I liked someone enough for me to be interested, I liked them too much to risk Jarrod or the Quad setting their sights on the.

Which drew my gaze over to Char and Tor.

They already know about the Quad, they've met Jarrod. They aren't afraid...

"Hurry up—next question," I said to hide the thought, to bury it deep down where neither observant man could read it.

"Last dirty dream," Char said with a smirk.

Tor hadn't asked as many questions, seeming to prefer answering to asking. The only part about that that disappointed me was that Char tended to ask questions he felt would bother me the most, like he enjoyed my embarrassment more than he did my answers.

"I'll answer first," Char offered. "It was, like, two weeks ago. I dreamed about some faceless girl I met in a bar, and we went into the bathroom, locked the door and I bent her over the sink."

"Gross," I muttered.

"What?"

"Do you know how dirty bar bathrooms are? That is *so* a man's fantasy because it doesn't even think about the girl who is apparently leaning all over a probably wet and filthy sink where people wash the taste of vomit from their mouths."

"You don't get it because *you* have no experience. In the moment? Things like that don't matter."

"Pretty sure vomit sinks *always* matter. So do all the weird STDs a person could get from that."

"Yeah, yeah." Char waved off my concerns. "Don't try to get out of answering by bitching about my dream. Your turn."

That wonderful brandy had made it easier to answer, made it feel less scary to admit such things to not just any two men, but ones who I wanted. "It was a week ago," I admitted, closing my eyes as I recalled it. "There wasn't much lead up, and it probably seems pretty boring to you. We were in a big bed with soft sheets and candles all around."

"Were there rose petals?" Char asked with a mocking tone.

"No, there weren't, thank you very much. I imagine those would stick to my skin and feel gross. The man kissed all over me, the touches soft, and he kept talking to me, reassuring me. He was careful, and he waited until I wanted him as much as he wanted me." I shivered at the memory, at the sweetness of all those caresses, the way they'd warmed my body until I'd grabbed his shoulders to pull him closer, ready to bed for more. "I woke up just before anything good happened, though. I *always* wake up before the good parts."

No one spoke at first, it made me open my eyes to find both Tor and Char staring hard at me. And *boy* did I recognize the lust in their eyes.

So maybe not so boring?

Char blinked quickly, seeming to wake first, and elbowed Tor. "Hurry it up, Steinbeck, make with your answer."

Tor picked up the pen, it slipping from his grasp at first, proof that my answer still affected him. Seeing him a bit ruffled was actually pretty nice.

He scribbled an answer, his writing far less neat than it had been when we'd started, before he'd drank.

It was two nights ago. I was sitting in a chair and a girl was on her knees in front of me.

Reading the words had my body heating, because without even meaning to, I put myself in that position. I pictured myself on my knees, looking up and into his steady gaze. I thought about undoing the fasten on his pants, the click of his zipper as I pulled it down, slowly, then the sight when I finally got to see him naked.

What would he look like? I wasn't so sheltered as to not know how a man looked naked, but I also hadn't exactly seen much in real life. I hadn't gotten to explore, to touch, to do anything like that.

I picked up the plum brandy and took a sip because my mouth had suddenly turned dry, and that was all I had. As soon as I tasted it, I regretted the decision. Alcohol did *not* help thirst, and after I swallowed and set the bottle down, I wiped my mouth with the back of my arm.

I opened my eyes, my gaze moving over Tor, his dream in my mind. I looked down his T-shirt, over his chest, his stomach, the loose fabric making it so I couldn't see the details. Thankfully, I'd seen it before, so I could imagine well enough.

My attention fell to his lap, the gray fabric of his sweatpants obscuring what I really wanted to see. I tried to ignore how perverted I felt, ogling a man just because of some dream he had, but I couldn't help it. The fact he was so stern, so hard to understand, that to think of him in a different way excited me.

How would he look if he were in that position? He could speak, softly, so would he groan? I recalled the sounds Hayden had made, and I wondered, would Tor do the same? Would he slide his fingers into my hair? Would he make me take more of him? To take him deeper? Or would he tease the strands as he let me do as I pleased?

"Seems our little kitten here is interested in that," Char said, making me realize they'd caught me.

"No idea what you're talking about," I muttered softly, but I *still* couldn't drag my gaze away. It was like my words and my body were on totally different wavelengths and not communicating at all.

"Really? Yet you're staring at his cock like you can see it through his pants." Char's voice didn't come from far away, as it had before, but instead from so close that his warm breath spilled across my ear. When he'd moved, I had no idea, but he'd ended up leaning in to whisper right to me.

I finally got the strength to jerk my gaze away, but strong fingers stopped me. Char reached around so his arm rested behind me, curling around to grip my chin and keep my gaze where it was. "Don't look away. How often do you get a chance like this? Besides, look *closely* and you'll see how he feels about you looking at him. Doesn't seem he minds at all."

I could have struggled or pulled away and Char would let me. He liked to push his luck, to see how far he could go, but he'd give if I really wanted him to.

The problem was that I didn't want him to let me go. The warmth and strength in his touch soaked into me, and after our conversations, after the talk about dirty dreams and our sex lives, I craved more of it.

So I did as he said and focused on where I'd looked before. It took a moment before I parted my lips on a soft gasp.

A new shadow appeared in the gray fabric of his sweats, and I licked my lips again as I realized it was because he was getting hard.

"Do you want to go back to your room, kitten?" Char asked. "You can go sleep off what we all drank, and we can all forget about this."

"Or?" My question came out soft, the sound so unlike my normal voice.

"Or you'll end up with a lot more of an education. I can't promise you romance or dates, but I can fulfill all that sweet, innocent curiosity you've got."

My answer — that I'd stay, that I wanted this — rested on my lips, but I couldn't quite say it. Despite Tor's physical reaction, he hadn't actually agreed, hadn't consented.

I somehow pulled my gaze from his hard cock and moved it up to his eyes. I didn't ask the question, not with words, instead using my expression to ask.

Tor swallowed hard, the gulp loud, and he winced slightly at the end, telling me it aggravated his throat. Just as I expected him to turn me down — I'd gotten used to not getting what I wanted, after all—he nodded.

Which was about the last thing I'd ever thought I'd get.

"So, seems like he's in. What about you? You staying or are you running away to go have another dream that ends before the good parts?"

"I'm staying," I whispered.

Char's lips touched my ear, the touch soft for only a moment before he nipped the lobe, leaving a sting behind. "Good girl."

And I had no idea just how hot those words could be.

Tor

I would have walked away if not for Char. Just seeing Kenz made me uneasy, had my heart beating faster and my palms sweating. She just looked so innocent, like something I never should sully with my touch.

In fact, it still felt as though, if I crossed that line, if I put these hands on her, I might just stain her.

However, Char proved he was an expert at manipulating people, because he knew *exactly* where to press to get others to do as he wanted. How long had he planned this?

I thought about the questions he'd asked during the game, how they'd ramped up and steered us in this direction, and I realized Kenz and I had both fallen prey to his trap.

And yet I have no desire to pull myself from it now.

"Sit up on your bed," Char told me.

For a reason I had to attribute to my own foolish lust, I followed his order. It wasn't that I would do whatever he said, so much as I wanted to see what would happen, what he had planned. Char might be shady and manipulative—no real might about it—but I had a feeling we both wanted the same thing this time.

Kenz.

I sat on the foot of the bed, the position allowing me to look down at Kenz and Char—boy did that take me back to that dream. It overlaid on top of this moment, the way the woman had crawled toward me.

The part I hadn't mentioned? That I'd kept to myself?

I had no doubt that the woman in my dream had been Kenz. The dark hair, the brown eyes, that wide-eyed and innocent look she got. It couldn't have been anyone else, and now, seeing her from that same position, my cock ached.

Char released his grip on Kenz's chin. "Get closer, kitten."

She didn't glare at him and his order as she normally would have, and my breath caught when she came closer, crawling on all fours after setting her brandy down. She wore her pajamas—a thin tank top and a pair of loose shorts—and it allowed me to see the way her shoulder blades shifted beneath the fabric as she crawled. The line of her back teased me, the dip near her waist, the sight of her hands out flat against the floor.

I wasn't the type to normally fantasize about a woman crawling like this. It just wasn't my thing, so why did this excite me so much?

Because it's her.

I suspected no matter what she wore or did, I'd want her.

She stopped when she knelt right in front of me, just inside the space between my spread thighs. Uncertainty colored her expression, but it didn't look like doubt. This wasn't her wondering if she wanted to be here so much as her being nervous about what to do.

And at that moment, I really wanted to show her. I wanted to be that man in her dreams, the one who had reassured her, who had touched her and taught her and shown her the things she wanted but didn't yet understand.

I glanced past her, at Char, because this sort of thing was done one-on-one in my rather limited experience. I certainly hadn't ever considered getting off while a man watched.

He smirked, as though to tell me the ball was in my court.

What a terrible saying at a time like this.

So I gathered my courage, hooked my thumbs into the waist of my sweats, and pulled them down. I'd thought about only taking them down a bit, but with Kenz seated as she was, that would make it awkward. Instead, I pulled them off entirely, then set them on the bed beside me. The cool air touched my heated dick, but I hardly noticed it because of the pounding of blood rushing through my veins.

When I forced myself to look down at Kenz, though, her gaze was on the floor instead of where I suspected she really wanted to look. That adorable side of her helped calm me and reminded me of how nervous she had to be. That made it my job to stay in control and confident.

"Come on, kitten, you didn't start this because you wanted to stare at the floor." Char pressed his lips to the side of her throat, leaving a gentle kiss then touching the spot with his tongue.

I expected some sort of jealousy over him touching her, but none came. Why was that? If anything, he felt like an extension of me, as though him touching her, the shiver he drew from her, was part of me, part of this.

Kenz lifted her gaze, dragging it up my legs, the motion so slow that by the time she looked directly at my cock, her entire body trembled. She parted her soft pink lips, her eyes widening in a way that was far too tempting.

I saw the dark inside of her mouth and without thinking about it, my hand wrapped around my shaft. I wanted to sink into that heat, to fill her mouth, the feel of that teasing tongue that often peeked out rubbing against my hard flesh. I wanted so much from her, but I had to hold back.

The last thing I wanted was to ruin this by scaring her.

So I made do with stroking my cock slowly, her gaze following the motions, a hungry look in her dark eyes.

"What do you think?" Char asked, his voice dark and coaxing. "Is this what you wanted?"

She nodded quickly, which was more than I'd have expected from her in this state. The alcohol may have gotten her to say more than she otherwise would have, but the lust would make any well-thought-out speech difficult.

It made me feel as though we were on solid footing for once—neither of us able to communicate with words.

"Do you want to touch him?" Char asked.

Kenz reached out with her hand, but Char caught it before she made contact, earning him a threatening glare from me.

Char didn't appear the least bit sorry, speaking to Kenz again. "Don't you remember his dream? I'm pretty sure he didn't use your hands, that time, did he?"

Kenz nodded, then shifted forward slightly, pressing in closer to me so her shoulders brushed the inside of my knees. It made it seem as though I'd captured her there, as though she were at my mercy.

Of course, the part that made it all the better was that she'd chosen this, that she was willingly trapped, that she could have put a stop to it at any time. *That* excited me all the more.

After all, our differences were obvious. I came from nothing, had lived my life in silence and darkness where she was the light. She was rich, from a respected and feared family — the complete opposite of me.

And yet, when the smart move would have been to run as fast as she could back to California, to leave me, the other men and Florida as a whole in the dust, to never look back, she didn't. Instead, she leaned in and pressed a gentle kiss to my knuckles.

It made my cock jerk despite the fact she hadn't touched the damned eager thing.

She moved her lips over my fingers, sliding her tongue along the seams. She trailed over each finger, moving up one by one, until the tip of her wet, warm tongue touched my shaft.

That brush of her against me had me releasing a heady groan, the sound quiet but still there just the same. How was it that this touch seared me so much deeper than anything before? I wasn't a virgin, even if I didn't jump into bed with people the way Vance or Char did, but I couldn't recall any of my one-night stands before, not compared to Kenz in this moment.

She didn't stop, either. Maybe the first touch broke the leash for her, shattered her nerves. She tipped her head to the side and pressed her lips directly against my cock with a gentle kiss, then trailed a string up my length until she reached the head. She kept her hands away, allowing me to grip the base of my cock and hold it still as she explored.

And explore was the best way to put it. Her breaths were hot and quick, escaping from her nose as she offered a line of reverent kisses over the thick edge of my cock, near the head. She licked there, tracing the line, following every detail she could find.

I'd had to deal with many challenges in my life, things that tested my confidence and discipline. I'd been interrogated, had to remain calm even in the most dangerous of situations, but never had I felt so close to breaking as I did right now.

It wasn't just the sensation, either. More than that was the sight. Kenz had the face of an angel, a girl so sweet that she seemed impossible. She smiled like the sun, could draw anyone to her, could make anyone forget their worries, and the sight of her teasing my cock with her tongue and those plump pink lips was too much.

"Lick the head, kitten," Char whispered, his voice like a dark narrator. As he spoke, he slipped his fingers up her back, following her spine, and she arched against each place he touched like the kitten he called her.

Kenz pulled back, staring for only a moment before rising higher on her knees to slide the flat of her tongue over the head of my cock. She paused for a moment, tasting the pre-cum beaded there. After a quick swallow, she leaned in again and repeated the motion with the tip of her tongue. It localized the sensation, made it more powerful. Worse, when she reached the hole, she circled and pressed against it.

Had *anyone* paid such close attention? Practiced motions were one thing, and they felt good all right, but her exploration and enthusiasm did so much more for me. Every thought she had played across her features, the excitement as she discovered something new, as she decided she liked it.

"What a good girl," Char praised her, slipping his hand around her to tease her breast through her top. "Now take it in. You don't have to go deep — not yet — but slide those pretty little lips of yours around his cock."

Even *I* struggled to hold back when Char's voice filled my senses. It felt like those internet videos of people whispering, the ones that were supposed to calm a person — except calm was the last thing I felt.

Instead, I fought against my release already, like some kid who had never had a girl touch him before. Who could blame me, though?

Kenz pressed one kiss against the tip of my cock, then a delicious, hot pressure surrounded the head. The sight was so unexpected that at first, my brain couldn't make sense of it. It wasn't just a matter of seeing a girl blowing me — I'd seen that before. I'd even fantasized about Kenz doing this exact thing, but none of those prepared me for reality.

A line appeared between her dark eyebrows, a sure sign that she was working hard, that she was figuring out how to do this. The slight wrinkles that normally covered her full lips had disappeared as my cock stretched her, and she rubbed her tongue against the sensitive underside of my shaft.

She went to pull away, but Char placed a hand on the back of her head, stopping her retreat. Her lovely, innocent eyes widened, but the tension inside her slid away as soon as he spoke. "You aren't choking, kitten, so you're fine. You want him to enjoy this, right? You've wanted this for a while. What a poor showing if you gave up so fast. Come on, look at him, right in the eyes, and *beg* him for what you've been dreaming of."

Her teeth grazed me, even that slight sting arousing, as she met my gaze. I lost myself in the darkness there, the trust, the need. I wanted to thrust so badly, to feel the friction all over my aching shaft. However, since that wasn't possible—the poor girl was overwhelmed with just the head, after all—I moved my hand instead. I stroked my cock from the base up to the point where my fist touched her lips.

She continued to tease me with her tongue just as she tightened her lips and sucked. It added another level of pleasure, and between that and her sexy little mouth, I had no hope of resisting any longer.

I refused to close my eyes, to miss a single moment of this as I came, as I gave in to that tightening sensation that had run through my thighs, my lower back, my balls. I spilled into her mouth, my thoughts too far to even think about whether or not she'd want me to finish there. Those were thoughts for people in their right mind, and I was nowhere close to that anymore.

I breathed heavily as I came down from the heights of my release, only then realizing my eyes had closed on their own. When I opened them, I found Char's hand still on the back of her head, not letting her pull away even as my cock started to soften in her warm mouth.

"Swallow your gift as a thank you," he told her.

Her tongue moved as she obeyed, as she swallowed my seed, even that sensation almost painful after I'd come. Still, I couldn't bring myself to tell her to stop, to risk ending this any sooner than we had to.

She yelped, the sound something between panic and plea, and I looked down her body to find Char's hand that wasn't still holding the back of her head had disappeared between her thighs.

And just like that, I knew just one round wouldn't be nearly enough to satisfy me.

Char

I'd never worried much about my kinks. For me, sex had usually occurred with my mask on, being someone other than who I was. I played the part I needed to, typically that of a doting, sweet man who gave the girl everything she wanted.

That was how I'd been with my wife. I'd touched her so gently, always asking her what she wanted, what she enjoyed, if she was okay. Roughness had no place in those masks, after all.

It was why I'd never thought about what *I* wanted, because that hadn't mattered. It hadn't been about me, but about whoever I was at that moment.

This time was different, though. Kenz already knew the real me, knew the ugly side, the person I hid from most people. So instead of being that perfect, vanilla gentleman, I was *me*.

And wasn't it a shock to find the real me was a pervert? Holding the back of her head, feeling the slight push as she tried to move away, excited me. My cock had been hard since the first order I'd whispered to her, the first time I'd told her to obey, and it had only worsened when she'd taken Tor's dick into her small mouth.

In fact, even though I hadn't actually been touched at all, I doubted any sex I'd ever had had felt half this satisfying. It was like feeding a starving beast inside of me, like hunger pangs finally going away.

I stroked my fingers along her cunt through her shorts and smiled. "You sure wore some thin fabric, kitten. Did you do that on purpose? Hoping this would happen? Because you also walk around in next to nothing — maybe you're just so desperate that you don't care who fucks you, just so long as one of us does?"

She whined, the sound muffled by Tor's cock. No doubt he was uncomfortable with the continued stimulation, but the hunger in his golden eyes suggested he'd happily endure it.

And I got off on even that.

No wonder I hide who I am — look at the real me. Who would want this?

I shook away the condemnation. I could wallow in self-loathing later. For now, I might as well enjoy this.

I moved my fingers to her clit, rubbing there as I slid my other hand to her hair to hold her still. She shifted her hips, moving her knees together to close her thighs.

The tiny act of rebellion made me laugh, and I didn't hide it from her. "You know the best thing about this position? Even if you close those thighs of yours, it doesn't do a thing." I made my point by letting go of her hair—she didn't seem to want to pull away anymore—and pressing at her lower back. It arched her, which exposed more of her pussy to me.

I rubbed her clit through her shorts, the action mocking. "You see? Your sweet little clit is still mine." I leaned in and nipped at her left ass cheek, doing it hard enough to leave a mark, then ran my fingers up, proving my point, stroking each place as I spoke.

"In fact, if I wanted to, I could fuck you, no matter how tight you press those thighs of yours together. Your tight pussy is totally exposed." I could have stopped there, but that darkness inside me wouldn't allow it. I moved my finger up farther, stroking between her ass cheeks, to press in at the most intimate part of her. "Even here, kitten, I could slide right into your ass and there isn't a thing you could do to stop it."

Tor let out another one of those sounds, surprising me as they had thus far. They weren't exactly moans, more breathless, rougher and quieter, but that didn't hide that they were clearly born of pleasure.

It seems he's able to go again quickly. Or more likely it was Kenz. She was far too attractive for her own good, after all. I doubted anyone could resist her.

Clearly I can't.

Just touching her through the fabric wasn't enough, not anymore. Even if I'd thought I could resist, that I could walk away without feeling her pussy clutching around my fingers as she came, I knew it wasn't possible anymore.

I grasped her hip in one hand to hold her still as I slipped my fingers into the baggy leg of her shorts. These things had tormented me already, the fabric hardly enough to cover her if she were alone, let alone bouncing around in a house of grown-ass men. I'd thought about this before, and getting to do it now was even better than if I'd stripped them off her fully.

She wore no underwear, which meant I found her bare, drenched pussy. I groaned at the feeling, the heat, the idea of being the first person to ever touch her like this.

"How is it possible you can be this wet?" I asked. "If you weren't wearing these shorts, you'd be dripping all over the place, wouldn't you? How lewd."

Her cunt twitched against my fingers, telling me she liked my words just as much as I did. I moved my gaze up her back, to her head. I found her moving again.

My lips curled into a smirk. "I didn't even have to tell you anything and there you are, sucking his cock already? You know, teaching you like this feels like training a pet. Is he hard again?"

She nodded, the motion small since she seemed reluctant to release him.

"Take him deeper, then. Open your mouth wider — watch the teeth — and stick your tongue out more. Show us just how badly you wanted this."

Tor reached out suddenly on a quick grasp, holding the back of her head, which told me she'd done as she was told. His gaze was locked on her face, no doubt enjoying the sight of her taking his cock deeper.

"Good kittens deserve treats, don't they?" I took that chance to slide two fingers into her cunt.

She took them so easily that I wouldn't have guessed she was a virgin. It didn't seem possible for a body this sensual, this sensitive to have never done this before. Her pussy was tight, but it didn't fight me at all. Maybe that went to show just how badly she'd wanted this.

I pulled out slightly, then thrust in again. "Your pussy grips me so tightly, like it doesn't want to let me go. Do you have *any* idea how badly it makes me want to just slide right into you? Do you think you could take me like that? Right now?" I twisted my wrist, ensuring that she felt my knuckles stroking against her, wishing I could get deeper, to feel more of her.

Her cry came out again, and she didn't pull away from me. She didn't try to avoid the way I fucked her with my fingers. Instead, she braced her hands on the ground and brought her hips backward, begging me with her body for the same thing I wanted.

Which made it clear I couldn't hold back anymore. I let go of her hip and yanked my pajama bottoms down, freeing my cock. I pulled my fingers from her cunt, rubbing the wetness over my length.

Tor's sharp gaze met mine, a warning there.

He really is overly protective, isn't he? I flashed him a smile to tell him not to worry. I wouldn't go too far no matter how badly I wanted to.

I ran the tip of my cock over her slit, through her shorts, pressing it against the giving spot where I'd aim if I were going to fuck her. The fabric kept me from plunging into her, but not from letting her feel the thick head of my dick.

"I'd love to pull these aside and do what we *both* want, but you'll have to earn that. For now? Well, I'm happy with training and fucking any part of you, pet." I moved back enough to line my cock up with her thighs, just below her cunt. Between the wetness I'd spread on myself and how drenched her thighs were, I slid easily into the space between her toned legs. "Keep your thighs tight, or I might just slip," I threatened.

She straightened, the muscles of her legs straining as she tried to obey. It wasn't as good as her cunt would have been, no doubt, but it was more than enough for me right now. I shifted down a bit, spreading my legs wider to angle myself better. It caused my shaft to rub against her clit, and her sharp breath said I'd aimed well.

I set both hands on her hips to hold her still, and Tor's hand in her hair kept her from getting knocked forward or choking on his cock.

Though I wouldn't mind hearing that sound. In fact, my fantasy supplied an idea of how she'd sound if she gagged, and a phantom sensation around my cock made me think that the feeling of her throat squeezing down on my dick would be amazing.

I thrust hard, able to go rougher than I could have if I'd actually slid into her. She was wet and desperate, but there was no way a virgin would be up to a fucking this rough her first time out. So I entertained myself with her body, getting off not only on the physical sensations but on how she gave it up to me, how she didn't struggle against it. After a lifetime of rejection, of expecting others to never accept me, her submission offered a heady feeling all its own.

Her breathing sped and she moved her hips, clearly walking that edge, wanting to come, striving for what she needed to fall into that pleasure.

And the darkness in me that she unleashed, that she'd unmasked, had me moving so I no longer stroked against her. "Not just yet, kitten. I get to come first." I let my voice drop low, knowing it came out like gravel. Denying her felt like another caress, another touch, another tool right then. Her sound of frustration was all

I needed to get off, especially as I stared down, the sight looking so much like I was actually fucking her.

I came hard, leaning forward, resting my forehead on her back as I leaned over her. *Fuck* it felt like she'd snatched my soul right out of my body, like she'd hollowed me out entirely with that orgasm, like I had nothing left inside me at all.

Her whine brought me back, though, so I nipped her back through her sweat-soaked tank top, then rose again. I slid by hands beneath her, finding her still needy cunt through the leg of her shorts with ease. I pressed three fingers into her, not warning her, enjoying the way she jumped before bringing her hips back toward me.

I moved my other hand over her stomach, capturing the cum I'd left there. It was warm and thick and I gathered it on two of my fingers.

The muscles of Tor's neck stood out, and I could see the fight inside him to not force her down on his cock, to not thrust his hips up and into the welcoming heat of her mouth. He neared another orgasm, and the desperate sight was fucking *sexy.*

Kenz's cunt squeezed down in warning, so I reached forward, over her, and slid my two cum-covered fingers into her mouth. I put them against her cheek, between her teeth, to keep her mouth open. It meant I also felt Tor's cock, the way she took it in just a bit, then out again in shallow movements.

"Come, kitten. You've more than earned it for being so good for us. I'm sure the taste of our cum is exactly what you wanted, isn't it?"

Kenz came in a rush, as though my words had broken the dam. Her cunt tightened into a vise, and a part of me was damned thankful I didn't have my cock in her right then. Even if I knew it wasn't possible, I wondered if she couldn't snap a man's dick with that sort of strength. Her teeth also closed — the action not under her control, I was sure — making me glad I'd thought about it.

I doubted Tor would be in a great mood if he got his cock bitten off, and an assassin was the last person someone wanted moody.

His hand tightened in her hair, no doubt pulling the strands until they stung, and his cock jerked against her tongue and my fingers as he came again.

He withdrew from her mouth, hissing when her lips stroked him. Then again, coming twice so quickly couldn't feel that great afterward. *And why is it that gets me in the mood again?*

I pushed that question away and pulled my fingers from her cunt, letting her hips fall so she was sitting instead of kneeling. I swirled my other fingers in her mouth, through the cum Tor had left, then withdrew those as well. She collapsed more, shifting so she was on one hip, leaning against Tor's naked thigh with her cheek. She looked back at me, her eyes lidded as if they were too heavy to keep fully open.

They might both appear exhausted, but I had a feeling I could have gone another couple rounds. I wasn't sure I'd felt this alive in…

Maybe ever.

So I lifted my hands and looked down at them. Kenz's juices covered the fingers on one hand, and a mixture of my cum and Tor's on the other. They looked different, but they drew me just the same. While both Tor and Kenz watched, I licked my fingers clean, swallowing down every drop I could find from both hands, savoring the way our flavors mixed.

Alcohol might have started this, might have let us indulge in a way we'd have hesitated over otherwise, but I knew it wasn't the true cause.

And just as strongly, I knew it wouldn't be the last time, because I couldn't imagine not feeling *this* again.

Chapter Fourteen

Hayden

I handed a beer to Tor before sitting on the tailgate of his truck in the driveway. Char stood with a beer of his own, and Vance drank something out of a glass since he tended to be too fancy to enjoy beer — especially straight from a bottle.

"She asleep?" Char asked.

"Yeah. She seems to be sleeping better now than she was before. The dark circles are about gone, in fact. I think days she does self-defense practice especially take it out of her, so she crashes pretty fast." That brought back the memory of her yawning as she'd crawled into her bed, half asleep before her head had even hit the pillow.

Did she fall asleep faster because she'd gotten more used to the house? Because she knew us better, so she trusted us more?

I'd like to think that, but I wasn't foolish enough to believe it had anything to do with us specifically.

I held the bottle against the edge of the truck bed, hooking the lid on it before hitting it down to open the bottle. The lid flew off, clicking as it hit the bed liner.

When was the last time we'd gathered like this? Had we ever, really?

Before Kenz, we all lived our own lives, only speaking as much as necessary for whatever task we had next, to share information we'd found. We'd eaten alone, exercised by ourselves, and sometimes gone weeks or even months without seeing each other despite living in the same house.

However, Kenz had changed all that. *She changed a lot more than that.* Now the house didn't feel so large or empty or lifeless. Hell, it almost felt like a home.

And now, when Kenz went to sleep early, the four of us tended to gather. Tonight, with the sweltering heat even after the sun had gone down, seemed the perfect time to have a cold beer.

"We need to talk," I said when I couldn't put it off anymore, guilt weighing heavily on me.

"What the hell? Is this a breakup talk?" Char asked with a chuckle. The laugh didn't sound like he was brushing my statement off, but rather an attempt to lighten the mood.

I took a big drink, using that as a way to delay the conversation and come to terms with my thoughts. I'd practiced this in my head a bunch of times, but it didn't seem nearly as simple when actually faced with the topic.

"You look like a kid who's admitting to their mom they stole cookies," Vance said.

No, it's worse.

"We all agreed we wouldn't touch Kenz," I started with, then stared down at the beer in my hand. "I agreed to it, too. I'm not the type who goes back on my word, so I need to admit to something." I took a deep breath, then blurted it out. Sometimes ripping the bandage off was the best way forward. "I crossed that line. Worse, I don't think I can say I wouldn't do it again. I know we made an agreement, that we trusted we'd all follow through on it, and I can't even say sorry since I think I'd do it again."

No one spoke, and I couldn't blame them.

We'd gone in on this together, swearing to work as a team to take down our common enemy. We faced someone so dangerous and deceitful that we *had* to be able to trust one another fully. Otherwise, how could we possibly think we had a chance against Lorien?

"I know I've betrayed you," I admitted, my voice soft. "We have to trust each other, and because of what I did, I broke that. I should have told you sooner, but I just didn't know how to do it. I've never broken a promise like this before, and I didn't know how to address it, how to deal with it, so I figured I should just come out and say it. I'm sorry, and I'll do whatever it takes to make you understand that you *can* trust me, even after this."

Still, no one spoke. My heart pounded so hard that they *had* to hear it.

Just before I forced myself to look up, to see the expressions of disappointment, a sound caught me.

It was Char's laughter. It started out as a chuckle, but he quickly lost control of it and bent forward, holding the edge of the truck for balance.

Vance swiped his beer before he dropped it.

"What's so funny?" I asked.

Char used the heel of his hand to rub over his eyes, collecting stray tears that had escaped from his laughing fit. "I just didn't expect this falling-on-your-sword thing. Fuck, you really are straitlaced, aren't you?"

"What are you talking about?"

"You really don't know? I thought we were all just accepting that such a stupid agreement wouldn't last. Was I supposed to do this, too?"

Do this, too? His words took a moment to work through, and when I did? I narrowed my eyes. "You mean *you* fooled around with her, too?"

Char shrugged, not appearing the least bit sorry or uncomfortable. "Well, seeing as I know how her pussy tastes, yeah."

I looked toward Tor, hoping for him to agree. "Can you believe this?"

Tor rubbed the back of his neck and avoided my gaze.

"Might want to look for someone who didn't get his dick sucked by her for backup," Char said.

"You what?" Vance asked. "I can't believe you all! I'm the man whore but I restrained myself!"

"Wait one minute," I interrupted. "You're trying to tell me that *Vance Moore,* who has screwed his way through almost every cover model out there, was the only one to keep his hands to himself?"

Vance shuffled his weight from foot to foot. "Well, not entirely to myself. There were *some* hand things happening, but it was second base at best, then I stopped myself. If I'd realized that you all would ignore our agreement, I wouldn't have bothered." He set down his drink and Char's beer on the tailgate between Tor and I before crossing his arms like a pouting child.

I rubbed my eyes, wondering why I'd been so damned worried. It seemed while I'd agonized over having crossed the line, everyone else had done far worse with no guilt at all.

It also forced me to think about Kenz, about how innocent she was, and picture the things they said. I doubted they were lying, and given that Kenz showed no fear of them, I was sure they had all been things Kenz wanted.

Besides, if I had the slightest suspicion that these men would have done something so reprehensible, that they'd force a woman to do anything, I wouldn't have let them within a mile of Kenz.

And just like that, my body stirred, some of the regret subsiding. My time with Kenz had been tainted by my guilt. Now that I knew differently — or rather, understood we'd all failed to keep our word — I could recall the way she'd looked lost to pleasure.

I shouldn't have held back, shouldn't have stopped myself from going further. I imagined how it would feel to cup her breasts, to slide my fingers into her, to have felt her squeeze down around me as she came.

Talk about a missed opportunity…

"So, now that we've all admitted to being degenerates who can't keep our word, what do we do?" Char asked.

My phone buzzed, and I glanced at the screen. *I'm not a degenerate.*

"I remember what happened, so I don't think you can tell me that," Char argued.

Coming from someone who decided to lick my cum off your fingers?

"That's right, so don't you think I'd know one?"

"Wait, you *what?*" Vance asked as he moved his gaze between his phone, Char and Tor as though he couldn't believe that.

Then again, the details do just seem to be getting more and more outrageous. They sounded less like normal sex and more like some kink video.

I never would have figured that the playboy would be the one on my side when it came to scolding Tor and Char for their behavior.

"And no one invited me?" Vance added on, making it clear I was the odd man out when it came to being modest or traditional. "I would have so been there if *someone* had called me to let me know!"

"Fine, fine," Char said with a dismissive wave. "I'll send you a text next time."

"Good." Vance picked his drink up again as though that resolved everything.

"So...what does this mean?" I asked, needing clarification. "Because we all decided not to touch her since we knew it would only hurt her. Now, what? Our cocks are suddenly more important than her wellbeing?"

At least the others had the decency to hesitate for a moment and think it over. I'd easily admit that she was tempting—obviously, since I'd fallen to her charms so easily—but that didn't mean I'd let us off the hook so easily.

My phone buzzed. *If we don't listen to her, how are we any better than Lorien, making her choices for her? We've been clear about this being temporary, so if she's okay with that, why ignore what she wants?*

"Because she's a kid," I said with a sigh. "And after what I did with her, that's a pretty terrible thing to say, huh?" I rubbed my hand over my face, unable to square the two facts.

Fact one—she was young and innocent and naïve, and I wanted to protect her from the big bad world.

Fact two—she was a sexy and sensual woman, and I wanted to treat her like one.

They opposed each other but were both still true.

"Did you ever think that we could be a good memory?" Char asked, his voice having lost the joking tone from before. The way he could switch gears so fast amazed me as ever. "I mean, we know what our future holds no matter what. We went into this with our eyes open, know what's waiting for us at the end, so we know what *her* future holds, too. If we keep rejecting her, how does that help her at all? We're gone and she ends up living not only with that but with the doubt because we turned her down. Maybe giving her some good memories is better than nothing at all?"

I swung one of my legs as it hung over the tailgate, unsure how to accept his words. Was that a real thing, or was it just a way to lie to ourselves, to get what we wanted while taking the blame off our own shoulders?

I peered to the side, toward the house, and stared up toward where her room sat. She laid in bed up there, sleeping soundly with no idea that we were out here, discussing her, talking about her future.

"Okay," I said softly.

"You agreed? I didn't expect that at all," Vance said. "I figured we'd have to work way harder to talk you into it."

I shrugged, dangling my beer from the neck between two fingers. "I know when I'm beat, and resisting hasn't done anything. In fact, maybe we were doing more harm than good by turning her down. I mean, she's sleeping soundly, she's been laughing more, seemed happier. I'm not the type to keep hitting my head against a wall if I'm not making progress, so if that wasn't doing any good for her, it's time to try something else."

"Does this mean it's open season?" Char asked.

"I don't like that phrasing," I admitted, "but if you mean we're not going to worry about telling her no for her own good? Yeah, I guess you're right."

Vance snorted softly, humor in the sound. "Trust me, I'm not going to stay in last place anymore. I have a reputation to uphold, after all."

I shook my head and pinched the bridge of my nose. Hopefully Kenz slept for a long time, because I had a feeling that girl was in for a mess when she woke up.

And yet, excitement grew inside me at the prospect, because I was pretty sure Kenz might be the only woman capable of handling four men like us.

* * * *

Kenz

I shifted in my chair, surprisingly nervous. It wasn't as though this was the first time I'd been in such a luxurious private room at a five-star restaurant before, but I didn't usually meet up with the people who ran the auction I was sold at, either. A moment of that horror washed over me once again, taking me back to when I'd woken in a cage. I recalled the helplessness, the fear, the way I'd felt less than human as the lights had poured over me and the auctioneer had started the bidding. It had brought me here, but I couldn't look back on it with anything but terror.

A warmth on my thigh made me jump, but a gentle squeeze reassured me. Hayden always did that, seemed able to tell when I started to lose my nerve and could pull me back just before I spiraled.

I'm not alone. Sure, I would see the man who had helped changed my entire life, would sit across from him, but I wasn't doing it on my own.

The men were here with me, and I knew they'd do anything they could to ensure this went well.

And to me, well only meant I left with Tor, Hayden, Vance and Char. My standards were exceedingly low, after all.

Finally, the door to the room opened, and Bradley walked in.

It wasn't the first time I'd seen him, but somehow my fear hadn't lessened at all. He was tall, dressed impeccably in a suit that made my father's expensive clothing look like thrift store cast-offs. A silver chain went from a button of his vest and disappeared into a pocket, telling me a watch rested at the end of it. He had no jacket on, but this was the sort of place that often took coats so the patrons were comfortable. He looked every bit the sort of man who would run black market auctions where a person could buy anything—including people.

"You're late," Vance said with a smirk.

Bradley pulled the silver chain and looked down at his watch. "Actually, I'm not." He turned the face of the watch just as the second hand hit the top and the hour hand moved to the six, showing he was exactly on time, right to the second.

And didn't that explain him to a T?

Bradley came to the table, pulled out a chair, then took a seat in a way that was amazingly graceful. How was it that everything he did could appear so smooth? He didn't pick up a menu, didn't even reach for one. Instead, when a server came in a moment later, he rattled off a quick order for a drink — sparkling water with two lime wedges — without glancing the server's way.

The rest of us ordered similarly, no one choosing an alcoholic drink.

Then again, the last time I drank...

My cheeks burned at the memory of my time with Tor and Char. When it was my time to give my order, I opened my mouth and did so without even thinking about it.

I only realized I might have said something strange when the eyes of every other person stared at me as though I'd lost my mind.

"One Shirley Temple," the server said with a chuckle that made me drop my gaze to my lap.

Everyone else had ordered adult things, and there I was, proving what a kid I was after all. The opening, then closing of the door said the server had left, but I kept staring at my lap instead of around the table. Somehow, Bradley still managed to make me feel like I was still in that cage, that I was locked up and stared at and had no idea how to escape.

Which was foolish. I *knew* that if I stood right now, if I walked out, no one would stop me. The men would follow me, of course, but they wouldn't force me to stay.

Yet somehow, Bradley messed with my mind and made it difficult to remember that I wasn't trapped anymore — at least not by him.

"You wanted to see us?" Hayden asked.

Bradley held up one finger. "We can discuss matters, but wait for one moment."

Before anyone needed to ask why, the door opened once more. A group of servers entered this time, with platters balanced on their hands, their movements almost like a well-practiced dance. The one who had taken the drink orders placed glasses before each of us with our selected items. The pink of my soda was bright and cheery through the glass and three red cherries floated on top.

The other servers brought lots of food we hadn't ordered. Bradley didn't appear the least bit surprised, suggesting he'd preordered a selection of dishes and appetizers.

Did that mean he expected this to take a while?

"Is there anything else you need?" the server who'd brought the drinks asked.

Bradley waved her off, still not looking her way. "No, nothing else. Thank you."

"Of course. I will ensure you are not disturbed. If you need anything, please press the button on the edge of the table." She then left, closing the door softly behind her.

It almost felt as though she took the oxygen with her, and even the scent of the food—as delicious as it looked—couldn't ease the tension.

"So, again, why did you call us here?" Hayden asked.

Bradley looked at me, then gestured at the food. "I had no idea what you might like, so I had them prepare a number of dishes. Please, eat."

I couldn't hold his gaze. The moment we made contact, I dropped my gaze again, feeling as though his eyes were a trap I might fall into. He was the sort of person who looked dangerous, but I knew it wasn't nearly as dangerous as he truly was. I knew it because I'd grown up around lethal people, could tell from the way they moved, the way they spoke, like a sense that most people never developed.

It was one reason I hated interacting with him so much.

He let out a soft huff as though he didn't appreciate my reaction.

If you don't want people to be afraid of you, maybe don't abduct and sell them!

Talk about the consequences of his own actions.

"She appears well."

"When you sell something, it no longer remains your problem, I thought," Vance said.

"It isn't, but that doesn't mean I wish to see harm come to anyone, especially innocent women."

I opened my mouth to smart off to him but snapped my lips together before it escaped. The last thing we needed was for me to piss him off. He was in a position to make things far worse for me and the men.

Instead, I picked up my drink and took a sip through the straw, rolling the sweet liquid around in my mouth to distract me.

"I called you to ask again if you have any plan to enter into negotiations with Lorien," Bradley said.

The mention of Lorien had me sitting up straight, my hand clenching around my glass, my heart speeding.

"I thought we already had this talk," Char said.

"We did. However it is my job to ensure our clients are happy, and this particular issue has caused a lot of problems for us. People in my position succeed by trust and reputation. The last thing I want are previous clients going around and ruining what I have spent my life building."

"And how does this little chat help that?" Vance asked.

"While it appears the direct conflicts have ended — there have been no more attacks so far as I know — the parties are not yet satisfied. I understand Lorien is continuing to contact you, and he still attempts to find a way for us to intervene."

"Your rules say you can't intervene, though, certainly not on his behalf. He has no rights to her."

"Technically, neither do you. Given that you *both* managed to cheat my system, neither of you have retained clear rights to the product. I would be fully within my rights to take her back and cancel the auction entirely."

"You could try," Hayden said, no hesitation in his tone.

Bradley smiled, but it lacked any warmth.

I didn't realize that 'fuck around and find out' had a look, but there it is.

Char spoke up before Hayden could go further, using his cheery, 'let's all get along,' tone. "You *could* do that, but then you would have to admit to the fact that two different people managed to interfere with your system. I would imagine that if you're worried about your reputation and the trust of your clients, that would be a bad thing."

Bradley stared at Char for a long moment, then nodded. "That's right, which is why I have tried to handle this delicately. However, the longer it drags out, the more likely that it causes me problems. The quickest way to a resolution would be to allow Lorien to take her."

"Not happening," Hayden said.

"I thought as much. Everything becomes so much more complicated when women are involved, does it not? What if we re-held the auction? We put her back up and allow a fair bidding war to occur. It would erase any doubts or issues with the previous sale, and you and the other party would agree to abide by the results."

"That sounds like it would help him but not us," Char pointed out. "Why would we do that?"

"Because he has agreed that if we do so, he will follow whatever happens. That means he will make no attempts to contact her if you win the bid."

That might have seemed like a good idea if it hadn't been for the fact that winning a bidding war against Lorien was one hell of a risk. From what I'd heard, he had all the money of his family at his disposal. The men had money, as well, but moving such large amounts quietly was the problem. Lorien could liquidate and use much bigger amounts of cash than anyone else since so many of his assets were already hidden. He didn't have to explain it to anyone, like good old Uncle Sam for tax purposes.

"In addition, because the auction house is partly responsible for this mess, we have agreed to pay thirty percent of the winning bid to the loser, should you agree to resolve this in such a way."

I pressed my lips together, an uncomfortable feeling gnawing at my insides. I thought about how much the men wanted their revenge, how much they deserved it. After what Lorien had done, he *should* be held accountable, but he'd avoided it thus far. He'd played games and stayed out of their reach and stolen so much from them.

I'd been a problem for the men, and they'd risked their lives to keep me safe. By keeping me around, they risked more than that. They all had things they wanted to protect, things that Lorien could use against them, and I struggled to see a downside to handing me over.

It didn't mean they couldn't deal with him in the future, that they couldn't keep going later to get him. In fact, with me there with him, it might even give them a better chance. Even after years with Lorien, I had no doubt that if they appeared, I'd still side with them, I'd still help them however I could.

I swallowed hard, the action hurting my throat as though I'd tried to force a baseball down my esophagus.

"Not a chance," Hayden said, managing to let me take a deep breath, as though he'd pulled me up from beneath the water. "I told you the last time that we weren't interested in handing her over or selling her off."

Bradley let out a big sigh, the sort of sound a parent made when they were over whatever nonsense their kids were pulling. "Fair enough. I didn't really expect you to agree. However, understand that this little standoff between you is thus far an annoyance. If you fail to resolve this, however, if it begins to cause me true problems, I have no issue solving it myself. I can assure you that *none* of you will be happy with the method I use to do so. I do not allow anything to affect my business, least of all petty games between cheaters."

Wow, I had to admit, Bradley could scold people better than the sternest principal at a school. He could put about anyone in their place with a tone like that.

"I wouldn't threaten me." Char's tone had dropped out of that cheerful one, giving a glimpse of that darker side of him he usually kept hidden. "Getting your people to do as we wanted wasn't that difficult. Underlings are notoriously unreliable, after all. It is *never* a good idea to overestimate your position, because getting the foundation kicked from beneath you causes one hell of a fall."

I jerked my gaze to Bradley, my eyes wide, because I'd never heard someone talk to Bradley like that. Beyond that, it was a very clear threat, and Bradley didn't strike me as the type to take that lying down.

He didn't react at first, staring back as though thinking. He didn't laugh, but neither did he seem angry. The room remained so silent that the ticking of a clock on the wall felt like gunshots, counting the seconds as they passed by.

Finally, Bradley nodded. "I can't say I expected anything different. However, I am a believer in offering people choices, especially to avoid violence. I prefer to give people that chance so that when things do happen, those people know that it's down to their own stubbornness. Now, before I leave, I ask a favor."

"Are you really in any position for a favor?" Vance asked.

"I believe I am, given I have yet to make a move against you. Besides, I don't take favors lightly and I always offer something equally valuable, since I don't like to owe others. Allow me to speak to the girl privately for a short time. In exchange, I will offer you some information I think you would be interested in."

"I thought your place as Auction Manager meant you wouldn't give anything up about clients?" Char asked.

"I can't give you anything obtained in the course of my business, which means no financials or contact information that a client has given me. However, as you know, running the auctions is far from my only source of information. I have gathered facts outside of that which I would be willing to share. I believe things such as a timeline of Lorien's *professional* jobs over the past five years might appeal to you?"

"We know what he's done," Hayden said.

"You know the main jobs, but I assure you, he has been busier than you realize. In addition, I have the times and dates of his travels over that time. If a studious person were to have all that, they may have a better chance of tracking down information about him. They might even manage to locate current images of him. I imagine that would be exceedingly useful."

A glance at Hayden showed his lips thinned into a tight line. Obviously, he was tempted. Bradley offered something that Hayden wanted, something that could go a long way toward identifying and potentially trapping Bradley. By knowing more about him, including a true timeline of events, they might even manage to locate him.

Hayden shook his head. "I'm not about to risk her, not even for that."

Bradley looked around the table. "And you all agree with that?"

Tor nodded, no hesitation at all.

"I agree with Hayden," Vance said.

"Same," Char added.

And just like that, the fear inside me went away. Even this, something so simple, something without much risk, they still put me first.

However, I couldn't let that happen. I'd done a lot to affect their lives — I wanted to give back, to protect them as well.

"I'll do it," I said softly.

The instant weight of the glares from Tor, Hayden, Char and Vance made me want to crawl under the table. Instead, I pulled my shoulders back and spoke, my gaze on the table so I didn't lose my nerve. "I'll speak to him. It's just a quick talk, and that information would help you, right?"

"You don't have to do this," Hayden said. "Even a small risk is too much. We can get that information some other way."

I shook my head, then forced myself to meet his dark eyes. "It's fine. If he wanted to do something, he could have already. Please? Let me do this."

He sighed heavily, but I knew I'd won. Once I asked, he had little chance to deny me. He turned his hard gaze back on Bradley. "We will step out for you to speak, but if you do *anything*, you will not like our reaction."

Bradley didn't appear the least bit bothered by his threat, only nodding. "Of course. I'd expect nothing less."

Hayden stood, the chair scraping hard against the floor. Tor, Char and Vance did the same, all of them giving Bradley glares that I was thankful weren't locked on me.

When they left, I still refused to lift my gaze to look directly at Bradley. That felt too dangerous, too close, so I took another drink of my soda and focused on the table in front of me.

"You look better than the last time I saw you," he said, his voice the same flat one I'd heard from him before. It was strange that he could say something like in the same tone he used when threatening people, as if the two things were no different to him.

I nodded, unsure how to respond to that. It reminded me of how Lorien asked me the same thing, reminded me how this all looked from the outside.

The men had cheated to buy me from an auction like property. They'd moved me into their home and refused to allow me to leave, escorted me everything I went. Those things didn't paint them in a favorable light.

Yet, that wasn't how *I* saw the men. These people had no idea the truth. They didn't know that Tor bought sugar-free treats for me just so I had them in the house. They had no idea that Vance ensured I had access to whatever art supplies I needed and always gave advice when I felt stuck. They didn't know that Hayden watched over me no matter what I did, had taken wounds meant for me without any hesitation. Even Char, who wasn't even close to what I'd call sweet, always listened to me, never made me feel alone.

We were all in a horrible situation, trying our best, and out of any of them, I trusted *my* men the most.

"You realize that things can't go on like this, don't you? Lorien and the men you are with are like two dog packs fighting over the same den. They may keep their distance at first, but eventually, they will clash if neither finds a way to back down."

"Yes, I know," I whispered.

"I am glad to know you understand that. Too often, normal people fail to recognize how bad things like this can get — for all involved. You may think me heartless for suggesting they turn you over, or that we re-auction you, but my goal is truly to make it through this with as little harm as possible."

"As little harm to you, you mean?" I spoke the words, but they came out soft.

"Not just me, no. If that was all I cared about, I could have sent my people to both parties and eliminated the entire bunch. My problems would be over then, but I dislike unnecessary bloodshed. I am trying hard to avoid such a thing. However, if we cannot bring this to a close in some way, if the two packs end up facing off directly…"

I shook my head, then lifted my head to look at him. My voice wasn't as strong as I would have liked it to be. It shook, fear causing it to rise and fall as I spoke, but I still forced myself to do it. "Everyone thinks Lorien is untouchable, they assume he'll win, but they don't know anything. They don't know how strong Hayden is, how crafty Char is, how determined Vance can be or how vicious Tor is. If I have to bet on anyone, it won't be on Lorien."

Bradley sat back in his seat, his expression still giving *nothing* away. "You have a lot of faith in them. This isn't the first time I have dealt with a person sold in one of my auctions, despite my best efforts to prevent it, but it is the first time I've seen someone so quickly taken in by her *owners*." The use of the words owners made my chest tighten.

Sure, I *knew* that they'd bought me, that they'd traded a lot of cash to buy me, but they'd never treated me like property.

Have they?

Bradley continued to speak, though the sharpness in his eyes said he'd caught my reaction. I had a feeling he missed very little. "Don't get me wrong, many do submit eventually. I think that is human nature, to make the best of the situation we find ourselves in. In my experience, people can adjust and even find enjoyment in nearly any circumstance if they are forced to. Still, your ability to acclimate so quickly… It makes me wonder if that is simply a part of your personality."

"What do you mean?"

"Some people fight everything. They dig their heels in and refuse to move no matter the risk or the damage. Those people do not adjust so easily. Others, however, are weaker. They prefer the path of least resistance. Those are the ones who meld into whatever happens, who give in quickly. Is that the type you are?"

I wanted to say no. I thought about Nem, about my mother, about the Quad, about Jarrod. I'd been around so many strong people who were that first time he'd spoken about. If they'd ended up where I was, they'd have fought no matter how useless it seemed, willing to die if it meant getting what they wanted.

I didn't feel as though I fit in with them, like I'd been the one dropped into a family that wasn't my own. No matter how much I wanted to deny his claim…he was right.

The fact that the men were good to me didn't change that I'd given in, that I *always* gave in to everyone. Whether they were good to me or not, whether I wanted to or not, I never held my ground.

I complained, I pushed back a little, but when it came down to it, I did as I was told.

If Lorien had bought me and not the men, would I be in the same position? Would I think I'd fallen for him? Would I have simply accepted whatever he said so I could survive, no matter what?

I closed my hands into fists because the only answer I had was one I didn't like.

"Maybe I am," I admitted. "Maybe I am weak, and maybe I don't stand up for myself, and maybe I do just do whatever others want."

"Aren't you sick of that? Doesn't it grow wearing eventually?"

"Some people are strong and some aren't. Wishing it was different doesn't change anything."

He nodded, as though accepting my statement. "You might be right, or perhaps the problem is a matter of definitions."

"What does that mean?"

"What is a common symbol of strength in the world? The lion, right? We picture the male with his long mane. However, I have seen so many times when the females of the pride run the male off. It proves that what we see as strength isn't always what ends up succeeding."

I frowned, trying to figure out his point. The words felt strange from him, not fitting the rest of what I knew about him.

Before I could make sense of his meaning, he rose. "I want you to take away one important point. When I warned you that this would end with bloodshed, I didn't intended to imply that Lorien would win. There is a good chance he would lose, but winning and losing are not the only things to consider. Lorien may well lose, but he will not do so easily, not without inflicting his own damage. The question you must ask yourself is how much are you willing to lose? How far will you allow this to go before you decide that the risk is too great?"

He took a card from his pocket and held it out to me, waiting until I gained the courage to take it. It was a business card with a phone number and no name on the white thick cardstock. "If you grow tired of this, please, contact me."

"You'll help me?"

"In a fashion. I am willing to do what it takes to reduce the bloodshed and problems, but that does not mean the help will be to your liking. One thing I've learned in such situations is that no one ends up getting quite what they want. Sometimes the best we can do is hope to reduce the damage and live with the results."

And no matter how depressing that thought was…I'd lived a life that had taught me the truth of it.

I might have wanted some happy ending, might have been naïve enough to even dream about it, but life had taught me no one got what they really wanted. The business card I tucked into my pocket was a physical reminder of that very lesson and a warning against hoping for too much.

Chapter Fifteen

Kenz

I took a deep breath as I stretched out in the grass, wetness soaking into the back of my shirt.

"You should put down a blanket," Hayden said, his shadow falling over me and blocking out the warm sun. "You'll get all wet."

I opened one eye to peek up at him and gave him a smile. "Lying in the grass is self-care. Also, clothes dry, so it's fine."

He sighed, but I could tell by the way he did so it was a surrender. Sure enough, he sat beside me. I fought against my desire to laugh.

He got way too embarrassed by things like that, which meant I didn't need to point out all the times his awkwardness charmed me. He did that all on his own already.

"I can't believe you dragged us all out here." Char had grumbled the entire trip, but he'd still come. That seemed pretty normal for the surly man—he often didn't like things, voiced his displeasure with them, but still went along. I'd learned to ignore him when he behaved like that.

"Some fresh air is good for us," Vance said and plopped down beside me on the grass area where we'd veered off the hiking path. "We've been in that house with little break for a while, now. The last thing we need is to end up going stir-crazy there."

Tor didn't say anything, as usual, but I expected him to rest against a rock on the outskirts. He often did that, remained slightly away from the rest of us, which was why it took me by surprise when he came over and sat just above where I had stretched out.

In fact, if I shifted just a bit to the left, I could have set my head in his lap.

And boy was that tempting...

"You're the only person who could drag me outside like this," Char said just before something touched my hand. When I glanced down, I found he'd set a water bottle in my hand without saying a word about it.

I sat up, charmed against my better instincts by the way he did such things. He might snap and snarl and bitch at me, but at the same time, he watched out for me in his own way. His kindness might not be easy to see all the time, but it was still there.

If I pointed it out, he'd only offer some sarcastic retort, so I only gave him a smile in thanks before unscrewing the lid and drinking some of the water. It was so refreshing after the long hike, where we'd made our way through the forested area, the humidity making my skin sticky.

Still, it felt nice to stretch my muscles and move around. I'd started to exercise at the house, practiced self-defense whenever I could, but getting to actually go somewhere refreshed my soul in a way that no amount of working out inside could.

"I can't believe I've lived here so long and never knew about this place," Hayden said.

"That happens when you live somewhere. I lived near San Diego for years but I almost never went to the beach." I thought back to the few trips we had made before my mother's death. "I remember one trip. My mother and father were busy—as usual—and I think I complained enough that the Quad gave up trying to ignore me. They brought me to the beach for the day. My sister was in tutoring, so it was just them and me. They set out this big blanket and an umbrella, and no one set up within twenty feet of us. It was hilarious, looking back, because the beach was so packed, but we had this huge ring of space around us."

"Are they that scary looking?" Hayden asked.

"Yeah, they really are. They just give off this, 'come close if you want to die,' vibe. Still, I never really noticed it, probably because I was used to it. Besides, they tried to make up for the fact I couldn't play with other kids much. I dug a big hole with Rune's help and we buried Dane in it. Probably not the first time Rune had buried a body."

I chuckled at my own joke despite knowing it wasn't really a joke... "We had ice cream and played in the water. I remember near the end when I looked over at another group and saw a kid with her parents. I'd had a moment of envy, where I wondered what it would feel like to be in a real family, to have parents who spent time with me, to be doted on like that. I remember sitting there, feeling sorry for myself, when Colton pointed out someone taking pictures. See, people would walk along the beach and offer their services for taking photos. They had the person come over and do a picture—the Quad and me—and it felt like a real family right then, like since it was in a picture, it made it real."

I laughed at how simple things had seemed back then. "I kept that picture under my pillow for years, taking it with me no matter how many times I moved, because at the end of the day, they were the only stable thing I ever had in my life, the only people I knew I could call at any time."

I glanced to the side, seeing the men who surrounded me, and a strange warmth filled my chest. It reminded me of that picture, of the sense of belonging I'd had back then. What did that mean?

It means you love these guys, but you already knew that.

It also meant I felt a sense of family here, especially because just like that beach trip, I had no doubt that my men had gone along with this because I'd wanted it. They hadn't gone hiking out of some need they'd had, but because I'd asked, and they'd wanted me happy.

I looked down at my water, my cheeks aching as I fought a smile. If they saw that, they'd only laugh at me for it.

"You ready to keep going?" Vance asked as he peered back toward the path. "It's going to be an uphill hike to get back to the car."

I shook my head, unwilling to lose this just yet. Sitting out here like this, Lorien wasn't a problem. They didn't need their revenge. I didn't have to think about who I was to the world. It was like when I'd gone to the beach with the Quad, when things had felt normal, when I didn't feel like I was from a different world from everyone else.

"Can we stay just a little longer?" I asked softly.

Vance bumped his shoulder against mine, then gave me a playful smile. "Sure, Kenz, we can stay."

And just like that, I didn't think I ever wanted to leave, to go back to the real world. This fantasy was so much better. If only I could make it real somehow...

* * * *

A few hours later, we neared the parking lot where we had left the car. We'd sat in that clearing for another hour or so before my stomach had rumbled, signaling time for us to head back.

The entire day felt like a dream, like a chance where we'd gotten to just be ourselves. Even Char had laughed a time or two — usually at my expense since he so enjoyed teasing me. Of course, I'd started not minding that. The words that felt cutting before now had a bit of affection in them, as though he had no idea how else to interact with me.

"Let's get pizza for dinner," I said. "We can get a couple big ones and eat them together at home."

"How does someone as little as you eat so badly?" Char asked.

"Good genes," I answered with a shrug. "Is that a no?"

"Anyone who says no to pizza shouldn't be trusted," Hayden said in a serious tone.

The easy atmosphere reminded me that the men were a group. Perhaps they hadn't always been one, hadn't started as one, weren't close in the way the Quad were, but they still had created a group among themselves. They trusted each other, relied on each other, had each other's backs.

And now I'd found a place with them as well.

The trees opened up as I hopped over a raised rock in the path. My ankle gave out when I landed, and I didn't have more than the chance to sigh as I prepared myself to hit the ground.

Except, a strong arm saved me, pulling me against a solid chest. "You are such a disaster," came Char's annoyed tone.

Annoyed or not, however, he'd still saved me. I glanced up and into his face, into those familiar dark eyes, his red hair even brighter as the sun had started to set. It lit it up, and before I knew what I was doing, I'd reached up to touch the strands, a few having fallen over his face.

He froze, as though I had a knife to his throat rather than just touching his bangs. Even still, he didn't stop me, so I brushed his hair from his face.

He really is handsome, isn't he? It hit me then, something I hadn't thought much about. Sure, he was attractive when he played his game, when he acted like the perfect gentleman, but now?

As surly and unreasonable as he was, I still wanted him.

I leaned closer, drawn by the sheen on his pink lips, wanting to taste them, to feel if they were just as soft as they seemed.

Before we made contact, however, something hit me. It pushed me just as pain seared through my arm and a loud bang echoed through the trees. My breath left in a rush as I hit the ground, Char along with me.

I turned my head to find Hayden above me, a gun in his hand, his gaze stoney and tracing the distance, searching. That told me how serious the situation was.

From around the car, I spotted a number of people stepping out — six, it looked like — all of them armed.

I peered down at the pain in my arm to find a red gash there, near the shoulder, clearly from a bullet graze.

Which meant my feeling that things were okay, that they were comfortable, that sense of safety had disappeared with just one bullet.

It only took one bullet to ruin everything.

Vance

The sight of six men headed our way was a very bad thing. I held a hand out, getting Kenz to her feet at the same time Char rose as well. I grasped Kenz's hand and tucked her tightly behind me.

Tor and Hayden stepped forward, toward the men. It reminded me that those two had *no* issues with violence. Even Char lifted his chin, an edge of danger on him that I rarely saw from him.

It made me feel slightly useless. I knew basic self-defense, and I was far from a weakling, but my life had been spent gathering information and living in the spotlight rather than fighting.

"What do you want?" Hayden asked.

"The girl," one of the men answered.

Like hell. My brain supplied the response before I had to think about it.

"Lorien wants her alive," Hayden snapped. "If you hurt her, let alone kill her, what exactly do you think he'll do to you?"

"Lorien's on his own," the man at the front said, a vicious glint in his eyes. "He hired me to send a few of my boys over for her. He said it'd be an easy job, that I didn't need to send many. Well, seems he didn't tell me the truth, and I lost a few of my best men on that one. Then the asshole said it was *our* fault and refused to pay." The man had a bat in his hand and twirled it like some athlete showing off before his turn at the plate. "Seems fair turnabout to make sure he doesn't get the girl at all."

Hayden narrowed his eyes, his hand not shaking in the least as he faced off against the man who had spoken the most. That astounded me, the way neither he nor Tor appeared thrown in the least.

They stood tall as if they weren't facing potential death, as if that didn't matter.

Kenz squeezed my hand, the action knocking loose that thought. There were four of us and six of them. I wasn't armed, but clearly Hayden was. I didn't see a weapon in Tor's hand, but I also knew him well enough to suspect he had one.

Even if he didn't, he didn't really need one, given his career.

And Char? Who the fuck knew what the guy knew or had. He was a mystery, but if I had to guess, he could at least hold his own.

It meant we were outnumbered, but not horribly so.

Hayden slipped his hand into his pocket, the motion hidden as he shifted toward Tor. When he withdrew it, something silver sat in his palm. With a quick but hidden motion, he tossed the item back to me.

Keys.

They were the car keys. Was this his point? That if it came down to it, I was to get Kenz out of here?

"You think Lorien will be okay with that?" Char asked, his tone light and joking despite the serious moment. "I mean, he doesn't strike me as the type who lets things like this go easily." Char turned his head slightly, talking to me. "Remember like a year ago? When someone stole his car? I don't think it was even his favorite car or anything."

I forced myself to smile, to ignore the tension in the space. It was time to play the game, and I could do that for an audience after a life in the public eye. "Yeah. Did they ever find all the parts of that guy?"

"They found, like…sixty percent maybe? Enough to identify him, at least." Char let out a soft laugh, as if it were the funniest thing. "If he does that over a car, I wonder what he'd do over a girl he says is his soulmate?"

"Oh, people won't find *anything* of someone dumb enough to hurt her," I agreed, nodding.

The man who had spoken moved his gaze between Char and me as though considering that. He pressed his lips together, his bat hanging loose in his hand and tapping against his thigh. "You're telling me that *this* one is really that important to him? She doesn't look like much."

I kept my mouth shut before I answered too honestly, telling that asshole that he'd be lucky if a girl like Kenz even looked his direction.

"You know rich folks — they're eccentric," Char said. "No accounting for taste in people like that."

The man shrugged. "Well, I guess that doesn't really matter. The thing is, if he's really as attached as you say, don't you think he'll be pissed about what's happened already?" He pointed toward Kenz's arm with the end of his bat.

"We could just all walk away and pretend like this never happened," Hayden said.

"We *could,* but that seems like putting me in a losing position yet again. I mean, I've lost out on the money Lorien was supposed to pay me, the reputation I lost by failing before and a few of my best guys." He shook his head. "No, I don't think that makes any sense at all. How about instead, you hand her over and we don't kill you?"

"Pass," Hayden said.

"I figured as much. Well, the next best thing then is for us to take the girl, kill the rest of you and hand her over ourselves. I get the payment I deserved before, probably a nice bonus and you all are out of my way. I'd prefer to do it without having to deal with getting rid of bodies, but in our world, that just isn't always possible." The man took a few steps closer, his lips curled into a smirk that turned my stomach. "So last chance. You want to do the smart thing or make this harder on us all?"

Hayden glanced to the side, meeting Tor's gaze. They seemed to exchange some conversation between them, as if they operated on the same wavelength and understood *exactly* what to do.

It was a language I didn't know, however. It meant the best I could do was hold the keys in my bad hand and clutch Kenz's hand with my other as we waited.

The first to move was Tor, and it sure as hell startled me. He was silent usually, and even when he communicated, it was always careful. He wasn't the type to threaten, to posture, not like the rest of us.

I played my games, and Char did his with ease. Hayden was less about posturing, but he was the first to use his size and strength when needed. Somehow, even knowing that Tor killed people for a living, it hadn't ever sunk in entirely.

It sure as hell did now, though.

He moved with a fluidity that came from practice, from having done this so many times that it had become second nature. He flew forward without a hint of what he would do, ducking low to avoid getting hit when one of the men pulled his gun and fired without aiming well. Tor caught the man's wrist and yanked forward, throwing him off balance and lifting his knee to catch the man in the face. He slid the gun from the man's grasp, twisting and raising it, firing a single bullet to land between another man's eyebrows.

Even when others reacted, it seemed no one could get ahead of Tor, could stop him, because he remained a few steps ahead.

Hayden pulled the trigger of his pistol, no hesitation in the action. While he might be a man who protected others for a living, he'd proven he had no problem killing to achieve that. The bullet struck a man near the back—the one who had fired at Kenz to start with. It made me wonder if he'd picked that target on purpose.

Of course, doing that gave the man at the front, who had done all the talking, the chance to swing his bat toward Hayden. Hayden raised his arm to block the hit, to prevent the bat from striking anything vital, but the crushing thud said it still hurt like a bitch.

And despite Char being smaller and thinner than the others, it only took a moment to see he was more than comfortable in a fight. One of the men grabbed the front of his shirt, no doubt expecting him to be easy prey. He proved them wrong when he jerked his hand up, striking the man in the chest.

The man fell forward, to his knees, and at first I didn't understand it. I couldn't believe he'd struck him hard enough for that reaction. It wasn't until Char stepped to the side that I saw the handle of a blade sticking out of the man's chest.

Right, makes sense that Char doesn't fight fair.

"Go," Hayden shouted to me. "Get her out of here."

I nodded and pulled Kenz along with me, going to flank the group who all seemed caught up with the three men causing them all the problems. Kenz went with me despite her wide eyes. I could read her expression easily, knew she didn't like the idea of leaving them, of running away, but that was too bad.

Just before we reached the car, someone hit my side, knocking me down. It felt like a tackle in the middle of a football game and knocked my breath from my lungs.

A crushing weight landed on top of me, and I let Kenz's hand go so I didn't yank her to the ground with me.

In my other hand I had the keys, and as I rolled to my back, I found a man on top of me. He was a hulking bear of a man with cauliflower ears—a sure sign that he'd spent plenty of time fighting. He lifted his arm, his hand clenched into a tight fist, which gave me two choices.

Try to block the hit or toss Kenz the keys. It took me back to how often people told me that my face was my only redeeming quality. Still an easy choice, though.

I tossed the car keys toward her just as my cheek exploded in pain. The hit fragmented my thoughts, making me wonder just how the hell the others could take a hit and keep moving so well.

Probably because they were used to it.

I tried to shake away the pain and when he went to strike me again, I lifted my hands to deflect the punch. Instead of his fist landing directly, it grazed my other cheek. I wanted to look to the side, to see Kenz getting into the car and gunning it, but I couldn't pull my gaze from the man above me.

The man was a fucking idiot who couldn't read a room, it seemed. Anyone with half a brain would have realized that I was nothing in the scheme of things. They'd come for Kenz, and they needed to grab her to succeed. Instead of going after her, though, he focused on me. When my face became too difficult a target, he shifted and struck me in the ribs.

I couldn't draw in air, the pain instant in a way that shocked me.

He chuckled, and the next thing I knew, silver flashed above me. He had a pocketknife in his hand and a crazy grin on his lips, neither of which signaled anything good for me.

He lifted the knife and tensed, no doubt ready to bury the thing into my stomach. I recalled Char having done the same thing earlier, but I sure hadn't thought I'd end up in the same position.

Except, just before he did it, as he savored that moment of triumph, something struck the side of his face, knocking him aside.

I didn't wait around to figure it out, taking the advantage, ignoring the pain in my side and the way I still struggled to draw air. I grabbed a rock from the ground, curling my fingers around it, and swung it as hard as I could at the man's head. The sickening crunch made my stomach uneasy, but I staggered to my feet, ready to do whatever I had to.

I turned, searching for the person who had knocked him off me, expecting Char or Hayden.

I didn't expect to find Kenz there, her hand in a tight fist with silver points showing from between her fingers. *The keys?* She'd tucked the car keys into her hands, each sharp point sticking out from her fist, drops of blood escaping from them.

"That's not why I gave you the keys!" I told her, hating how strained my voice came out.

"Well next time, be more specific!" she yelled back.

And I couldn't help it. I walked up and caught her by the back of her neck, pulling her close, not caring that my lip ached or that I could taste blood. The thought of her endangering herself for me pissed me off, and I couldn't think of any other way to deal with that frustration.

"I told you I'd wait, so tell me no."

She blinked, staring up at me with eyes I'd completely fallen for. I expected her to say nothing, to be passive, but why was it that she never did what I expected?

Kenz curled her fingers into my shirt and leaned up to take my lips in a clumsy, messy kiss. It wasn't sweet or practiced or with any finesse at all. Instead, it felt as hungry as my own.

"This is *not* the time!" Hayden's harsh words forced my mind to work again because, no matter how little I liked the reminder, he was right.

I pulled away, peering down at Kenz's flushed face, a red spot on her lip from my blood.

Right. Focus.

I took her wrist in my hand and extracted the keys from her grasp, which she easier gave me. "Next time, you run when you're told to."

"And leave you? Think again."

I narrowed my eyes but let it go. We could argue later. *And we sure as hell will!*

I reached for the handle of the car, but a bullet bouncing off the door made me freeze.

"Not so fast."

I turned to find the man who had spoken first with a pistol pointed directly at Kenz, his cheek red and swollen, his gait not nearly as good as it had been when he'd swaggered around with that bat of his. It seemed the others had done a number on him.

Not enough, though, given he still breathed.

"This is over," the man snapped. "I'm taking her."

"No, you aren't."

He walked up and pressed the muzzle of his gun to my forehead. Even still, I didn't pull away, I took the threat and kept Kenz behind me.

"Do you want to die?"

"Not yet," I answered.

"Then let me have her. I'm done playing this game, done fucking around. You hand her over or you get a bullet. That's it."

Kenz released my hand, the action a surrender, like she already knew my answer. Even if I hadn't been ready for this before, however, her doing that made the choice easy.

I grasped her hand tighter, squeezing hard, hoping she understood what I meant.

"I pick the bullet."

Chapter Sixteen

Tor

Blood on my hands was far from unusual. Somehow, at times like this, I didn't even feel like myself. Or, perhaps, it was more accurate to say I felt more like myself than ever?

Whatever the option, it wasn't how I felt at other times. When I fought, when I killed, I became something else, something driven by instinct, something that only saw action and reaction. It meant when one person moved, I immediately moved in response, countering.

And the trail of bodies I left proved my skill with such arts.

I panted hard, but to someone looking at me, it might not seem it. When the man before me dropped, I peered around to take note of the situation.

In short? We'd won. Six weren't really a big deal — I could have dealt with them all on my own if I didn't have to deal with protecting anyone else. Char and Hayden remained on their feet, each nearly finished with their own adversaries.

Then my gaze caught on the first thing to cause me any real spark of fear. Vance stood near the car, Kenz with him, their hands grasping each other, and the leader with his gun pressed to Vance's forehead.

And the look on the man's face? I *knew* that look. It was someone ready to pull the trigger, someone prepared to spill blood. My body moved faster than my thoughts, my steps light, as I reached into my jacket to wrap my fingers around the handle of a thin, sharp blade.

That man was the last standing — outside of the ones Hayden and Char finished off. Still, one tiny jerk of his finger on the trigger would be it.

Even I couldn't stop a bullet fired from that range.

Vance didn't flinch, didn't do anything but stand straight, his blue eyes hard. Seeing him like that felt like seeing a different man from the one I'd come to know. He was often unreliable, selfish, the epitome of a rich, spoiled brat. He'd taken the damage to his hand as the end of his life, and he'd lost most joy and pleasure in his life.

Even when he spent the nights with random women, I never saw any true contentment or enjoyment from it for him.

However, it wasn't the spoiled brat there — it was a man willing to stand tall no matter what came at him.

And the reason was clear — it was the woman with him, the one whose eyes were peeled wide as though she couldn't believe what rested before her.

I shook away those things, focusing instead on details. The man's arm held straight, but his posture slightly to the side—courtesy of his tangling with Hayden, no doubt. His hold on the gun implied he was comfortable with the weapon, that he used it enough, which meant firing it would be second nature to him.

Situations like this were always a gamble, no matter how little I liked that. I could approach this as perfectly as possible, but one twitch of his finger and I couldn't counter that.

Which forced me to move, to do it knowing it might not work out. This was too important to hold back, to regroup, to wait. I slipped behind the man, not even the shifting of his gaze implying he noticed me at all. Then again, that was one of my best skills—my ability to get up close.

Some killers preferred sniper rifles, but not me. I tended to remain quiet, get close and end targets with my own hands.

I did that now, moved quickly into place, my actions precise. I grasped his wrist with my free hand, shifting the barrel just a few inches to the side. Sure enough, his finger moved, the kickback of the pistol strong.

I brought the blade up between his ribs from the back on the right side, the sharpness allowing it to slide in with little resistance. His hand opened, the gun dropping to the sidewalk, his weight pulling as his knees gave out.

Then again, piercing the heart through the ribs like this tended to end any fight in a person quickly, which was exactly why I preferred such methods.

I allowed him to collapse, reaching past him to take the gun from the ground. Any person used to dealing with people and weapons learned quickly to not leave guns on the battlefield. There was nothing worse than an opponent who I'd thought was done grabbing one. That sort of wound ended up horribly embarrassing.

I looked around, finding Hayden and Char headed over, all the enemies down. Vance stood beside Kenz, and after one big breath, he seemed to be okay.

Kenz, on the other hand, had the expression of a woman about half a moment from collapsing. Not that it was a shock—normal people didn't tolerate scenes like this. Their minds rebelled against the sight of blood or death. The primitive parts of our minds didn't like that, since it signaled danger.

Kenz may have lived a hard life, but exposure to *this* level of danger and violence was different. I reached out, reach to catch her when her brain shut down in response.

Except, she didn't. She wavered just a bit, but before she went over, she pulled in a shaky breath and regained her balance. *Tough woman.*

"Vance, Char, get Kenz back to the house. Tor, let's clean up here to ensure there's no evidence left." Hayden had that take-charge tone of voice he often used, the one that told everyone things would be fine.

I nodded in agreement—Hayden and I were the best options for taking care of the scene, after all. Even if I hated the idea, even if I didn't want Kenz out of my sight after this, I remained still as Char slid into the driver seat and Vance got Kenz into the backseat.

The car pulled out quickly, leaving Hayden, myself, six bodies and a lot of blood.

"Well fuck," Hayden muttered, the curse word uncommon but completely fair.

I nodded, then sighed. After such a nice day, dealing with corpses wasn't the way I'd wanted it to end.

* * * *

Kenz

A knock on my door had me automatically calling for the person to enter. Honestly, it had taken longer for someone to bother me than I'd expected.

After Char and Vance had gotten us back, we'd all taken showers. Between the hiking and the fight, sweat, dirt and blood covered us all. After my shower, though, I'd yet to leave again.

I couldn't wrap my mind around what had happened, around the way Vance had stood against that man and so easily picked a bullet. It caused a squeezing around my heart that hurt each time I moved, each time I breathed, as though a corset had been laced far too tightly around me.

The crushing loss and grief from my mother's death, from grieving for my sister, even from the loss of my father, they all came back to me and threatened to pull me under.

The door opened, and Tor walked in first. His hair was wet and pushed back, telling me he'd showered as well. *How long have I been in here?*

Looking at a clock felt like far too much work, like spending energy I didn't have, so I pushed the worry away. Whether it had been thirty minutes or six hours, what did it change? What did it matter?

My gaze dropped to Tor's hands, finding them clean this time.

He tucked them into the front pocket of his sweater, and when I glanced up at his golden eyes, he didn't look right at me. Clearly that was a sore spot.

On his heels, Hayden walked in. Char and Vance followed, suggesting they'd all been together, probably all waiting. I could almost picture them in the living room, trying to figure out how long they had to wait before checking in on me.

That might have charmed me before, but right now? Right now I couldn't find it in me to like it, to feel anything positive at all. Instead, all I saw was that gun pushed against Vance's forehead and the fact that he'd almost died.

They'd *all* almost died, right before my eyes.

I lifted my hands and rubbed my palms against my face, trying to clear that away.

"Deep breaths," Hayden said, a heavy hand coming to rest on my back that I *knew* was his. He rubbed gently, as though calming me. Hell, it might have worked at any other time. "You're safe now."

A thin laugh escaped me as I dropped my hands from my face. *I'm safe?* He really didn't get it, did he?

"I know that was scary," Vance said as the bed dipped to my side from his weight. "It's over now, though. It's okay now."

"You think this is about *me?*" How could they misunderstand so fully?

"You've seen stuff like this before," Char said. "I know it's scary, but you've been through worse. We kept you safe because we always will."

His words snapped the chain on my mouth. I rolled my shoulder to knock Hayden's hand from my back. "Do you *really* not get this? Not understand why I'm upset?"

The expressions on each of the men's faces said no, they really didn't understand at all.

Just seeing how clueless they were drove my temper higher.

"Vance, you just *stood* there, with a gun to your head, and you chose a bullet! What the hell were you thinking?"

He blinked slowly, then frowned as if my words made no sense. "What else was I supposed to do?"

"What were you supposed to do?" I shoved his chest hard, unable to stop myself when he appeared so damned clueless. "You were supposed to value your *own* life, too! You're supposed to think that your own life matters and work to protect it as well!"

I rose then took a few steps backward, feeling the way they all stared at me as though I'd lost my mind. I couldn't really disagree with them about that one, though. It was like the frustration inside me, that helplessness, it had grown to the point where I felt entirely stuck and lashed out at everyone around me.

Or, in this case, at the people who were causing *this* part of the anger.

"Of course I've seen violence before. I've seen people killed, I've been in danger before, I've had guns pointed at me. Hell, I've been *shot*. I've seen bodies and blood and death lots of times. Those things don't bother me, but watching you four fight with no care for your own wellbeing? *That* is my problem."

"We didn't—" Hayden started to say.

I cut him off by pointing my finger at him. "You did. You've done it before. We've *had* this talk before! Even when the Quad fought, when I saw them kill, they never did it as recklessly as what I just saw. You all seem like you don't even care if you live." Admitting that made my stomach drop, the truth that I'd tried not to see.

The way they fought, the way they'd lived for the past five years, the way they pushed me away, it all came together to point to that one horrible truth. I swallowed, trying not to cry, not to lose it. They needed to hear me, to talk to me, and that couldn't happen if I let myself fall to my own pain.

No one spoke at first, and when someone finally did, it was Char. That fact startled me more than anything else. "I lost my wife five years ago because of Lorien. He stole the only thing I'd really wanted, the thing I'd wanted to protect, the entire life I'd built. When we all decided to go after him, we did it knowing we wouldn't survive, that there was no way this would end with us alive. We're going up against someone that dangerous, that vicious, and we went into it accepting that we wouldn't make it out alive."

His words were exactly what I'd suspected, but somehow hearing it hurt worse than I'd thought possible. I'd thought they'd only thought I was more important, but now I realized it was deeper than that. They not only didn't expect to come out alive—they didn't want to.

Vance's soft voice came next, and he stared down at his right hand as he spoke. "If anyone understands, I'd think it'd be you. It wasn't *just* my hand he took, it was a piece of my soul. I see things in my head, feel this need to create, but because of Lorien's actions, I *can't.* I'll never be able to again. My family thinks I'm useless, and all I've ever had in my life that I cared about, that I was proud of, was what I could create. I've lived the last five years only because I want to punish the person who did that to me. After that?" He shook his head. "Once Lorien is gone, even if that doesn't kill me, I don't think I can go on knowing I'll never paint again."

My legs trembled, my knees only seconds from giving way. Even if I'd suspected this some of the time, hearing them talk about themselves in this way *hurt*. They'd felt like my solid place, like a foundation for me, but now I discovered that I didn't have that. They'd crumble away the moment they got what they wanted.

Hayden hunched forward, setting his elbows on his knees, looking almost broken. It was strange to see him like that when he normally seemed invincible. "I've spent my entire life willing to trade my life for my clients, working to protect people. I've been willing to take life to do it, but it's always been to save others, always a last resort. That day, when Lorien bombed that building, he didn't *just* take the life of that client. He made me realize that sometimes sitting back and just waiting isn't enough. He took away my trust that I could do anything to save people, made me willing to strike first. He turned me into something I don't recognize, someone willing to kill in revenge, and that person isn't someone I want to be anymore."

I stared at the floor, and a pair of dark bare feet came into view. I lifted my gaze to find Tor in front of me, but I still didn't look him in the eyes. I couldn't. If I did, I knew I'd lose the tenuous hold I had on my boiling emotions.

I expected to hear the buzz of my phone, but instead, he leaned in so close that his lips nearly brushed my ear. I'd only heard his voice once, when he called my name, but I'd never forget that raspy, quiet quality of it.

"You saw what I really am today. I dropped man after man, ended up with blood all over my hands. I'm a killer, Kenz, but I thought before that sticking with targets who harmed people made it okay. Seeing

Lorien take that contract, seeing all the pain he caused, it made it clear that I'm not really any better. I can't pretend what I do is okay because I don't allow for collateral damage, because I try not to take any contracts for innocents. I've got too much blood on my hands and that weight is just too heavy now. I want to do one good thing before the end. It won't balance the scales, but getting rid of Lorien will mean I did *something* positive."

"This is why you all push me away, right? All the other stuff, about me being young or innocent or any of that, those aren't really the reason, are they?"

"I don't want to leave you hurting any more than you have to," Hayden said. "You got dragged into this mess, are going to have to live with what happens, but I want you harmed as little as possible. I want you to go back to your life afterward and have a good life, to do the things you want, to be happy."

He set his palm on my cheek, as though pleading with me to understand. "You've got a long life in front of you, and I want to make sure you get to live it the way you want."

I knocked his hand away, his touch like acid on my skin. The fact he wanted me to understand, that he gave me that bullshit, it made it all worse. "How dare you," I said, my voice steady and low, reminding me of the tone Nem had used, the one my mother had used when pushed past a breaking point.

It was the first time I felt any true connection between those strong women and myself. I wanted to say I wasn't so different from them, but I knew that wasn't true. They would have stepped up and fixed this somehow, would have done more, would have saved these men. Me, on the other hand, I could only complain.

"I know exactly what it feels like to lose people I love, to keep living when they're gone. I know that guilt, that pain that never fully goes away as I wonder why I couldn't do more, why I couldn't save them, why I'm still here and they aren't. I remember the night I found out about my mother and sister, when I lay in bed and couldn't even cry because I just wanted to be with them, whatever that meant." The pain from that loss, the memory of that hopelessness, I stopped pushing it down.

I stopped trying to hide from it, stopped trying to pretend to be okay, and let them see the depth and breadth of that agony. The tears I'd kept in, the ones I'd ignored, they spilled down my cheeks. Each one was another night that I'd spent alone, another doubt, another desire that I was dead instead of those I cared about.

"So fuck you all! What, do you think you'll die, and I'll just forget? That I'll move on like none of this ever happened? You already know that I love you, even if you try to ignore that or pretend like I don't know what I'm talking about, but that doesn't change it at all. Do you have any idea how much I'd suffer if I lost you all? Especially if it's just because you didn't think sticking around for me was worth it?" I shook, the anger mixing with the pain until I felt like a bomb with a short fuse.

"Kenz," Vance said softly, but I knew his tone. It was an apology, but not for what he planned to do. He was trying to comfort me, not offering to change his view. A glance at each of them showed the same resolve.

"So I'm not enough to even make you want to live, huh?" I laughed through the tears that ran down my cheeks. "I've spent my life not being good enough, losing those around me, and here I am going through it all again. So you know what? Fuck you all. How dare you sit there and talk about how you care about me, how you want the best for me, when you won't think for even a moment about what that would do to me?" I couldn't stand there anymore, couldn't listen to them, refused to even *hear* what they wanted to say about it anymore.

I turned away, but Hayden's sharp voice stopped me. "I know you're angry, but you can't leave — it isn't safe."

"So now you care about me, huh? Don't worry, I'm not leaving. I'm just going to the backyard because I can't stand the idea of even looking at any of you right now."

With that, I walked out, unable to stop the tears that ran down my face.

Chapter Seventeen

Kenz

My eyes ached from the tears I'd cried the night before. I'd fallen asleep outside, against the raised flowerbed, but I'd woken in my bed.

I had no idea who had brought me back in and I honestly lacked the energy to wonder about it. Breakfast had been made by the time I'd woken, but no one had spoken to me.

They'd stayed around me, as if giving me the opportunity to speak if I wanted to, but they hadn't pressed the issue. It told me what I'd already known. Even that night hadn't changed a damn thing. All the tears I'd cried, the pain I'd shown them, it hadn't changed their minds.

After breakfast, Hayden had taken me to school. It wasn't for a class, but I needed to work, and I couldn't bring myself to do so in the house. That house had felt so safe before, like my own little oasis, but it didn't seem the same way anymore.

Now, it felt stifling, like living in a mausoleum before the bodies were brought there. Each time I looked at the men, I saw walking corpses, and I hated it.

I worked in one of the small rooms of the library, and at least Hayden had left me be. He sat outside in the main library, and I could feel his gaze through the window as he watched over me. Still, I worked at the piece, the painting of me in the wedding dress, putting in the details. One of the things about art that had surprised me was just how long it took to really finish a piece. The start came together quickly, the rough sketch, the basic colors, but the shading and details took hours of painstaking work. This one alone would take days and days more.

My phone vibrated, so I set down the paintbrush and sighed at the name.

"You don't normally call during the day," I said.

"I heard about what happened yesterday and wanted to check in," Lorien said, his voice holding a strange sense of anxiety. It was one of the times when I remembered that as terrible as he was, he did have some strange obsession with me. "Are you okay?"

"I'm fine," I assured him, even if I didn't feel like it. A bandage on my arm had fixed the graze, and I hardly noticed it as of today.

"You don't sound fine."

I sat in a chair in the room, sighing softly. "I hate this feeling of being trapped."

"Everyone is trapped. Our names, our families, our future—the whole world traps us. I did *not* send those men to attack you, though. You know that, right?"

"Yeah, I know. They were mad that you hadn't paid them for their last failed attempt."

He was silent for a moment, one that made my anxiety increase. It was one of those times when I was forced to remember that this man was dangerous, that he was a killer. "I see. I wasn't sure what exactly had happened. I received word a few minutes ago from the next in line in that group who called to apologize about the incident. They had few details, only knowing that they had left to find you. I wanted to call to ensure you were truly safe. It seems this was my fault, then, even if I hadn't directly sent them."

"People are jerks sometimes. You can't help that." My gaze sought Hayden at that comment, finding him with his eyes locked on me through the glass.

Yeah, you're the jerk I mean right now.

I sighed and shook my head. "It's fine, really. I'm not hurt."

"And your saviors?"

"Sorry to say, not hurt, either."

"I'm not that sorry about that."

"Really? I figured you'd be happy if they were killed so you didn't have to wait any longer."

"I'm surprisingly patient when the prize is right. I'm fine with adding pressure to help you make up your mind, but I have no wish to win by default. If that happened, you'd forever be thinking of *them,* forever seeing me as second."

"So what do you want?"

"I told you—I want you to pick me. I want you to see me for what I am, which is your perfect match. I want to give you the chance to fall for me the right way. I am curious, however, what is it about them?"

"What do you mean?"

"You cling to them. I've seen pictures, heard how you speak about them. They are important to you, and I am curious as to why."

I glanced at the picture I'd painted, my gaze tracing the lines while I thought about the best way to explain it.

"They watch out for me," I said softly.

"So? I would do the same. When you choose me, I'll ensure no harm ever comes to you. You may not like my more vicious side, but the opposite side of that coin of that is that I would keep you safe. Nothing in the world would touch you. What happened yesterday? It would never have happened if you were in my care."

"It's easy to say that. People always like to say how they'd do things so much better when they aren't in the situation."

"You think my words are empty? Because just prior to calling you, I sent my own men to deal with the rest of that group who targeted you."

"Why would you do that? They weren't involved..."

"Because they should have stopped the others. They were complicit. They knew what the others would do and allowed it, so they're just as at fault."

"Please, don't," I asked, my voice softening as I thought about the death he was talking about, about the useless taking of life. Already there were six people dead, and I didn't want any more on top of that.

"I do not take threats to you lightly," he assured me.

"You want me to fall for you, right? Then show me by doing this for me."

He sighed, the sound drawn out. "I knew relationships would mean compromise, but I find I do not like this. However, as proof of my seriousness, I will do so. I will call them back and let those others live.

You, however, are far too soft. Perhaps it's fortunate that you have me — otherwise, I suspect you would get eaten alive by this world. I wonder sometimes how you survived in California, how you survived surrounded by Mafia families and killers. You remind me of something too soft and too sweet, that would be crushed beneath the feet of those around you."

I shuddered in relief at the fact he'd given in. The last thing I wanted was people dying just for me.

The speaker in the corner of the room clicked on and a staticky voice filled the small room. It announced an event starting in the large auditorium, making me wince because it was far too loud for the size of the room.

"I will let you go now, since I have to call to make arrangements and stop my men," Lorien said. However, as his voice spoke above the announcement, I frowned at a strange sound in the background.

I'd grown so used to hearing him through the voice changer that it sounded normal to me. It altered all the sound that came through, twisting it slightly so the sound of a horn honking would change to something mostly unrecognizable. Usually he seemed to place himself somewhere quiet, mostly due to the calls occurring at night, which meant I rarely heard anything in the background.

This time it was different, though. Around his voice, something else came through, a background noise buzzy and unclear.

An uneasy feeling filled me, an idea that I couldn't quite believe.

"Can I call you back in a few minutes?" I asked. "I want to know for sure that you stopped those men."

"You doubt me?" He had a laugh in his voice, as though my worries amused him. "Like I would deny you speaking to me. Of course. Give me ten minutes to ensure I finish the task." He didn't wait for my response before hanging up.

I stared at the phone, fear creeping through me. I thought about what Hayden had said before, what I'd thought. He had to know me, right? If he'd fallen for me, if in his twisted mind he loved me, he had to have met me.

I'd assumed that it had been in my old life, but what if I was wrong?

I left the painting where it was, gripping my phone, leaving my purse behind. Nothing mattered except the idea in my head, the one I couldn't shake.

I left the small room, Hayden already on his feet and approaching me as I headed through the library.

He said nothing until we left the quiet space, but even when he spoke to me, I didn't answer. I couldn't. My brain couldn't keep up with anything except for what was in my head even as I told myself I was wrong.

Please, let me be wrong...

Ten minutes later, I stood outside a door, my stomach wrapped into knots so tight that I feared I'd throw up on the spot. I tried to breathe, but I couldn't draw it deep enough to help.

Hayden still hadn't spoken, just followed me as a familiar, steady shadow.

I hit the button on my phone to call Lorien. After a single ring, he answered, his familiar voice floating through the line. "As you asked me to, I did it. They won't be harmed, even if they deserve it. I hope that garners me a little trust and affection."

I closed my eyes for a moment, then twisted the handle of the door, not bothering to knock. *Please, let me be wrong. Let me walk in and see nothing, to have to explain why I barged in.*

Except, when the door opened, I found what I feared. There, the familiar man in the room stared back at me, his phone to his ear. At least a flash of surprise said I'd tricked him, that I'd outsmarted him, that I'd done something he hadn't thought me capable of.

"And here I wondered how you survived your old life. It seems you are far more clever than I expected, Kenz." He hung up the call and set his phone on his desk, staring at me with eyes that made my knees want to give way.

Grisham, my student adviser, was Lorien...

Want to see more from this author? Here's a taster for you to enjoy!

Black Heart Auctions: Taking Chances
Jayce Carter

Excerpt

Kenz

Sometimes my brain stopped working—it took one look at the situation I found myself in and just fucked right off. It had happened when I'd found out about the murder of my mother and sister, again when my father had tried to kill me and it happened again now, as I faced a man I'd trusted, one I'd relied on, only to realize that he'd been behind everything I'd suffered recently.

"So we officially meet," Grisham said, taking his phone from his ear, a soft smile on his face as though he didn't truly mind being exposed. "I didn't expect you to be the one to figure it out."

"How could you?" I whispered, trembles running through my body, fear swamping me as I tried to connect the man who had helped me so often with the monster I'd heard about, the nightmare from my dreams.

He tilted his head, making no attempt to rise or do anything but stare back at me. "I've already told you—you just didn't read between the lines. I saw your work at the entrance exhibit, and I knew, right away, that you were the one for me."

I took two steps closer and slammed my palm on the top of his desk. "You didn't even *know* me! If you actually gave a damn, why didn't you do something normal like ask me out? What sort of psychotic idiot have their soulmate abducted and sold at an auction?"

His chuckle came out soft and unconcerned. It forced me to look into his eyes, the ones I thought I'd known, and recognize an overwhelming emptiness in them. They seemed to lack a part, as though a vital piece of him had gone missing at some point.

Or maybe he'd never had that piece at all.

"I tried to get closer, but you never allowed anyone near. You had a wall up no matter what I did, kept me at a distance that I couldn't cross. We are *soulmates*, Kenz, and if you only give yourself the time and space to recognize it, you'll see it, too."

A click behind me made me freeze. The safety of a gun flipping off was a sound no person ever really forgot.

Grisham — *Lorien?* — peered over my shoulder but no change to his expression suggested he worried at all.

"It was you all along?" Hayden asked, rage in his voice that terrified me as much as the man before me.

"You were so close," Lorien said with a laugh, "but you never saw it. You never managed to put the pieces together to find me. Sometimes, I wondered if you and the others' incompetence was a sign that you didn't really want to find me. The four of you should have managed it, yet in five years, you've never gotten close enough for it to matter."

"Who cares?" Hayden fully entered the office, then shut the door without ever removing his gaze from

Grisham. "A bullet between your eyes doesn't require much time, after all."

Grisham shrugged and sat back in his chair. "You won't shoot me."

"Do you really think that? After what you've done? After I've chased you this long?"

"You're smarter than that. If you couldn't find solid proof about me, do you think the police will? Or do you think that if you kill me here, in my office, in a place where others will come quickly at the noise, *you'll* be held responsible as a murderer?"

"So? I'm ready to throw my life away," Hayden assured him, no hesitation in his voice.

It brought back the same crushing pain from last night, the realization that the men I loved didn't value or even want their lives.

"But are you ready to throw hers away?" Grisham gestured toward me.

He sure knows where to aim that threat.

Hayden hesitated, his lips pressing together, but he didn't lower his gun.

Grisham's smile spread wider. "Kenz has enjoyed a quiet life this last year because her existence isn't widely known. If anything happens to me, her identity will get out. I have ensured that every person who might wish to make use of her will know *everything* about her. Her ability to live as she wishes will disappear if that happens, assuming she survives it."

Hayden lifted his lip, a look of pure disgust on his face. "And you claim you love her, that you're soulmates, but you would do that to her?"

"I'm a practical man. We're soulmates, and that means if I go, her time should come soon after. Besides, if something happens to me, do you think my mother would sit back quietly? She may be a meek woman, but mothers are notoriously vicious. If I'm harmed, she will set her sights not only on Kenz herself, but on those Kenz cares about as well. I know you don't value your own life, but you are far too easy to predict, and you'll value the life of others."

My stomach rolled as I thought about Nem in danger because of me. Not just her — she was tough, as were the Quad — but others. What about Sasha? What about those who worked for my sister? I'd lived in this world long enough to know exactly how much death came from a real war, when there were no innocents — just the victors and the dead.

Hayden still didn't lower his gun, but the look in his gaze said he'd taken the threat seriously. "So what now?"

"Now we appear to be at an impasse, don't we? We both have something to hold over the head of the other. It seems we are at a standoff at the moment." Grisham moved his gaze from Hayden to me, and I had to fight the desire to take a step away from the intensity of it. "I am not backing down. I *will* have Kenz."

"I'm not something to own," I whispered.

Grisham gave me an indulgent smile. "Everyone is something to own. Even me. And don't mistake me, you will have me as well. If I wanted a slave, I could have that. Instead, I've given you time to get to know me, to realize we're meant to be. My patience has limits, however. I suggest you do not push me to that point." His threat sent a shiver through me.

"This isn't over," Hayden said.

"Of course it isn't. However, I will admit, this is the most fun I've had in a while. Jobs are too easy anymore, no challenge, no real risk, nothing to make them interesting. At least this has become interesting. So go on, and think carefully, Kenz. The longer you draw this out, the riskier it gets. I don't care who dies, who suffers as we drag this you, but I have a feeling *you* do."

I swallowed hard, my throat tight and dry. So many faces flashed through my mind, all the people who might pay the price for this, not the least of which were the men I loved.

Was I really worth risking so many people?

* * * *

Char

I rubbed my eyes, exhausted after all the hours I'd spent on the phone and staring at my bright screen of my laptop.

I was used to research—it was a necessary evil in my line of work—but I wasn't sure it had ever mattered quite this much, that I'd ever done it with so much focus.

A water landed in my lap, and I groaned when it smacked me in the groin. A glance up showed Vance without an ounce of regret.

Instead of snapping at him—he'd only enjoy annoying me, after all—I gave him my best fake smile. "Thanks."

"Anytime." He twisted the lid off his own and tipped it back, gulping it down.

Despite the sun having set a little while before, the heat hadn't let up. Sweat had soaked into the back of my shirt, and when I moved my hair from my face, I found droplets on my forehead. The cold water was a welcome treat, though I could have done without the crotch-shot.

"Anything new?" Vance asked.

"Just a lot of bad," I admitted. "Even if there was a doubt before, there isn't now. Grisham is Lorien."

"How did he land a job at a college? That's a hard background to fake."

"Looks like his mother and father made sure he was never connected to them by anything official. So, officially, from birth, he's been Grisham. He went to college under that name, got his degree in Fine Arts and the History of Art. If you follow his official name, he's lived a perfectly normal life."

"Why would they do that?"

"It's not that uncommon, especially for second kids. It lets them hide an heir," I explained. "If no one knows who he is, no one can target him."

"But with his brother and father gone, he's set to take over, so why keep hiding him?"

"I get the feeling he likes it, that he wants his other life more than he wants to lead. In fact, I think the only reason he's taken an interest in his family business at all is so they don't stop him. I doubt he wants to run it."

Someone sat beside me, and I fought the urge to jump.

Damn Tor, the sneaky bastard. I wondered at times if he just enjoyed freaking people out by sneaking up on them. It was like a reminder that if he wanted to slit my throat, he could.

He set a hand behind him and leaned back, his gaze going up to the dark sky. After hearing his voice the other day, it still echoed in my head. It was quiet, but it was there.

Given I lived my life by talking, by twisting facts and people into useful forms, by twisting *myself* into whatever I had to be, his silence always unnerved me a bit. Yet, there was something oddly comforting in that quiet, as though I didn't have to be on during that time.

"Water?" Hayden huffed softly as he shut the slider behind him. "I figured tonight would be a night for alcohol." Even as he made the joke, however, he held water as well.

I suspected none of us wanted to let our guard down, not tonight, not now that we realized just how close the danger to Kenz really stood.

Instead of Lorien being some faceless voice over a phone, a name without form, we'd discovered he was closer than we'd ever thought. The idea that Kenz had met with him right under our noses, that we'd never even thought to suspect him, ate at me.

I was supposed to read people well, to know when they lied, and yet I hadn't even considered he could be the one we searched for.

"How's Kenz?" Vance asked Hayden.

Hayden pulled a chair over from the seating area and sat in it. "She's okay. She showered, barely ate, but she's sleeping now. Hopefully a full eight hours will help her feel more ready to deal with this tomorrow."

"What's there to deal with?" I muttered. At their looks, I let out a rough breath. "He's got us, doesn't he? He knows that we can't move against him, not as long as he threatens Kenz. We're stuck."

"He can't move, either," Hayden pointed out. "Now that we know who he really is, he can't attack her directly or we tear apart his life."

My phone buzzed, and just like Hayden and Vance, I pulled it out to peer at the screen. *Even if we don't have proof to turn him over to the authorities, we know plenty of enemies of his who would love to get his real name.*

"That doesn't help," I snapped. "It means we're both stuck right here, at a place we can't stay. Kenz is still in the middle, and no one can move, can do anything. We can't get our revenge, he can't get Kenz, so what? We just stay like this until we die?" I carded my fingers through my hair, pushing it out of my face so roughly that I accidently yanked at least a strand or two.

I made my life by reading others, by tricking them, by creating plans that got me what I wanted, but I couldn't figure out a plan right now.

I couldn't see a way forward, a path to what we wanted most. Each time I went down another rabbit hole, each time I explored some new method, it led to the same.

Kenz paying the price for our revenge.

I rubbed my palm over my face as I let out a humorless laugh.

"What's so funny?" Hayden asked.

"I was thinking about that first night Kenz got here. Remember how scared she was? I took one look at her and was ready to do whatever it took to get what we wanted. The idea of using her didn't bother me at all, and if she got hurt because of it?" I shrugged. "Funny how that changed, how now the idea of her left holding the bag just isn't acceptable."

"I know what you mean," Vance said. "I've spent five years wanting nothing more than revenge. I wanted to make Lorien pay for what he'd done, and each time I saw my mangled hand, it only made me more desperate for that. Now?" He shook his head. "I go days without thinking much about it. Even when I look at that hand, I don't feel the same hatred I did before. Hell, sometimes I wonder if I couldn't just walk away from it all, if I couldn't move on."

I nearly scoffed and said there was no way that was possible.

However, I couldn't quite get that out.

I used to see my wife's smiling face in my dreams. I used to dream of her almost every night, waking up panting, having to remind myself she was gone. The anger and sorrow that would overcome me at times like those had only been soothed by my thoughts of revenge.

However, those dreams had slowly been replaced by something else, something calmer. I'd started to dream about Kenz, to see her sweet face, to hear her laugh in my mind, to think of her. Worse, a part of me even had fantasized about a future, about what could occur in the future with her.

It wasn't that I'd forgotten my wife so much as Kenz had built a foundation beneath me, had allowed me to stand instead of drown, and I wasn't sure what that meant.

"It doesn't matter if we'd be willing to give up our revenge," Hayden pointed out, his voice soft. "Lorien wants her, and he's willing to get her killed if he can't have her. Even if we were willing to walk away from this all, we can't. We started on this path and the only way Kenz can be safe anymore will be to deal with Lorien and the threat he poses."

Nice idea, but we still don't know how to do that, Tor wrote.

"I have an idea," Vance said.

I lifted an eyebrow in his direction. Of all the people who might have an idea on what to do, I sure would have placed Vance last. He was smart, of course, and his network of information was impressive. His connections due to his art and family meant if we needed to know someone, if we needed to get close to someone, he could manage it. Still, he'd never been the type to plot much, especially when it came to situations like this. "Oh yeah?" I asked, not expecting much.

He snorted softly, the sound implying he could guess my line of thought. "Yeah. Why does Lorien's threat matter?"

"Because of Kenz," I said.

Vance shook his head. "No. I mean why specifically does it matter if he threatens Kenz?"

Because he can carry it out, Tor wrote.

"That's right. See, Lorien has the backing to do what he says. Grisham doesn't have much power, but Lorien does, and he has that because of his family. He's dangerous as an individual, sure, but he's only dangerous the way a man is. It's his family that gives him the power to threaten Kenz, though. His leverage is there because of his mother, because she'll follow through on his wishes if something happens to him."

It hit me then, and I cursed at myself for why I hadn't thought about that before. Worse, the fact that Vance had beat me to such an obvious solution bothered me. "The way to deal with an enemy is to cut off their resources."

Vance nodded. "That's right. If we can strain that relationship, if we can sow doubt between them, it lessens his ability to carry out his threat."

"She's his mother," Hayden said. "Mothers don't just abandon their kids, no matter how terrible those kids are."

"Are you sure about that?" Vance asked. "Because as someone who constantly gets threatened to be disowned, I can assure you that parents aren't quite as perfect as we like to pretend. Besides, we don't need her to throw him to the wolves, exactly, just to withdraw her support of him. Without her backing, his threats mean nothing. He's made his life on his own, worked on his own, only using her connections, so without her, he's got no one to help him carry out his plan. If we want to take him out and not risk Kenz, we've got to split him from his mother."

I thought about it, trying to come up with a reason why it wouldn't work, but I couldn't come up with anything. It wasn't that it would be easy, of course, but it was something.

It was a hell of a lot more than we'd had before, at least.

I glanced up at the house, toward Kenz's dark window. She'd been the key to find him, to get this far, but at the same time, she was the thing standing in the way of ending it quickly.

And for the first time, I wished we could all just walk away, could forget this all, but a tightness in my chest assured me it wasn't possible.

Maybe this was all my punishment for wanting things I didn't deserve. I might not get what I wanted, but I'd do whatever it took to make sure Kenz could have what she wanted.

She deserved at least that much.

About the Author

Jayce Carter lives in Southern California with her husband and two spawns. She originally wanted to take over the world but realized that would require wearing pants. This led her to choosing writing, a completely pants-free occupation. She has a fear of heights yet rock climbs for fun and enjoys making up excuses for not going out and socializing.

Jayce loves to hear from readers. You can find her contact information, website details and author profile page at https://www.totallybound.com

Home of Erotic Romance

Sign up for our newsletter and find out about all our romance book releases, eBook sales and promotions, sneak peeks and FREE romance books!